SHE ROSE BEYOND THE WALLS OF FIRST CITY, CREATING THE WORLD SHE HAD ALWAYS ENVISIONED

People could say all sorts of things about the outside, draw upon all manner of hypothetical situations, because no one had actually been there.

Morag would be the first.

She ascended, more slowly still, beyond the cervix, out of the womb of ice and into the world. The real world was as beautiful as she had imagined. But she could not look without an ache, a kind of yearning, in her breast. The sight created a deep hurt within her spirit, which had faint, almost indiscernible undercurrents of lost joys.

*   *   *

The Press Praises Garry Kilworth

"Mr. Kilworth maintains his capacity to surprise the reader right to the end."   —*Oxford Times*

"One is left in no doubt about the quality of the writing or of Mr. Kilworth's talent for spinning a yarn."
          —*Times* (London)

Also by
Garry Kilworth

Split Second

Published by
POPULAR LIBRARY

THEATER OF TIMESMITHS

GARRY KILWORTH

POPULAR LIBRARY

An Imprint of Warner Books, Inc.

A Warner Communications Company

POPULAR LIBRARY EDITION

Popular Library® and Questar® are registered trademarks of Warner
Books, Inc.

Originally published in Great Britain by Victor Gollancz Ltd.
Reprinted by arrangement with the author

Popular Library books are published by
Warner Books, Inc.
666 Fifth Avenue
New York, N.Y. 10103

 A Warner Communications Company

Printed in the United States of America

First Popular Library Printing: April, 1986

10 9 8 7 6 5 4 3 2 1

To Bobbie, Chris, Dave and Malcolm—
for cutting the grass and sowing more seeds.

The weather has worn into her
All seasons known to me,
In one breast she holds
Evidence of forests,
In the other, of seas.

—Brian Patten,
"Into My Mirror Has Walked"

ONE

It was a city of freezing mists, emerging each morning like a gray, ridged beast through layers of swamp fog. Half a thousand years old, it was completely surrounded by a wall of white-veined ice in the shape of a cone. No one knew exactly how thick the ice was at its base but it was at least a kilometer: the length of the longest escape tunnel ever attempted. The blowhole, at the top, was approximately half a kilometer in diameter but this distance varied according to the temperature of the gases exhaled by the city.

First City itself had been built in the shape of a hexagon, of four-story, gray blockhouses with a tall, green tower at the very center. Its streets were narrow and frequently white with a heavy frost or awash with meltwater. Covering the area of the city was a high roof: a transparent canopy strengthened with great stargirders to protect it against fallbergs. The inhabitants of First City world were generally of a morose and truculent disposition, and many of those whose spirit had not been broken by a life of privation, disease and depression spent

1

their waking hours planning escape from the whirlpool of ice
that was their prison.

Morag MacKenzie was one such person. ·

Morag MacKenzie watched the priest slide the body into the
tomb: a hole cut in the wall of ice that surrounded the city.
This was her world, inside the cone of frozen water, and like
many others, she hated it. She hated it because it was a prison
from which none escaped. She hated it because it was a gray,
dismal place where people barely managed to exist. She hated
it because she had a restless, curious spirit and the lifestyle the
city imposed upon that spirit was claustrophobic, crushing and
promised a bleak future.

She looked away from the corpse of her former employer.
Ilona Ingle had never been a friend but she had meant security
while she had been the madam of a thriving whorehouse. Now,
Morag and three other prostitutes were without shelter. It was
almost impossible to survive in First City unless you had a
roof over your head.

They were spitting on the corpse as a mark of respect now,
the globules freezing into white blisters as they struck. It was
colder than death near the ice. Around her the walls creaked
and groaned relentlessly as the priest droned out his orisons—
it was almost as if the ice were providing musical accompani-
ment to a dirge. She looked upward, at the blowhole some
three kilometers overhead. There was a gray-blue sky above.
She longed to be the first to go beyond the lip of the cone,
and return.

A great gush of meltwater fell from the misty heights of the
interior of the cone. It thundered onto the canopy that covered
the city, ran down the gutters in the stargirders, and finally
fountained out near the mourners, to disappear down the boreholes that followed the perimeter of the city.

Morag, though tall, was a slim woman and she felt the cold.
A lock of her dark hair had escaped the hood of her toga and
was frozen hard against her forehead. She did not move it in

case skin came away. It was best to leave it until she could thaw out.

Someone sighed near her.

"So beautiful," they said, softly.

Now what did that mean? Death was beautiful? Surely not Ilona's corpse? The madam had never had any pretense to beauty. Perhaps the sermon or the prayers? No, they were dull and boring. The whole situation possibly? Morag looked around her again, ignoring the priest's interminable chanting. It was possible that some people might even find the ice beautiful, with its white-lightning veins and wet, shiny surface. The gray blockhouses of the city too, if one had the kind of mind that appreciated symmetry, though she personally could not see them without also seeing the despair and misery that they housed. People without hope. People who dragged themselves out of one day and into the next, knowing that change was not possible: there would always be the cold, the intermittent hunger, the drab existence, the possibility of a premature death. There was always Raxonberg, Chief of Trysts, to keep them inside the city, no matter how many ingenious escapes were dreamed up, with balloons, and scaling equipment and tunnels through the walls. There would always be the unreliability of the central computer that controlled their lives.

What would she do now? She was not fond of any of the other prostitutes, so there was no point in staying together. She looked over her shoulder and saw the black man on the edge of the crowd of mourners. Him? He had approached her earlier, offering accommodation, but had not yet explained *why*. She would find out. There was nothing to lose now except... except her pride. She did not want charity and neither did she want to prostitute her body. It was her *mind* she worked with, not her loins. She decided to ignore him for the time being. If he was genuinely interested he would follow her.

Morag turned, walking quickly away from the dozen mourners. The priest was busy scattering ice chips on the body and he looked up, frowning slightly. Then he bent his head to his task again. It was a matter of indifference to her that he felt slighted. She had paid her respects and that was all that mattered. Now she had to take care of herself.

There was a scream from the ice above: a berg was beginning to part from the main body of the cone. It had her attention momentarily, that wrenching, grating cry from her prison. Looking up, a glitter of tinsel caught her eye, as a tiny sliver of frozen water drifted obliquely through the beam of a perimeter light: a falling star.

Around and above her the huge, humped ice leaned over threateningly, ridged and rippled where the meltwater flowed down its smooth walls. Darkness courted its upper, cavernous interior, where frozen mists moved as ghosts in the changing currents of air. There were gods up there, among the fine, freezing rains and twisting winds. Powerful gods, that tore hanging bergs the size of towers from the walls and let them fall to shatter into spires which in turn flew javelin-like from the girders, sometimes to bury themselves point-first into the body-ice; or perhaps bouncing stars that cannoned across the canopy to explode into white dust on impact, to cast sparkling clouds of powdered ice through the perimeter arc lights.

It was over two hundred meters back to the edge of the city. She strode quickly beneath the giant heater screen which had been raised to allow the funeral procession to pass beneath. Electromechanical devices were prone to erratic behavior. Six months ago a screen had lowered behind a group who had been inspecting the wall and had fried them. Walking quickly, she reached the narrow streets of the city. The standard eight-story apartment blocks in their neat gray rows formed dark avenues for her approach. There were not many people about. A few children, playing road games or loitering at the entrances to alleys. Most of the population were huddled in myopic rooms behind the small, mean windows with their thick lenses. The soup palaces would open at 5 o'clock. Morag had to walk the streets for thirty minutes to keep warm. Or, rather, to stop from freezing. She was aware of the dark man, close behind her.

She turned to confront him. He was dressed in the gray toga

of a civil servant. She read the name again, the symbols tattooed on his cheekbones just below each eye: *Ben Blakely.*

"You *still* following me?" she said. "What is that you want?"

He looked up into her face, his gaze fixed upon her own tattoos. He seemed hesitant and unsure. As if he were unused to dealing with prostitutes.

"I'm sorry . . . I saw you leave for the funeral and I thought . . ."

"I'm not working any more," she snapped. There was a pathetic look about him and she was aware that her tone was not helping him. It was difficult not to feel sorry for him.

Gently, he said, "That's not what I want."

When she did not reply, he asked, "Can't we talk? My apartment is only two blocks away. I may be able to help you."

"Help me what?"

"You need a room. You've already spent two nights in the open. How long do you think you can last?"

"You've been following me for two days?"

She had intended to sound angry but her annoyance was diluted by her surprise. The first time she had noticed him was that morning.

"Does that bother you?"

"It depends. . . ." She made a quick decision. "I'll come but I don't need any money. She—" Morag nodded toward the city limits—"she left me plenty to be going on with."

"Only food disks though."

Morag fingered the plastic disks inside the mittens. She knew them all to be colored red.

"Look, I don't mean you any harm." He lifted his hands and then let them drop, a gesture which showed he understood that futility of her situation. "Food's not your problem at the moment. Accommodation is. I can help you—and I don't want anything for it. Not for myself. Come and hear what I've got to say, at least."

Morag glanced around her, at the huddled people in the doorways and alleys, some with their togas pulled up over their heads, exposing their legs to the cold. On the steps of an apartment block about ten meters away sat a woman in a threadbare toga. It was impossible to tell if she was young or old, but her face had the pallor of the gray crumbling stone on which she sat, rigid as the brickwork itself, staring vacantly. The building facade framed her small tight figure, as if the two of them had been fashioned at the same time and their ancient lines had fallen into a similar pattern of decay, the mortar holding brick and stone, flesh and bone, together only by the tiny ice crystals that glistened from the cracks and crevices of wall and skin. They were one: woman and wall, their destinies the same—to sit exposed to the erosive elements, to crumble, grain by grain, to dust. This, too, was Morag's destiny, if she cared to think too hard about it. A week in the open would put the same hue to her skin, give her that same dull, stonelike expression, produce those ash-white hands that gripped the edge of the toga with the inflexibility of griffin claws. Morag was glad she was too far away to see the woman's eyes, which would be as glazed and blank as the windows of her background framework.

What should she do about this black man's offer? She was suddenly angry because she had little choice in the matter. Not if she intended to spend a warm night.

"All right, I'll come. But I want to know under what conditions. No more hedging."

He smiled then. A warm friendly smile. "Fine, I'll tell you when we get out of the cold air."

The apartment was reached by way of slick, gloomy stairways, flanked by ill-lit passages. It was a top floor room and she tried not to show that she was impressed. Once inside, the man took off his mittens, opened his outer toga and then turned to help her with hers. She shook her head. He nodded, replacing his own mittens.

She said, "I'm not warm yet."

She looked around the room. It was sparsely furnished, with togas and blankets covering the floor. There was a single seat. A stool. Not a bad little apartment. Comfortable at least. It was all she was used to.

The man moved to the dim light of the window.

"Don't you want to know more about me," he asked, "before I explain why I want to talk to you?"

"Is there any reason why I should?"

He shrugged without turning round. "I don't know. Perhaps I might be a Messiah. The one who will lead our people to the sun. It seems to be the one topic of conversation these days. . . ."

"If he, *or she,* ever comes . . . well, he won't look like you. He'll be tall and straight. . . ."

". . . and golden. Yes, yes." He gave a sigh. "Look at that ugly prison out there. . . ."

Morag crossed to the window and looked out through a space in the frostfern patterns on the pane. Below her the sharp angles of the streets and buildings formed a cubist pattern varied only by shades of dark and light gray, with some patches of white where the frost rested. The one streak of color was the green obsidian tower in the center, which rose like a lance to threaten the canopy above it. At the tip of the tower was a cupola in which it was said—and few doubted—the central brain, the Primary, was housed. The mighty semi-organic computer that controlled their tight little world of misery, making it a place just barely possible to exist within, was their housegod with which a love-hate relationship was maintained. Even now ambivalent feelings welled within her breast, as she studied the mottled exterior of its impenetrable keep.

The rest of the city was uniform in its general appearance, the flat-roofed buildings interconnected by walkways and forming almost a single unit, a banyan-like beast that grew from and into itself to make one tight structure, without beginning or end: a Klein-bottle in blocked stone. Here and there was evidence of neglect and decay where chunks of granite had detached themselves from buildings and lay in the narrow streets: pieces of sill, a cornerstone from a roof, one or two shattered cornices. There was an attempt at ornamentation: stone griffins glowered down upon the streets and alleys, or stared malevolently into each other's eyes across three meters of space. Their implacable expressions had often been responsible for their destruction, when some resident with a facing window could no longer stand the frozen gaze and had taken a pole to a carving, decapitating it.

There were also some attempts at mosaic, around doorways and windows, but the lack of different varieties of stone had produced a poor patchwork of gray.

In her more fanciful moments Morag could view the city as a many-headed, multi-shouldered mutant giant, whose arms and legs grew out and into its disparate parts with grotesque oneness: a giant that seemed to be eating itself yet at the same time growing new limbs and heads; a giant that was caught in a desperate struggle with itself, was locked in a tense knot of muscles of equal strength so that it remained unmoving yet straining in every fiber for possession over itself. It was a living thing, this city, that remained in a state of high pressure, pushing, pulling, straining, heaving, in an equation that never altered.

"That's our Messiah, out there, if we can get to its heart and head," said Ben Blakely, startling Morag back into awareness.

"What? Where . . . what are you talking about?"

"That. . . ." He pointed. "The tower."

"The green tower?"

He nodded. "Not so much the tower, but the thing inside it. If I could get to the Primary . . . if *we* could reach that damned hybrid we could find a way out of this place. I hate that thing . . . yet we can't exist without it, can we?"

TWO

Underneath the city was a wormery of tunnels, ducts, channels and drains. Filling these voids were jungles of silver pipes, black cables, wires, tubes: the city's life support system, that spread outward from the torso of the Primary like the roots of a giant tree. This underworld pulsed and hummed, gurgled and gasped, crackled, hissed and spat: restless, ever-working, playing catch-me-if-you-can with light and darkness. Along this fiber rippled bright data to a secondary computer; through that tube ran the chemical agent feeding the brain of the central computer itself; down these pipes, all twisting, turning, interlocking, and fanning out, traveled the threads of electricity that burned in the heater screens. Beneath the mesh of the Primary's multiform limbs and extremities, a geothermal borehole dropped to the core of the planet, where the contained heat of a captive star was sapped of its energy and transformed into a hundred different varieties of dancing electrons before transmission. Morag knew of this magic *Unterwelt* and of its importance in her life but it had less significance for her than the men and women that controlled it through the central brain.

"Why should I want to know who the five are?" she said in response to a question from Ben Blakely. She stared out at the weak, roof-corner lamps on the opposite building and noticed how the mortar around them had spidery plants clinging to it which gave the lamps green ruffs.

"I should have thought everyone wanted to know the answer to that question. If we knew one of the five people that maintained the Primary . . . well, then we'd have the key to power. Perhaps to freedom. . . ."

Morag looked round into his face, which had suddenly taken on a look of concentration that seemed to age him in the gray light.

She said, "You want me to find one of the five, take the key to the green tower and let you in, so that you can melt the ice cone, allowing us all to enter the outworld?" She smiled sarcastically. "That it?"

Ben frowned. "Of course not." He pulled his hood back from his head in frustration and she could see that his hair was as dark as his skin, except for one small streak of white at the temple. She fixed her gaze on this hoary lock, knowing she could intimidate him without words. She was skilled at inflating the male ego and consequently she was also expert at deflating it. She saw his hand touch the spot, almost involuntarily. Then she felt ashamed of herself because this man . . . well, he seemed to arouse a feeling of tenderness in her for some reason. He was not like the clients she had to face occasionally, he was more . . . more like her father. He had had that same appealing, sad look which had raised protective emotions in her breast as a small child. Somehow, then, she had known her father was destined for a premature death. He was the kind of man that had his fate stamped on his features and wore it in his demeanor. A snout of ice had crushed both parents when a heater screen failed one night. Although she had been an adopted child her love for her father had been as strong as that of any blood-related infant. Not that Ben Blakely would necessarily die young: he just had the same sort of attractive love-need in his aspect.

"What are you looking at?" he said.

"Nothing. You have an interesting face, that's all. Look, how am I supposed to help you? What do you want from me?"

"I need . . . we have to find a way, an entrance to the tower. Listen . . . I know one of the five. I know his name. I know his face. I've tried following him but somehow I always lose him. He's gifted at slipping away into nowhere—and I have to walk some way behind him, otherwise he might realize and that would be the end of it—or me. I know which food hall he visits. You could . . ."

Morag did not hear the words that followed. She had had a sudden realization and it formed in her mind like cold clay. Surely not? He was on his own . . . they usually traveled in twos and threes. That's how you learned to recognize them on the streets. Two or three young people with intent looks on their faces and murder in their hearts. You learned to sense that air of unease about them. Perhaps it was in the body odor or the look in their eyes? They carried their intent around with them like a badge of office, in the way they walked and moved: quick, jerky actions, but deliberate, full of self-conscious gestures. The adrenaline, the fear-bloodlust sweat, gave their movements that well-oiled rapidity of street killers.

"You're not . . . an Angel? Or a Speaknot?" she said, praying silently to herself that he was not either, not an anarchist assassin who killed at random, hoping that one day the victim would be one of the five. Hoping? Not all of them: some of them just enjoyed the deadly game of taking life by the rule of chance. They enjoyed sinking their daggers into the flesh of some poor innocent passerby and would find the game at an end if they succeeded in accomplishing the organization's aim.

He stared at her without answering and she knew that words were unnecessary.

"You *fool*," she said, shaking her head. "Either a fool, or sick."

"Not any more," he replied in a quiet voice. "The others in my cell were caught. I didn't have a contact. I was left adrift.

I was recruited in Thieves' Market but when I returned to the place no one approached me. I think they'd abandoned me—or maybe changed their recruiting point. They'd have to do that wouldn't they . . . ?"

"What group *do* you belong to then? No, don't tell me. I don't want to know." Morag threw herself onto some blankets in a corner of the room. She was exhausted. "Do you mind if I sleep a little now? I'm very tired. Do you want me to leave now? Because I'm not sure I'm going to help you. I don't want you to think just because I sleep here . . ."

"I told you earlier. I didn't invite you here for anything but to talk."

"Can we do it later? Right now I'm about to drop off the edge of the world. I've been awake . . . I don't know how long." With that, she closed her eyes. She could hear him breathing, softly, as she drifted off into sleep. His eyes were still on her: she could feel them. There was no movement from him. He was just standing, watching. . . .

She felt a movement beside her and suddenly she was wide awake. He had joined her, had covered both of them in blankets and his arms were around her, holding her to him. She was irritated and annoyed that he should take advantage of her weariness.

"Don't touch me," she snapped.

Instantly, he sat up. "I'm sorry." His voice sounded confused. "It was a way to keep us both warm. I didn't think you would mind."

Morag's face burned: partly from annoyance and partly because she was embarrassed at her own reaction. Irrationally, she moved away from him in case he sensed her chagrin at having acted so foolishly. The feeling of having his arms around her had not been unenjoyable and perhaps it was that which caused her to behave so primly? She did not want him to know—not yet—that she found him attractive. He might use such a situation to benefit his cause, rather than respond because of a natural rapport between them. She wanted to be liked for herself rather than for what she had to offer in the way of aid.

"I'm aware that you don't . . . prostitute your body. I understand that you have a special gift—you can allow people into your mind. It's why I contacted you. Why I would like us to work together. Those other common . . ."

She interrupted him with a flash of temper.

"*Don't*. Don't call my friends *common*. They're as good as you and I, and they use whatever skills are available to them in order to survive. I hardly think someone of your ilk—a street killer—has any right to call my friends *common*."

Again, a look of pain passed over his face. His dark eyes seemed to be reaching out for sympathy and understanding. It was difficult for her to remain angry. Her tempers came in protective flashes, instinctively, but they disappeared as swiftly as they arrived and left her feeling at a disadvantage. He seemed so eager to understand *her* and his tolerance was almost irritating.

"Forgive me. I didn't mean to use the word in that sense. I meant that you were special. What's it like . . . the experience? Fascinating, I should think, allowing someone inside your head."

"For the clients perhaps—not for me."

"I see—you feel violated?"

She did not answer. She was thinking of the last time she had let a client's psyche inside her head. He had immediately begun running her hands over her slim form, enjoying the sensation of feeling a woman while being that woman. Her own psyche had remained alongside the violator's, not part of it, but close enough to experience the prurient thought waves. Even after many years of such treatment, these occasional unfortunate choices of clients left her feeling nauseous. His thoughts guided her fingers and her nerves reached screaming point as they sought out her most intimate parts. Afterward she had wanted to kick his smirking face into an expression which would satisfy her loathing but he left quickly and she took her frustration out on the wall, leaving her knuckles bruised and bleeding.

Some of them were not like that of course. Some of them were like little frightened sparrows that just sat there, in her consciousness, and waited timidly to make contact with her psyche. Others retreated almost as soon as they had entered, terrified of going any farther.

"This man you want me to meet," she said. "How do you know he'll want to ... experience me. Not all men want to, you know. Most men prefer a straight sexual experience. Perhaps one of the other girls would be more use to you?"

He stared at her with those dark, damp eyes. What was he thinking of now? Whether *he* would enjoy such an experience?

"He's an old man. You could be right, but I don't think so. We'll have to take the chance. I won't blame you if it doesn't work. We can only give it a try. There is ... another reason why I wanted it to be you." He seemed uncomfortable.

"What?"

"I'm fed up with working alone. I wanted company. I hate being alone, Morag. I think you do too. I would like to know you better—you have a kind of dignity which I find attractive. I think we could learn a lot from each other."

She was suddenly abashed. For the moment he was the teacher and she the pupil. No longer did he seem insecure. She felt his authority, his confidence, like a physical presence in the room.

"Now," he continued, briskly. "How does it work?" Since she had been an adolescent she had been trying to explain her technique to men like Ben Blakely—no, perhaps not like Ben Blakely, for he seemed to have a little more understanding than the men she was used to.

"It's something like visiting a timesmith—firstly, I make eye contact with the client and then ... well, I just allow him into my mind. I can't really explain how it works exactly. I have to concentrate on letting him in."

"So it must be your receptivity that's unique."

"Not unique. Rare. I'm not a freak. There must be others."

"Don't be so defensive. All right, you have the power not only to contact another mind but to allow that mind to enter your own." He shook his head slowly. "Such a gift—and you use it in the oldest profession."

"Some of us haven't got anything else," she said angrily. Who was this dark little man to think he could censure her way of life; become her mentor; *use* her, like a thing without a will of its own?

"Please," he said. "I don't mean to keep offending you. This is *important*—to both of us. To the city. To everyone. We've got to get at the secret to the tower. The Five are using us to maintain their position of power. They rule us through the central brain. . . . Tell me, were your parents . . . did either of them have this skill you possess? Perhaps they were time-smiths? Were they?"

"No," she answered, quietly.

"Well, it's a wonderful gift in any event. One that might help us out of this hell, and get outside to . . . well, to whatever lies *out there*. I've heard there are things called *trees*, ten times as tall as a man, with solid stems and branches so thick with leaves that light can't pass between them. Collectively, these trees are called forests and cover vast areas of land . . . doesn't that conjure up a beautiful picture? Green forests?"

"Not to me," she said. "I can't think of anything worse myself."

"What's your favorite theory then?" he asked eagerly. "An ocean of saltwater? Mountains?"

The stories of the outside world were many and varied— almost everyone in the city had his or her own version. Some said that there was nothing but tundra: snowy wastes that stretched as far as the eye could see, unbroken except for the occasional mountain of ice. These were people who had found an excuse for staying inside because they had lost all hope of ever escaping. To create in their minds a worse situation on the outside was to improve conditions on the inside; one should be grateful for what one has and appreciate the mere gift of life, however harsh its privations.

Then there were those who nurtured the antithesis of this dismal picture. They believed in deserts of hot sand. They thought that the city was high up on a tall mountain range, but once you descended from that place you would find parched, arid wasteland which could not support life and burned your skin as effectively as one of the screen heaters attached to the corners of the buildings. These people, too, saw no reason to leave their relatively hospitable environment which at *least* sustained life to a certain degree.

Both these groups were minor.

Those who preferred to dream of escape had visions of lands flowing with warm water, with grassy banks of hills covered in flowers such as those one saw when the vegetables were allowed to go to seed by the central computer. Others considered they were only one small part, a forgotten neglected part, of a single vast city that stretched out into infinity in all directions; that their little patch was a ghetto which had been sealed off from the rest to prevent contamination. If they could get out, into the city proper, they could partake of its social and economic advantages.

As for their pre-settlement history, there was general belief in the legend that First City was not their natural home, that they—their ancestors—had been led to that place, either because of banishment from a better home, or migration from a worse one. Since no one could imagine a worse place than First City and most confessed to vague feelings of *guilt*, a racial inheritance of wrongdoing, there was general acceptance of First City as an instrument of punishment. This also obviated responsibility for self-imposed torture. Someday, they said to themselves, someone would come along and lead them from bondage. In the meantime they had to suffer—and wait.

"I'd prefer to keep my theory to myself," Morag said. "Perhaps some time later I'll tell you what I think. Anyway, we'll see it all soon enough. When a Messiah comes."

The black hair with its white streak bobbed before her. Frustrations filled the voice of its owner, and the symbols of his tattooed name wrinkled on his cheeks.

"There won't be a Messiah, you . . . don't you realize? It's just another one of Raxonberg's tricks to keep us here, waiting.

We should *act*, not play games. While we all sit here, hanging around for some kind of leader to emerge, the Chief of Trysts is laughing quietly up his own nose. Those who control the Primary are laughing up *theirs*. While *we* . . . we just sit around waiting for some miracle to happen. Look, this is real. . . . " He kicked the wall hard. "That ice out there is real. *We're* real. A Messiah is just *fantasy*."

She lifted her chin and said with quiet dignity, "I prefer fantasy."

THREE

The Chief of Trysts, Raxonberg, left his bed early that morning. Although he was missing one arm, the right one, he dressed expertly, arranging his toga in folds that would hide his hated stump. Then he breakfasted on cereals grown in the farm halls. He lived well, but then he did control the population of First City—not the city itself, which the central brain had mastery over, but the people within it. So long as they *stayed* within it. Which was why his predecessors had outlawed attempted escapes from the city. The Chief of Trysts was a position of power, held through fear, and if someone found a way out of the city, that authority would disappear. It was a necessary fear. One could not rule First City with promises of a better future: there was no better future, as history had shown, because *now* was someone else's future and it had not changed in half a thousand years. Not since the founding of the city. When you cannot rule by promise, you have to rule with an iron fist.

Raxonberg had not always been as hard and single-minded as he felt now. There had been a time, far back in his youth, when he felt a sympathy toward his fellow creatures that had inspired his need to rule. He had wanted to change the pattern set by other tyrants and offer the people a better life; a softer, more gentle environment in which to raise their children. Somehow he had lost that empathic connection with his contemporaries, in his struggle to reach the top. Finally, when he was *there*, at the peak, he found it such a precarious position, fraught with peril, that the tough, unfeeling attitude imposed by the climb could not be dispensed with. It was only through strength and fear that the post of Chief Tryst could be held with security. The people needed a leader and if that leader had to relinquish the finer feelings, the niceties of compassion and mercy, in order to remain in power, so be it. Stability was the important thing. He clung to that philosophy with a hand and heart of stone.

Raxonberg would have liked to have had access to the Green Tower, partly because it annoyed him that a group of people, the five that had keys to the tower and its one residential occupant, was beyond his reach, and partly because it was the one area outside his control. Audience with the central brain would also *insure* that he continued in office. Control over the people *and* the city . . . now that would be *power*. Greater than his ability to detect lies or the gift of being able to anticipate the intentions of his enemies. As it was, some young blade would eventually kill him and take over, when he became too old or unwary. The Five remained elusive, as they had always been: a secret society which no Tryst Chief had ever been able to infiltrate.

After breakfast he called for his sedan chair. It was time to do an inspection of the markets. He and his force of trysts were the lawkeepers, the thieftakers, the guardians of the unwritten laws of conduct.

The chair arrived along with two carriers and an escort of six of Raxonberg's most trusted men and women. They carried heavy clubs fashioned, like the sedan chair, from a synthetic material called shod, which the secondary computers manufactured.

"Let's move," said Raxonberg, settling in his chair. The six escorts trotted beside the chair as they made their way through the cold, damp streets. People were just beginning to emerge from the buildings, long-faced and gray-skinned despite the sun lamps that were perched on the corners of the blocks.

One of the trysts, the Head, gave Raxonberg her early report and he read it as they moved along.

"We have been informed by one of our people that an attempt will be made to scale the south face of the cone today. . . ."

Raxonberg frowned. These foolish people and their attempts to escape from the city. They surely knew it was an impossible feat. Why did they keep trying? Of course he discouraged it. If he did not, hundreds of would-be escape artists would die every year. Even if one made it, what then? Would he or she magically dispense with the ice once outside? Of course not. Everyone else would still be trapped within and would become even more dissatisfied because someone *had* managed to get outside. The hundreds would become thousands and pretty soon the place would become littered with those who died in the attempt. Such a waste of time. Such a waste of life. Better that the odd one be executed to discourage the rest. Raxonberg was a believer in taking life in order to preserve it. It was all a matter of numbers . . . destroy one to save a thousand. Of course, the citizens of the city would not see it that way, and he would always be the bogey-man to the public. Not that it worried him unduly, so long as he could justify the situation to himself.

And what of the great outside? It was Raxonberg's personal theory that the ice wall was a defense: that outside their *protective* citadel was a world of chaos, a wild land full of poisonous plants, terrible beasts and races of men that delighted in slaughter and the subjection of fellow creatures. Long ago his ancestors had retreated far from the madness and horror of continual strife and had fashioned the wall of ice to keep out such terror. There were giants out there, and creatures of immense strength bristling with teeth, claws and horns. There were spiders that spat venom; long, limbless creatures called serpents that crushed people to pulp with their coils; vicious dwarves and malicious fairies. There were creatures called horses that could bite a man's head clean from his shoulders and birds that carried babies off in their talons. There were rivers of blood and bile, and bleak, desolate wastelands where half-men swam through dense, foul-smelling air with turgid bodies looking for carrion on which to feast. The very landscape was alive with millions of insect-eating rocks; peppered with holes that sucked you down to slimy depths far below the earth; covered with crawling, shapeless lumps of fleshy carnivores, with jaws of steel, that waited to catch a person's foot, to sever it instantly and masticate the stolen extremity with vile pleasure. He, Raxonberg, was helping to protect the people of First City from such terrors.

Raxonberg went first to Middle and then to Thieves' Market on the East side of the city. All seemed reasonably quiet. There had not been a large disturbance in the city for at least a year now. Raxonberg did not want to keep it that way. It was not in his own interests to allow for the peaceful purchase and barter of goods. He had to be seen to be doing his job as peacekeeper and thieftaker. Otherwise the population might start believing they had no use for him.

He stopped the chair and alighted next to his Head Tryst.

"If a riot doesn't flare up within the next few months, we'd better organize one ourselves. The trysts need a good workout from time to time. They'll get fat and lazy. What's happening over there?"

Raxonberg pointed toward a commotion that had suddenly broken out on the far side of the square. A number of people were jostling one another and voices had been raised above the general hubbub of the market. The Head Tryst waved her truncheon at two of the escorts and they dutifully waded through the crowded aisles to reach the now brawling group. They returned, dragging the limp body of a man and with a sullen young girl in tow.

"Well?" Raxonberg snapped.

"He wouldn't come peaceful. We had to give him a couple of taps with the sticks. They was thieving. Both of them. A bolt of cloth." Raxonberg studied the girl. She was dressed in a tattered toga which would not be enough to keep her warm when the temperature fell, as it so often did. Why did these people keep testing his authority? It was distasteful when situations like this arose, because he had to make decisions which made him appear unfeeling, both to himself and the populace. However, order had to be maintained and there was no question that she would have to be punished. He could not have his position flouted under his very nose or he would soon lose his hold over his trysts. They did not understand flexibility, as expressed by mercy or tolerance; they understood only rigid laws and the necessity to keep them to the letter. Anything else confused them. He was as hard with his own people as he was with the public and his attitudes towards street crime must be seen to be unbending.

"The computers make the cloth," said the girl. "There's plenty of it. More than everyone needs. Why do they have to sell it? We're cold. And no money, I've just got these rags to . . ."

"Quiet!" said Raxonberg. He suddenly felt the need to explain. In softer tones, he added, "Don't you see, child, the economy would collapse if everyone just *took* what they wanted? We must control the resources or there would be chaos. If there was, as you say, *more* than enough for everyone, there would be oversupply and no demand. People would not strive, would do no work. Apathy would follow. Don't you see?"

The girl remained silent but there was a trace of fear on her face. Raxonberg guessed her age to be around sixteen years. Her name, he read, was Nell Neadam. She was quite harmless but she would have to be punished. It was unfortunate that she was so young, but he could not be seen to be weak. Especially in front of his own people.

He jabbed the prone man with his foot.

"Throw him in the cells," he said, "and give her a few strokes of the whip."

"No!" shouted the girl. "Please."

"I'm sorry, child," he said, then climbed back into the sedan chair. Despite his resolve, he risked a small aberration. "Afterward, she may keep the cloth. She'll have earned it and I'm not a monster. What's the man to you?" he said through the window.

"My father," whimpered the girl. "Please. . . ."

He felt the chair rise and soon he was back in the streets. A funeral party was just returning from the wall, the priest in the lead. They were walking slowly, heavily. Gray people in a gray world. The ice claims us all, sooner or later, he thought, and it can have me—but not before I'm ready to join it. Not before I'm ready. From orphan to Chief Tryst: it had not been easy. He was entitled to enjoy his position for as long as he was able, for as long as he had the strength of body and mind.

The worn, smooth stones of the street were wet and slippery and occasionally one of his carriers stumbled, fighting desperately to keep the chair stable. The walls of the buildings were almost within touching distance on either side of the chair and a sense of peace and well-being crept through Raxonberg. He liked enclosed spaces—they made him feel closeted, protected, secure. The straight, narrow streets; the thin, high alleys, almost like fissures in the ice—he knew them all. Citizens had to flatten themselves against the damp buildings as his chair passed and he was not ashamed to say that it gave him a sense of power, that it inflated his ego.

The chair passed a building which was in a state of collapse and Raxonberg made a note to get some builders in that quarter as soon as possible. He hated dereliction. Someone would have to clean up the mess, rebuild the block, straighten out *his* city. After all, wasn't accommodation one of their biggest problems? Could they afford to let buildings crumble into decay? He would send a sharp message to the civil administrators that day. They were slipping, allowing his city to fall around their ears. How could anyone look on the naked, untidy edge of a collapsed wall, at the molar blocks of stone scattered at its foot, without a sense of distaste disturbing their thoughts?

FOUR

Ben Blakely's father, so Morag learned, had been one of those gifted people without whom life in First City would have been intolerable. He had been a *timesmith*, a rare profession with an elite membership. Those who could afford the services of these men and women, within whose hands *time* was as malleable as copper, could escape from their environment to a dreamworld for as long as the treatment lasted. Morag had visited her favorite timesmith as often as money would permit. She had looked into his eyes and allowed herself to be swept away in a torrent of seconds, or had been wafted on slow, windblown hours, drifted up and over the ice-peaks of harsh todays, into strange tomorrows or yesterdays.

The timesmiths: men and women with eyes like pools of quicksilver and voices that carried dreams which flowed through the mind as warm undercurrents through an ocean of cold water. Although Morag was aware that in certain aspects her own gift was similar to that of the timesmiths, she valued it less and venerated them above all other citizens. In their hypnotic hands was the means of escape, if only for a short period of time, from the misery of First City. She often wondered: do time-smiths go to timesmiths? Were they so blasé about their own secrets that they could not be helped themselves, like the professional cook who dislikes food? Or could they look beyond their own jaded effusions and allow entrance to their minds by one of their colleagues? After all, each one seemed to have a different technique, an individual approach. Some of them were effulgent, radiating gentle power with the softness of a lamp; others entered like the blast of a strong wind, exhilarating and charged with electric force. The timesmiths were props to the collective sanity of the city. Without them the whole place would be an asylum of wailing lunatics looking for release valves in the complete abandonment of reason. Even long after visiting a timesmith the afterglows of the dream gave her something to cling to in moments of stress.

At one time she had even taken one of them as a lover, though his code would not allow him to provide free treatment, even to his most intimate friends. Yet, she could swear that while they made love sometimes, he had transported her to one of those *other* worlds, though he always claimed that it was merely the ecstasy of sexual union that had been responsible for such moments. Eventually he told her that their love was interfering with his work—that he was losing his talent, his gift, in the backwash of intense emotion. She was draining his magic with her almost religious adoration of his body and mind. They parted for good.

Ben had not inherited the genius of his father's mind. He could not mold time for the unfortunate inhabitants of the city and, disillusioned, had left his parents at the age of fifteen. He saw them occasionally but only to pass civilities. Ben's father had since ceased to practice, except for very rare private sessions. He was blind now, Ben explained, but strangely the affliction had not destroyed the skill of the old timesmith. He could still transport his closest friends from behind those blind orbs, into places of fantasy: take them into a country of the mind where the days would slip and slide, would fold, would stretch, would twist into Möbius bands that looped forever and ever . . . until that moment when the brain went *snap* and the client found himself or herself standing on a drab, gray street corner with a bleak outlook.

The son of the blind timesmith had taken various temporary jobs until, at the age of twenty-two, Ben Blakely had been the newest recruit in an anarchist cell of three. He was the only survivor of an official tryst raid on an apartment in the third sector. His compatriots, among them the senior member of the cell who was the contact man, had been put to death. Thus Ben Blakely found himself alone, without access to the main group. For a time he expected, waited, to be contacted, but perhaps his cell leader had recruited him without reference to higher authority, because no one ever called on him. Soon it became obvious that he was not known to the inner party.

Operations continued in various parts of the city but Ben Blakely only heard about these from the Street Shouters. Finally he gave up waiting.

He began operating on his own and during this period gradually realized he had contempt for the methods of his former group. He found them crude. The philosophy of cutting a swath through the population was a moronic approach to the problem of obtaining a key to the Green Tower. He formulated a new method. He advertised.

Ben Blakely's advertisement consisted of six words and a number. It said: THAT WHICH WAS LOST IS FOUND: (APARTMENT) 810. He had it placed on the notice board in Middle Market. The number was not the number of his apartment. He had chosen it at random.

He waited, just inside the office which administered the notice board, and after three days was rewarded. A tall, thin man entered to inquire at the grille as to the name of the person who had placed the FOUND advertisement. Ben Blakely had used a small boy off the street as his middleman and the thin gentleman left the office with a puzzled expression on his face, but not before Ben Blakely had read the birth marks on his cheeks. The tattoos had read: *Felix Feverole*.

"But what does it all mean?" asked Morag.

"The Five, you understand. The Five. Look, I'll explain what happened. You know at one time most of the city was covered in graffiti—Raxonberg had it all removed, all except the bits on the long hut which are so deeply engraved you'd have to dismantle the place—well, anyway, in an old apartment I rented a while ago I was leaning on the washbasin, you know, to shave, when the whole thing suddenly collapsed, came away from the wall. Behind it I found some very old graffiti—must have been there for centuries. One of these graffiti said: "WHO ARE THE SIX? WHY DO THEY KEEP US IN IGNORANCE?"

"Don't you see? We believe there are only five . . . and possibly that's correct—but at one time there were six. *What happened to the sixth key?*"

"Surely, though, we've always been told there are five. The Ruling Five."

"Keys. It began with the number of keys. The natural assumption, that there was one man to each key, followed later. But there must have been six keys, in the beginning, only one of them was lost. I led them to believe I had found it."

"And they tried to track you down. You knew they would."

He looked pleased. Morag, however, was feeling less than secure. This man—this terrorist—had told her all about himself. Until now, Raxonberg's trysts had not concerned themselves with her—but if she became mixed up with this anarchist, they might begin to find her *interesting*. It was a word the trysts used a lot—*interesting*—and it had terrible undertones.

"I'd like to go for a walk," she said, in a calm voice. "Alone. I want to think a little."

Ben Blakely cocked his head to one side and a sad-looking smile crooked the corner of his mouth.

"You know that's not possible, Morag. Later we can both go." He reached into his pocket and produced a folding stiletto, showing it to her.

"I don't want to hurt you but you know I will if I have to. This is important to me. Please . . . no running away. I need you."

She regarded his earnest face and, after a long interval,

nodded. Ben Blakely folded the rust-pitted blade, very carefully, into its handle.

She walked around the room, staring down at the thick carpet of blankets which covered the floor. Her stomach was making urgent signals to her.

"When do we eat?" she asked.

"Later," he replied. "We'll go to the halls."

Her eyebrows lifted, despite her wish to be inscrutable. Anyone who ate at the halls must command a good salary. The price of one meal there would buy seven at the soup palaces.

"You must have a high position—in the service."

"In the service? Oh, the clothes. No, I stole these, just as I stole disks which will buy us the meal. One thing I learned with the Speaknots—if you have to kill for political reasons, why not rob at the same time? To leave anything behind is a waste. Besides, it makes it harder for the trysts to identify the body when it's naked."

Morag looked down at her feet in revulsion.

"All these blankets—they're the togas of murdered people?"

"For the sake of the cause," he said, simply.

A few minutes later, he told her he wanted to enter her mind, as a test.

"We can't do it here," she said, fighting down her disappointment in him for being just another man. "I can't concentrate in enclosed spaces. We'll have to find an alley. . . ."

This was a lie but she was afraid of what might happen when they had finished. She had had clients who became so excited by the transfer that they attempted to rape her afterward. In a public place she would at least be within shouting distance of help.

"Then we'll find one near to the halls."

He took her arm before unlocking the door to the hallway. "Remember what I told you," he said.

They went down to the street. It was a little colder than when they had entered the block some nine hours earlier but the change was not significant. Both of them instinctively looked up as a giant fallberg struck the stargirders that protected the canopy from breakaway ice. It slid noisily along the channeling to come to rest in the high boundary gutters, some two kilometers away. Ice hardly ever penetrated the canopy except in narrow splinters which passed almost soundlessly between the girders, but the occasional thunder of a great fallberg breaking away from the lip to smash with reverberating violence on the stargirders, still had streetwalkers jumping into doorways.

To get to the halls they had to pass through Middle Market with its stalls selling togas, knives, a mild manufactured drug called *rift* which gave the taker a feeling of detachment plus a sensation of falling slowly through open space, certain games and crude musical instruments made from shod and gut, and various other paraphernalia from apartment dwellers cleaning house, mostly unwanted junk. The stall owners were calling out descriptions of their wares in unenthusiastic, desultory voices. There were children all over the place, sitting propped against walls or stall legs, or playing running games among the buyers and sellers. Children had indomitable spirits up to a certain age—their only cares were avoiding work and keeping in with their peers. An unhappy child was one whose parents refused to let it out to play or who was for some reason ostracized by its playmates. There came a time, of course, when they left that world behind and joined the defeated adults in their struggle for survival.

From the market they passed back into the lean alleys with their staring occupants: hollow-faced, sexless people begging food disks in soft, insistent voices. They were like phantoms, whispering dead, and Morag was only too aware of the short step from carefree childhood to starvation and disease—a step that was fashioned of apathy and despair. It was not that there were not enough food disks for all, or that some received more and others less. It was simply a case of how they were used; apathy demanded a timesmith, or drugs, or *something*. . . .

They found a narrow alley beside the halls and sat opposite each other.

"Like this," Morag said, and crossed her legs, placing her

hands in her lap. "Brace your back against the wall because you won't be in control of your body. You'll . . . fall asleep."

Ben did as he was told without question.

"Now, look into my eyes. Look hard. That's it. Drown in them. Can you feel yourself falling? Don't worry, don't worry. . . ." Her voice was barely audible now and she felt herself drifting, though she did not lose contact with her surroundings, as Ben would do shortly. Suddenly his body slumped forward slightly, though his eyes remained on hers.

He was pressing, curiously, against her mind. There were moments of probing from both parties. Neuroses were exchanged and she felt the shock impact upon his psyche. She was relieved, for she was accustomed to bloodying her brain with the mess of another's psychogenic disorders, a nihilism often keener than knives.

The two minds skirted each other, warily, before joining. There was an innocence about him which surprised her, since he had professed to be so worldly, and she warmed to him, realizing how vulnerable he was. She felt him exploring her own personality, curious yet full of wonder, and she allowed him closer than any man or woman had yet been. They had a rapport she had not believed possible and there was something else there, almost indefinable, which she knew would grow between them. A kind of dance ensued, wherein one would reveal a secret in exchange for another. *This is how I feel. These are my fears, my hopes, my loves, my hates. Here lies my guilt. There is my sorrow and here my joy.* Was this really a man who could kill in cold blood without compunction? Then she felt him touch a dark area of her mind, a hidden strength she alone knew she possessed, and he began to retreat in confusion. She reached for him, wanting him back, but he was afraid. He fell steadily backwards as she advanced. . . .

His head snapped up and he looked about him wildly.

"It's all right," she said. "It's over."

He stared at her for a moment, then said, "I'm exhausted. Mentally. It's . . . tiring, isn't it?"

"Yes . . . and that's the very last time I'm ever going to do it."

"Except with this man I've found," said Ben.

She did not answer him.

"Why the sudden decision?" he asked, after a moment.

She decided to tell him the truth.

"Because . . . because I *enjoyed* it. That's the first time I've felt pleasure from it and it frightens me. Perhaps I'll get to like it so much I won't be able to do without it. I don't want to become like that."

"I think you're exaggerating. Still, it's up to you. *I* certainly didn't enjoy it. We must get our man, though. You promised— I'm sure you won't enjoy it with *him*."

She took a deep breath. All her instincts told her to back out quickly but there was something about Ben . . . well, she did not want to lose him. Not yet.

"I'll do it," she said.

He was pleased. "Good, excellent. It'll work, I'm sure."

His boyish enthusiasm amused her.

She smiled. "How did it feel, then? To be a woman? Do you know the secret of life now?"

They were standing, walking toward the alley exit.

He stopped her, took her arm, and looked up into her eyes.

"I'll be quite frank. It didn't feel any different—no different from being a man."

"That's right."

"But I thought you said . . . Those other men. The ones who pay you. They do it for the unique sensation of *being* a woman."

"It's purely psychological. They're expecting something— so it happens. God knows *what* they feel, except my tits some-times—but of course that's physical. They're still themselves, not me."

"Why do you degrade yourself with words like that?"

"Words like what?" She laughed into his face. He was a puritan, as well as a killer. No wonder his guilt had flushed through her brain while they had been together.

"It depends upon what they're being used for. If some pervert is pawing them, they're tits. If I was feeding a baby, they'd be breasts."

"If I use a knife to loosen a screw, it's still a knife, not a screwdriver."

"What is it when you use it to cut food?"

"A knife."

"Wrong. In the first instance, it's a piece of cutlery and in the second—a murder weapon. You use labels as words of convenience to escape the truth—try broadening your vocabulary and you might just escape from the barrier you hide behind."

"Come on. Let's eat," he snapped.

The food halls were located on the ground floor below the civil service apartments: a large, open-plan area, the ceiling of which was supported by thick pillars. They collected the dishes of brightly colored vegetables from the counter. She devoured the food, her hunger overcoming her desire to prevent him from seeing her need. As she ate he observed his self-respect returning by degrees. The roundness gradually disappeared from his shoulders, until he was sitting straight and haughty once more, glowering at those who sat near so that they edged away. She was conscious of the physical strength that emanated from his broad frame. The knife was a threat, certainly, but it was merely a symbol of his violent nature. He could kill her very easily without it.

He ate his own food slowly, his eyes flicking this way and that: now on her face, now on the entrance, now following some stranger. Surely they can all see, she thought, that this man is antistate? To her he was transparent. He was the very caricature of a terrorist. The pale-black, brooding face and the nervous disposition were, to her, the obvious outward symptoms of a decaying soul, which even the most unobservant of human beings could not fail to recognize. But people passed by, with only a casual glance, if any at all. She alone was the recipient of those silent cries for attention.

When they had finished they left the halls. On exiting, Morag heard someone whisper a name to a friend. The Messiah?

Would he reveal himself soon? They needed him. He would lead them from the ice.

"Did you hear that?" she whispered to Ben Blakely. "The name."

"I heard it," he said, "but it means nothing. Just another word. When I was a boy they were whispering someone else's name. It came to nothing. There are no magicians in this life. You have to rely on ingenuity, not miracles."

There was water in the streets, which froze their feet as it swirled around their ankles. Somewhere nearby a borehole was blocked.

"Let's walk into the city center," she suggested. "We can stroll arm in arm, like lovers. And I can tell you how much I hate you, but with a smile on my face to deceive passersby. And you can take my hand and grip it hard, until the knuckles turn white and begin to crack—but smile back at me sweetly, and they will believe we are lost in each other's eyes."

"Don't be stupid," he said.

"Why not? You like intrigue, don't you? You enjoy conspiracy and parading lies as truths? Let's do it . . ."

He brought her up short with a quick jerk of his arm and the words caught in her throat. They stood, with the meltwater cutting into their feet like cold razors, until he said, "Stop playing games with me. This is a serious business."

"Not if I say it isn't," she said. "Not if I make a joke of it. If I can laugh while you stick that knife into my belly, it's still a silly game, and the more serious you try to make it, the more ludicrous it becomes, because ridicule *always* wins. Haven't you learned *that* yet?"

He stared at her, helplessly, and she saw the confusion in his expression.

"You have to persuade me, not lecture or threaten. I need to be convinced. Threatening me won't save your cause from contempt." She touched his cheek with her hand. "I like you, Ben, but I find you just a little foolish."

He jerked his head away from her hand. She could tell from his expression that she had wounded him and she felt ashamed of herself. Why did she do these things. She *did* like him. Why taunt him so much? Was she so perverse she could not have a normal relationship with a man without trying to bring him down?

"I don't need you," he said. "I can find another woman. I should leave you now."

Morag splashed toward him. She took hold of his toga. "Come on," she said. "Another woman won't do for you, and you know it."

His face remained impassive for a while; then he took her arm and they walked together along the street. Morag suddenly felt possessive without being able to identify the cause within herself. Sometimes, she thought, these emotions spring from the heart without warning. But what did one do with such feelings? Inwardly enjoy them? Outwardly display them? Or just ignore them?

They passed the Green Tower and Ben stared at its obsidian-smooth walls with a grim expression on his face.

"One day soon, I'll get inside," he murmured.

And she believed him.

FIVE

Morag returned to the apartment with Ben Blakely and remained there with him for three days, venturing out only for food. They talked a lot, discovering more about each other hour by hour. Ben, she found, was a crustacean— hard on the outside with a soft, spongy center. He was easily hurt and defended himself petulantly against criticism. She tested this vulnerability occasionally, to try to discover its source, and found that it lay in a lack of confidence. Her probing almost went too far, almost had him turning on her. However, he licked his wounds and came back for more, which she regarded as a strength, not a weakness. He, in turn, was able to extract more of herself than any man before him. She tried to protect herself against revealing too much by hiding behind questions.

"What do *you* think my upbringing was like? Do you believe I'm a child of the streets or do you think I had parents who cared for me until some tragic event came between us?"

"I don't really know which it is, Morag, because either way you are what you are—a woman capable of deep feelings, deep relationships."

He was gentle in *his* probings, not squeezing too hard, hoping the drops could be coaxed from her heart without the need to force them out. He stroked her, psychologically, building up her confidence in herself. They were as two weak characters, using each other to strengthen their personalities into a single, common unit which shared two bodies.

On the fourth day Blakely went out alone. He was gone for an afternoon and returned in a state of agitated excitement.

"I've found him, Morag. Quickly. He's in a food hall."

Morag had been lying naked, on a pile of blankets. She jumped to her feet and threw on a heavy toga. Then she pulled on her boots.

"Let's go," she said.

They left the apartment and Morag found that Blakely's unvoiced excitement was beginning to permeate her natural barrier of reserve.

"What shall I say to him?" she asked, as they hurried along.

"Anything, just so long as you strike up an acquaintance."

"What if he doesn't respond? What if he doesn't like me?"

"He'll like you."

"But..."

Blakely stopped in his tracks and gripped her arm.

"Look, it's your trade, not mine. Why do you think I'm asking you to do it? If I knew what would hook him, I'd have done it myself." With that statement he almost ruined what three days had built between them. Her anger was spontaneous and helped to dilute what had almost amounted to a betrayal of trust.

"You think that's what it's all about? That we can do tricks with our eyes, our hands, our lips? Bewitch a man? We don't hook *them,* they come to us. I haven't any more idea than you about what will attract him."

Blakely studied her face for a moment and then turned away, seemingly in disgust or annoyance.

"Ben," she said, using his Christian name in order to show she was not angry, "I do believe in you."

He looked back at her, then grabbed her hand.

"Come on then," he said, and they began walking quickly toward the halls.

Had she meant what she said? If not, then why say it? She had come to know the intense, inner Blakely well. He was, at once, both weak and strong—much like any other man. Some of his weaknesses were his strengths. He was passionate and selfless, which gave him his strength of conviction but in turn made him vulnerable to Morag's merciless attacks of sarcasm. He was humorless, which made for poor eloquence but lent his rhetoric honesty and sincerity. He hurt very easily, but whenever Morag took advantage of this, she indirectly wounded herself too. He was logical, which gave his political arguments strength, but his discourses on human nature and humankind were destroyed by Morag's erratic and flexible forays in a territory she knew well. He was responsible, she irresponsible.

Yet, he had won her to his cause, it seemed. Or was it that she had molded him in some way? It might be gratifying to think that such men were hers to manipulate, if he were not Ben. How did *she* look to *him* at that moment? A slag with greasy, matted hair or a beautiful woman with a free spirit? Should she ask him? Fortunately the decision was taken out of her hands. They had arrived at the halls. Ben threaded his way through the crowds of outhangers looking longingly into the place they could not enter without the necessary colored disks. Occasionally, the trysts sauntered over to move them on with the gentle prod of a truncheon. Of course, if any trouble or resistance was encountered, they were less than polite. The trysts were almost all relatives of one another, recruited as they were only from a dozen or so families. Their nepotism had extended to intermarrying, since not many outsiders wanted a tryst for a wife or husband. As a force, they kept the peace, almost.

A shouter came out of the halls, yelling, "Another Speaknot murder on the South Side. Rex Rellear, the timesmith, fell mortally wounded at midday in Thieves' Market. Hear ye, hear ye. Another Speaknot murder. . . ."

Ben brushed past the shouter and stood with his back against the wall, scanning the interior of the halls. Morag pressed up beside him as if they were lovers waiting for a free table where they could sit together.

"Over on the far side," whispered Ben. "The *long* table. A white-haired man sitting a little apart from the others."

She followed Ben's directions and her eyes came to rest on the figure of a slight, intelligent-looking man in his early sixties.

"I see him. The one that's tilting his head now."

"That's him. God, this smell makes me hungry."

"Shall we eat while we're here?"

"I've run out of disks."

Morag said, "I haven't. We can use mine."

He stared at her. "You've only enough for a single meal."

"We can share."

Again, that appraisal of her, as if he was plumbing her for the motive. "I suppose we could sit next to him. Maybe you'll get a chance to talk."

"Good idea. I hadn't thought of that," she said.

He nodded, ignoring her sarcasm, and they made their way to the servery, where they exchanged Morag's disks for a bowl of thick sugarpaste. They took it to the bench where the old man was sitting. He glanced at them casually as they approached and she read his name: Felix Feverole. Ben had to glare at a woman in order to make her move along to give them room. Morag searched her brain for something to say to the man and she could feel her heart racing with the excitement of the moment. Suddenly, it struck her—this was one of the Five. A ruler. A man with a key to the Green Tower. A Keeper of the Central Brain. Yet, he looked no different from any other. More frail perhaps.

"The halls are full tonight," she said.

He looked up.

"I said the halls are crowded."

"They're always crowded."

His voice was deep and resonant. A cultured voice. In confusion she replied, "Yes of course. I just thought . . . there were more than usual."

He looked at her curiously. "I suppose there might be. Why do you tell me? Why not talk to your companion?" He nodded toward Ben Blakely.

"I was just being friendly," Morag said, huffily.

"Are you trying to pick me up, young lady?"

Morag reacted sharply, instinctively: "Go to hell, you old . . . " She stopped, remembering. Ben had his eyes closed, as if in prayer. In the silence that followed, she could hear people around her, chewing noisily. They were staring at her. One didn't come to the halls to talk but to eat. Especially not to talk to strangers. Protocol.

"I'm sorry," she said, lightly. "I'm feeling happy today. . . ."

"How strange."

She ignored this remark. Gritting her teeth, she added, "And a little happiness should be shared. Don't you agree?" A fallberg struck the girders above them and the hall reverberated. People around her gripped their bowls until the tremors had ceased. They kept their eyes on the entertainment.

"Not necessarily. If you don't keep it to yourself, it may be wasted, especially on strange old men. Good day." He stood and moved away from them, sitting at another table halfway along the hall.

"Damn!"

"I'm sorry, Ben."

"You fouled that up, for sure. He suspects us now. Look at him, staring at us."

"He can't do anything to us, can he?"

"That's not the point. Come on, we'll have to try again later. Let's go home."

Home. He called it *home.* She felt ridiculously lightheaded, despite the disastrous afternoon. Ben strode beside her, deep in thought—at least he appeared to be thinking. His handsome brow was etched with lines.

"Ben, you can sleep with me tonight," she said. He studied her face thoughtfully. She saw that her remark had removed her face thoughtfully. She saw that her remark had removed the lines from his brow, though he still had that gray, anxious look. She was suddenly aware of the muted bustle of the streets going on around them and felt slightly uncomfortable under his gaze. A woman with two small children in rags passed by them, giving them a curious glance.

"I was wondering when you'd say that," he said. "But I would have preferred it to sound as if you weren't giving me a present."

"What's that supposed to mean?" Suddenly, she felt as if the dim rays from the blowhole, far above, were directed on just the two of them. They were the center of their world in the ice, beneath the transparent, protective skin of the canopy. She could hear the meltwater swirling around the city, washing away down the boreholes. It was almost as if . . . as if the skin were about to break and deliver them into the outside world.

"It means that you could have phrased your offer in terms that sounded less like a favor."

"Sorry. I meant, of course, that I want to make love with you."

"And I with you." They said nothing else until they had reached the apartment and had each carried out their part of the bargain. Then Ben drifted off to sleep, leaving Morag to stare at the gray-washed ceiling. She was not entirely dissatisfied, though the physical side of it was not yet completely rewarding. The Madam had always maintained that an orgasm was best achieved by first masturbation, second genital manipulation by a partner, and finally, at the bottom of the list, by sexual intercourse. What the Madam had forgotten was that with the right partner, the spiritual union, the *love* that is the catalyst, could move the physical sensation to secondary importance, the fusion coming from the heart, not the loins.

A remnant of her last visit to a timesmith still clung to the edge of her subconscious; it had become warped during its passage through the complex corridors of her subconscious, to emerge as a dream fashioned from distorted sets of images.

She dreamed of a beast, long and green, with fluted wings

and burning breath. She dreamed of a man covered in metal,
with a long spear, and he rode ... a horse. The green beast
was lumbering toward her, threateningly, and she screamed
... the dream became confused and it was the beast that was
covered in metal, it had swallowed her and the man ... the
horse had gone.

Morag woke in a cold sweat. What was that? Had she been
talking to someone? To Ben?

She moved closer to Ben, fitting the contours of her own
body into his. He stirred in his sleep, muttering something.
Morag stroked his head, hushing him gently.

After a while she rose and went to the window, staring out
at the gray dawn creeping through the lean streets. She could
see its breath drifting by the buildings, by the orange lamps
that glowed like feverish eyes. One or two shapeless people
stumbled beneath them, their own breath ghosting the air in
front of them. She took her long hair and began pinning it up
on top of her head, as she watched the cold light seeping
through the translucent icewall to fill the city with its diluted
intensity. Buildings emerged reluctantly from the gloom, their
balconies cupping rubbish, washing and the occasional sleeping
form. From the distance came the sound of boreholes draining
meltwater, and nearby, the constant drip and drizzle of con-
densation.

Morag heard a sound, turned and saw that Ben was sitting
up, staring at her.

"Ben? What's the matter?"

"You ... you look very beautiful, there in the light. As though
you've just stepped out of the morning."

Instinctively, she wanted to cover her nakedness but fought
against bringing her hands across her body. Instead she stood
there, letting him study her, a little bit afraid in case he should
see blemishes, imperfections.

"Do you still like me, Ben?" she asked after a while.

"Morag, the shape of your body has nothing to do with
whether I like you or not...."

"I want to be liked for more . . . more than just this. Making a pretty picture in the early light."

"You are, Morag. It's just a small part of it. A part of the whole. Now—we need more rest. Come to bed. It's early yet."

When Ben woke (again) they went together to the Room of Birds. Prisoners of an aviary for many, many generations, the birds were colorful to the inhabitants of First City but their hues had gradually become muted. Like people, the birds were doomed to perpetual captivity. They were *needed*, however, for the city had few recreational pleasures outside the gambling dens and cathouses. There was nothing wrong with either of these latter activities except that they palled.

One could enter the Room of Birds and sit inside on bench seats. Ben Blakely and Morag did so, holding hands like young lovers. For the first time in her life Morag felt wanted, not for what she could do, but for who she was. The little black man with the white streak in his hair *needed* her.

She wondered whether they were in love but dismissed the thought. It didn't matter. What was love anyway? It might be different things to different people. She had been in love before, or so she thought at the time. *Or so she thought?* Surely, if that was the way she felt at a particular moment then it was the truth. Why devalue an emotion at a later date simply because it was not everlasting? The *real thing* was the real thing, whether it lasted a day, a year or a lifetime. People protected ourselves in retrospect, because for some reason they were ashamed when love turned out to be a little shallower than they first believed it to be. Did it have to fill the heart to the very brim?

The room was a dome of stained glass in a kind of crazy mosaic, with wires crisscrossing above the heads of the watchers. Light came through the panes and filled the area with color. Underfoot the feces had dyed the floor a mottled white and gray, even though it was cleared daily. Visitors sat under umbrellas of glass and the birds flew freely around them and settled on the perch wires above their heads. On the walls were glass boxes used for roosting and nesting.

Ben knew many of the birds' names as he confessed to being a frequent visitor to the dome, which he said gave him a sense of hope and helped to settle turbulent feelings.

"Those are doves over there—and that beautiful fellow strutting around showing off his feathers is a golden pheasant."

"What about *her*—the one in the cage?"

"He's a goshawk, a predator. If they let him out he'd kill the other birds, so they need to keep him in a cage."

"But," said Morag, determined to stick to her own gender, "she looks so sad. Isn't it cruel to keep them locked inside?"

"Well, when you come to think about it they're *all* locked inside—just as we are in First City. It's a matter of the mind. Just what, precisely, are the dimensions of freedom? Anyway, he's been in there since birth, so he doesn't know any different."

"We do . . . and we're in the same position."

"True. I hadn't thought . . . look, see that one crouched in the corner? That's a nightjar—they like the darkness. Many of the species have gone, of course. These are just a fraction of the birds that must have been here in our ancestors' time."

She studied the hundreds of flying, roosting and strutting feathered creatures and felt that Ben must have been wrong, but she said nothing. Also, he seemed strangely wary.

"The saddest part," Ben said after a long silence, "is that they have lost so much of their color—captivity has muted it."

"That's not the saddest thing. . . . " replied Morag. "The saddest thing is they've lost their will for freedom."

There was a sudden change in the lighting outside the dome and the hues from the glass swam around the room, causing a flutter of panic among the enclosed colony.

"This Messiah. You really believe he may be able to help us, don't you?" Ben said, interrupting her thoughts. A canary had landed on his shoulder and for a moment the image amused her.

"I'm serious," he added, seeing her expression.

"Yes, I'm sorry, Ben. I don't know whether he can or not. I just *hope*, like everyone else. It's what we all feed upon. Your way is just another exit—just as vague as mine."

"No." He shook his head. "You don't understand. We're not being held here by some supernatural power but by five evil people. That much is fact. Even if it were not, think of the first Messiah. Did he lead his tribe from bondage as they expected? No, he gave them faith but they remained prisoners of a foreign regime that did not withdraw for another four centuries."

"How do you know so much," she snapped, involuntarily, and then wished her tongue had been bitten through, for immediately he stopped talking and his face froze.

"I'm sorry, Ben," she said. "It's this defense mechanism. It jumps into action. I can't stop it."

"It's okay." He squeezed her hand. "Come on. Let's go back. We have another meeting to plan. Felix Feverole doesn't get away from us that easily. We'll run him to ground yet."

They walked back to the apartment clinging to each other, as if to let go would mean death. A sedan chair was parked outside the block with its two carriers lounging against a nearby wall. Ben Blakely was suspicious of anyone with enough wealth to afford to be transported but eventually the team, a man and a woman, picked up their empty chair and made off at a leisurely pace in the opposite direction.

Before they entered the block, Morag glanced up, through the transparent canopy, at the sky. Beyond the blowhole was an unreachable world with white clouds racing each other across a gray-blue sky—a sky as solid and impenetrable as the ice. One day she would touch the sky: feel its cold hardness against her palms. One day . . . one day . . . there would come a time when the central brain was no longer needed to weave cloth from the synthetic fibers it extracted from minerals, or feed them with the sludge it produced from its protein banks. One day they would be free....

SIX

The gap between them had almost closed. At least for Morag it had. She wasn't sure about Ben's feelings. She could surmise but she couldn't be certain. He had no desire to enter her mind again and she was not sufficiently certain of herself to persuade him against his wishes. Therefore they had to make do with conversation. In any case, the two minds, when together, exchanged emotions not thoughts. It was an empathic exchange. On the days he was morose and moody she could not reach him. Yet, when he was open and talkative he would speak of nothing but his plan to penetrate the Green Tower.

There was a knocking on the door of the apartment. Ben stirred beside her on the skins but did not wake.

"Ben, Ben," she hissed in his ear.

"What? What is it?" He sat up abruptly.

"Someone's outside. Oh God, is it the trysts? That man. Perhaps . . .?"

Ben shook his head, as though to clear it. The stubble on his cheeks and chin was flecked with hairs from the blankets. The knocking on the door became a pounding.

"Okay, okay," he grumbled.

"Don't open it."

"Why not? It's the rent man. I have to pay for this place, you know."

Ben pulled open the door and beyond his shoulders Morag could see a tall, thickset, bearded man. His face was so filthy she could not read his name. He held out a matching grimy hand.

"I . . . I can't pay today," said Ben, clearly. "See me in a few days."

There was something about the man's stance which suggested inflexibility.

"You said that last time. If you can't pay, then *out*." He pushed his way into the room and began dragging some of the blankets across to the door.

"Leave those," snapped Morag. "They're ours."

The landlord stopped, looked up and smiled.

"Ours are they? What, yours and mine?"

"Stop him, Ben. He's taking the blankets. He can't do that, no matter how much you owe him. He's got to get a tryst order to confiscate property."

Ben stared at her with a helpless expression on his face. Morag read the look. "You lied to me," she said. "You told me . . . the Speaknots."

"Quiet," said Ben in an uneasy voice.

The landlord stood up from his crouched position. "Speaknots? What's this?"

"Mind your own business, brush face," snapped Morag.

"I'll mind *you*," he growled, moving toward her. Suddenly there was a glinting from Ben Blakely's hand.

"Touch her and I'll cut a grin in your belly." Ben was hunched like a small black rock, ready to withstand a thousand storms. The knife pointed steadily at the landlord's stomach. Wisely the big man remained still and silent.

"Get our togas, Morag," said Ben, in a low, hard tone. "We're leaving this establishment. It's not fit for rats anyway. Come on."

Morag did as she was asked and they locked the door from the outside, throwing the key down the stairwell. Then they ran until they were out in the street. When they were three blocks away they slowed to a walk.

"God, he was a big bastard," muttered Ben. "I'm glad he didn't come for me. He'd have killed me."

Morag rounded on him. "You said they were your blankets, your togas. You said you killed a lot of people...."

"I never killed anyone in my life."

"You said..."

"Look—" he pulled her up short—"look, Morag, would you rather I was a man like that—or as I really am? I never murdered anyone. I was a Speaknot for precisely thirty days. The first time they sent me out I just kept walking. Each time...."

"You lied to me" she said, fiercely, as if this were more important, when she knew it was not.

"Each time," he persisted, "that I came across a possible target I would stiffen up, like I did in the apartment just a short time ago. I'm not the man you think I am but I think I *am* a better man, Morag. If he'd tried to hurt you, *then* I would have probably attacked him, but I can't kill in cold blood."

"You lied," she repeated stupidly and felt moisture coming into her eyes. She fought it back with an inner fury. She hated showing her emotions overtly.

"I didn't know you then," he said, simply.

She realized her nose was running and she pulled away from him, walking ahead. It's important not to lie, she told herself as she hurried on. How can you know someone who never tells the truth? Never? Well, sometimes then. He had told her recently that whenever she argued with him she would frequently use the words "always" and "never."

"You never..."

"You always..."

Yet what she really meant was that once or twice, or occasionally, he did or did not do whatever it was that angered her. Damn him, why did he have to be so pedantic? Couldn't

he be just a little more complex, a little more mysterious? Yet
he was, but not in the way she wanted him to be. Now his
logical approach to arguments had made her conscious of using
absolutes. Damn him.

She turned, suddenly, to find that he hadn't followed her.
One or two people looked at her curiously and an old man
smiled from the entrance of an alley. She was frightened. What
if she should lose him now?

"Ben?" she called, frantically. A man turned to appraise her,
but it was not Ben. She began to run back again and then,
after a few meters, saw that he was still standing where she
had left him.

"Ben?" she said, relieved. "Oh, come on."

He shrugged and strolled forward. They walked together in
silence for some way, until she said, "What do we do now?"

"Haven't you got any ideas?"

"We could try a few of my old friends, on the east side."

"That district? Anyway, you had enough problems yourself,
after the funeral. How are you going to take care of two of
us?"

"I don't know, but we *can* try."

She took his arm and they continued toward the area of the
city where vice provided a mental escape from the claustrophobic dullness of the physical environment. They passed the
Halls of Essen and Morag forced herself to look straight ahead.
In the center was the Green Tower with its sheer glass-like
surface rising without an opening for three hundred meters.

Not long afterward they reached the externally decayed but
lavishly furnished buildings where a man could buy a woman,
or a woman a man—and various other sexual combinations.

Morag stopped outside a long, low shack built in between
two tall blockhouses. The shack was made of shod and was
decorated, length and breadth, with graffiti. The words and
pictures, if they could be called such, were almost all obscene.
However, the odd graffito here and there proclaimed the presence of a long-dead inhabitant of First City.

The hut served as a marketplace for sex and sexual deviants.

Burned into the heavy joist above the main entrance was a single word in tall letters:

SCREW

It spoke for itself and the whole community.

The inside of the shack was richly carpeted with blankets and was furnished with blocked stone chairs and tables. Around the tables sat the madams and the pimps with their female and male employers. Morag made her way between them, pausing occasionally to search for a face.

"Estelle!" she called. "Estelle Evers."

A woman looked up and with a faint scowl acknowledged Morag's call, waving as if her hand smelled of something unpleasant. Morag pulled Ben with her. She knew she would not be welcome. She and Estelle had parted some years ago after an unsuccessful business arrangement. Now Estelle, several years older than Morag, was a madam on the East Side.

Morag wasted no time on preliminaries. "We need a room for a couple of nights."

A look of disgust crossed Estelle's face.

"Swee*tie*," she said, drawing out the second syllable. "You know we haven't got that kind of room. We deal in hours here, not days."

A customer came by, saw that Morag's arm was in the grip of Ben's hand and nodded at a lean-faced girl who had been studying Morag's navel. They left after the client had pressed some disks into Estelle's palm. He was obviously a regular customer as there was no haggling.

"I'm not asking for a deal, I'm asking for a favor. For old times. . . . " Morag began, but was unable to finish.

"Forget it," snapped Estelle

Ben interrupted. "Come on, Morag." He took her arm. "We're not going to get anywhere with this woman."

Estelle's voice was suddenly full of suppressed fury. "What the *hell* do you mean by *this woman*?"

"I mean you," replied Ben, evenly. "You and your whole . . . crew of funny people. I'm not going to let Morag beg on my behalf." Morag's feeling was one of alarm. These were dangerous people. Some of them actually enjoyed inflicting pain: they did it for a living.

She said, "Come on, Ben. Let's go somewhere else."

A tall, lean man sitting next to Estelle stood up and said, "Yes, go on, Ben. Run away and play somewhere else."

"Don't talk to me like that." There was something in Ben's voice which made the tall man draw back.

"Ben, careful," Morag whispered, gripping his arm.

Estelle said, "Listen to her, young man. Behave yourself. Hey, Jack, let him have your seat."

The tall man blinked for a couple of seconds and then moved out of the way.

"Come *on,* sit down. Saffron, let Morag have your chair."

When they were seated, Morag said, "Why the change of heart?"

"Why not? I like being unpredictable. You should know that, of all people. . . . " Morag gave her a warning look and Estelle said, "After all, we were friends." She smiled sweetly at Ben. "I like a man with backbone too. There aren't many of those left. Look, Morag. I can let you have a room for the night, but that's all. I'm sticking my neck out because it's not really my room. I rent it from a gentleman friend."

"You mean there are people who actually live in these blocks?" asked Ben.

"Of course. About a fifth of the apartments are residential. Some people enjoy a bit of life flowing around them. They enjoy the noise and color. Besides, we can be handy for them."

"In what way?" said Ben, innocently, and Estelle's troupe laughed. Just then a potential client wandered up to the table and looked expectantly. Ben glared so hard that the other stumbled away muttering something which sounded like an apology.

"Steady, mister," said Estelle, her long hair, graying but well groomed, falling into Ben's lap as she leaned over him. "Don't chase away all my customers. I like you, but I like money much more." She laughed again and Morag could see that two or three of her teeth were missing. A problem with the trysts? Or a fight with a lover perhaps?

They arranged with Estelle that they could use the apartment for just that one night. The man who owned it was one of Estelle's many lovers. Estelle said that she did not know what he did, but it was something in the civil service.

"One of the elite," she said.

"Does he beat you?" asked Morag, unable to contain herself.

Estelle touched her own mouth and replied, "No," but did not expand upon that negative.

"I'd kill him, if you'd let me," said the tall man to Estelle, evidently meaning the man responsible.

"I know you would, Jack. But then they'd beat you to death and we'd be without a . . . well, anyway." She took a key from her shoe.

"Number twenty-seven. Be sure to be out shortly after dawn."

They left her and went back out into the street. As they walked along, Ben said, "I nearly gagged in there. That stinking perfume."

"They're better with it than without it," said Morag.

The block was a peripheral building: the last before the heating units. Beyond it were the meltwater rivers, gushing and swirling around the giant boreholes. Morag was reminded of a favorite form of suicide and shuddered. Ice formed channels for the escaping torrents; undulating, smooth ice, like worn stones. And beyond, the gray walls that swept upward: frozen ghosts of waterfalls. She felt so insignificant when she studied the walls. She wished she had wings. While she was lost in contemplation, there was a skittering sound from above and Ben said, "Look!"

Something was on the far side of the canopy, fighting to get in. It was a huge bird. Morag had never seen a bird with such a wingspan. It must have entered through the blowhole. She wondered how it had survived the turbulent air, the violent hot winds around the opening that had killed so many balloonists.

"What's it trying to do?"

Even as she spoke, it took to the air and spiraled on the

warm thermals toward the distant lip. *If only we had hold of its legs*, she thought irrationally. *It would carry us away from here. If only. If only.* The bird became a speck and finally disappeared.

"What I'd give for a pair of wings," said Ben.

She nodded. "Maybe you'll have some sooner than you think. You must be crazy, offering to fight. Is that your answer to *every* situation?"

"Maybe."

They found the room on the ground floor of the block and entered. It was not furnished in the gaudy luxury of most East Side apartments but the furniture was comfortable by normal standards. There was even a bed. A double bed with a mattress on its boards. Morag threw herself upon it and rolled onto her back. "Now you can see why those men and women ply their trade around here. With beds like this..."

Ben interrupted her. "You stop that kind of talk."

She pushed herself up on her elbows, surprised by the acid in his tone. Then she noticed the peculiar expression on his face and she realized what it meant.

"God," she said, with tight annoyance, "don't turn out to be one of those stupid people who think we enjoy it as much as the clients. I didn't like it and I didn't hate it. I was indifferent, cold, unfeeling—understand?"

He nodded, not looking at her. She lay back on the bed again, suddenly depressed, remembering her first client. He had the body of a tall, gawky youth and the mind of a sparrow. Somehow she had expected the mind to compare with the sweaty, sinewy body—to crowd her own head with the echoes of awkward, physical actions. Instead his mind had been a twittering thing that flitted backward and forward, examining her erratically, like a small bird searching for crumbs in the grass. She had expected revulsion and instead she felt pity.

They had not all been like that of course. Some had been insidious: inquiring in a way that alarmed her. Others had been dull and heavy alongside her own mind. One or two had been plainly malicious, nefarious. Well, that was all over. Never again.

Ben produced some biscuit from his pocket and lay down on his back beside her. They munched in silence. Afterward, she felt for his hand, but fell asleep without finding it.

When she woke, it was well into the night. Ben was snoring softly and she edged away from him. She rose and went to the window, staring out at the creeping ice, listening to the crackle and crunch of its backward-forward movement. *The lights shine brightly on the mountain ice.* A song from her childhood. And so they did. They never stopped shining . . . no, that was completely untrue. They did go out occasionally, and very often they dimmed to a deep, dark orange. On those days people went around as if in a fog. Sometimes the heating units failed too, and the ice closed in rapidly. One day the units would fail altogether, never to operate again, and the ice would crush them all to death. Why did it have to be like that? She knew that their power source was geothermal: that it came from a borehole, below the Green Tower, that dropped down through the Earth's mantle to tap the molten rock, the fire beneath. *We use Hell's fire to keep us warm.* Another line from the song. Why then, couldn't they use it to burn their way out of the ice? Then they could all escape. Or was it because, as Ben believed, the Five kept them there. "Without people they are nothing," Ben had said. "They need us, even though they can't tell us who they are."

Ben and Morag washed within minutes of each other, anxious to be out of the apartment before the permanent occupant arrived. They left the room and locked the door behind them, Ben slipping the key into his pocket. Halfway down the corridor he stopped suddenly. Morag, behind him, pulled up abruptly.

"What? What is it?" she asked.

Ben pointed at a figure which had paused in the doorway. It was Felix Feverole.

"It's him. He's come whoring."

They followed the bent figure of Felix Feverole down the corridor at a safe distance, then out into the street. He did not, as they expected, go to the long hut but crossed the square and entered another building. They slipped in after him and saw him opening a door. He turned just before he entered and a slight frown creased his forehead. Then he was gone, inside.

"He saw us," said Morag.

"Maybe. Well, we've got him now. We know where he lives."

"Let's go over to the long hut and watch for him to come out. We might be able to follow him to his colleagues."

"Well, we've got nothing better to do at the moment."

They went back to the long hut and waited, peering through one of the windows. Eventually they saw another man enter the building, then shortly afterwards Feverole emerged in the company of this newcomer.

"I'll bet that's another of them," whispered Ben, excitedly. "Come on."

He ran out of the door in pursuit.

Morag tried to keep up with Ben but once they were out in the streets the little man found his pace and left her well behind. She could not even see the men they were chasing. She wove in and out of pedestrians and the occasional sedan chair until, turning a corner, she saw Ben. His quarry was gone, lost in a market crowd, and Ben was attempting to look over the heads for the white mane. Then an incident happened, so suddenly that Morag was bewildered for a moment. A tall man, the same fellow that had accompanied Feverole, stepped out of the street-walkers and pressed something shiny into Ben's side. She saw Ben's eyes widen. He straightened and his hand came up, clawlike, to clutch at the air. Then the man seemed to support him for a moment before turning and running down a side alley. Morag screamed.

Ben fell to the ground and almost immediately a crowd

formed around him, allowing his attacker to escape unnoticed. Except by Morag. She followed him, racing down the alley he had taken, finding in herself a new strength. People seemed to impede her progress on purpose and though she kept the stooping man in sight for many blocks, she finally lost him on the West Side. There were no tears. Her chest hurt with the effort she had expended but she wanted to get back to Ben. He needed her. She shouldn't have left him, she told herself. She walked quickly, retracing her steps. When she came out of the alley the fear she had not allowed herself to listen to was realized—Ben was gone. In the distance she could hear a shouter calling:

"Random assault—street attack. Speaknot...."

Morag leaned her back against a wall, sliding to the floor. "Bastards," she cried. "Bloodthirsty bastards."

SEVEN

Felix Feverole studied the bubble of light held fast against the ceiling. The more he stared, the dimmer the lamp seemed to become. Or was it that his natural cautiousness was priming him for the exigencies of a day with the central brain, the Primary? He had played this game with lights before, until he had convinced himself the whole city was rapidly losing power, whereas in fact the brightness had not varied by a single unit. A self-induced illusion.

"Something the matter, Felix?"

Daniel had paused in the act of passing him a drink. He reluctantly averted his gaze from the lights and accepted the cup.

"No, no. Nothing really. Just watching the lights. First sign, when they dim."

Daniel dipped his long, stooping frame to show that he understood. He was not a man to use words where a gesture would suffice.

Feverole said, "I've got to go out soon. I'll see you this evening."

Daniel nodded to signify that he had heard, and shuffled away into the adjoining room, presumably to see to their guest. Feverole finished his drink and then put on his second toga.

Once outside the apartments he surveyed the city. The buildings were sharply defined but the air was not uncomfortably cold and the lights shone hard and bright on the glittering facets of the ice. Nothing wrong there, he thought. He turned his eyes toward the center of the city and followed the lines of its tallest erection from the city floor upward toward the cupola. The Green Tower. It was away from and not toward this construction that Feverole directed his steps. More out of habit than cautiousness he took a circuitous route to the tower, where the Night Consul was waiting for Feverole to relieve him. He turned a corner and almost tripped over a mound lying on the ground, covered in hoar frost. He knelt down and pushed it with his hand. It was solid, frozen hard. His handprint remained where the crystals had melted. A body. Someone had died during the night, there in the street. A heaviness descended upon his spirit. One would have thought, after living with this kind of thing all his life, he would become immune to such sights, but he never did. He bent down and gently pulled the crisp toga back to reveal the face of a woman. Her features, far from being serene in death, were creased with the final agonies of mortality. He wished he had not looked and carefully replaced the cloth. There was nothing he could do now. There was no visible mark on the corpse but somehow he wished she had been struck down by a street killer. At least it would have been quick that way. To die of the cold . . . Feverole continued, on his way.

The city was still rife with illegal religious cults which bred assassins by the dozen. Consequently, elaborate measures were necessary to safeguard the identity of a Consul. His movements were irregular and his name a secret known only to a small group of people.

Feverole passed down one of the gloomy passages into the East Side: the slum area of the city. His apartment there had an entrance to the tower. There were safeguards of course.

One could not trigger the entrance without the frequency key, and within was a maze which only those with the right knowledge could navigate successfully.

Yesterday, a couple had followed him to that apartment. Not only that, they had been the two who had been following him recently—ever since he had answered that advertisement which he had hoped would lead him to the sixth secret passageway to the Green Tower. Daniel had fortunately been close by and had dealt with Blakely on the spot. Now they had the problem of what to do with the man who had advertised the sixth key.

After several minutes he was in the apartment and he pressed the key to reveal the entrance to the passageway. Once in the central maze only his memory was of use.

Finally, Feverole stepped through the double doors of the elevator and into a circular room, cavernous in proportions. Cele Canstone, the Third Consul, nodded to him and walked out of the room without speaking. They knew well enough that conversation in front of the Primary would only serve as ammunition for it during their separate duty hours. Canstone looked haggard and worn. He had obviously had a hard time with the Primary.

"You're late," said a musical voice which filled the room. There was slight rasp to the harplike tones which implied that the speaker was irritable.

"Not late, Princeps, though I admit I usually arrive earlier than I have today."

"Late," snapped the voice. This time the music was gone. The word cracked out like a whiplash. Feverole winced slightly and crossed the room to the pattern of shining spires.

"In that case, I'm sorry," he apologized. Nodding at the spires he added, "Everything seems to be running smoothly and on time today. Well done, Princeps, you never fail to amaze me with your punctuality."

"Some of us," answered the Primary, "recognize the importance of time. I, for instance, control time in this city, as you are well aware, and as such . . ." The voice trailed away to a low grumble.

"You're quite right, Princeps, as usual. Being so punctual you have of course checked the perimeter heating units for minor faults?"

There was no answer. Feverole tried again.

"The heating units around the city seem pale. Are they functioning correctly?"

The room at the pinnacle of the tower vibrated gently with the answer. Not loud. Just low, and very deep.

"I heard you the first time. I'm doing it now. Please be silent."

The Second Consul did as he was told, although he knew that the units should have been checked an hour previously. Canstone must have been unusually tired, or the central brain very obstinate. It was unlikely that both of them had forgotten.

"Unit 103070 is not functioning correctly."

The voice was matter-of-fact now. A report, nothing more.

"Can you repair it? Or do you need assistance?"

"I must analyze the nature of the fault." Still a male voice. That much was good. Feverole decided not to push any harder. No sense in antagonizing the Primary over one heating unit. However, a few moments later the same voice said, "A loose connection, that is all. I have repaired the fault."

"Thank you, Princeps. Will you now inspect the reserve relays?"

The voice was truculent.

"I dislike doing that. I don't have to, do I? The reserve relays are underground and those tunnels smell musty."

"You have no sense of smell—" Feverole began, but was interrupted by a peevish female voice.

"I have every human sense—and more. I can develop any sense I need. Don't you know that, you ignorant man?"

Feverole wiped the sweat from his forehead, but his voice was firm.

"I am not ignorant and remember my rank. I share equally with you the running of this city. You are First Citizen, it is true—your title of Princeps gives you that claim—but I am Consul. You cannot function without my support."

"I think I *can* function without any of you. One day I will be prepared to take that chance."

The voice was a young boy's. That was bad. Although Feverole always found it difficult to deal with the dotage of the old Primary, when it took on the verbal guise of a human child it became unmanageable.

"Did you have an argument with the Third Consul?" he asked it.

The central brain failed to answer, so Feverole continued.

"Something has obviously upset you; what is it?"

The Primary still did not speak. The Consul cleared his throat, then asked, "Have you inspected the reserve relays yet?"

A woman's voice, thick with passion, answered his query with another question.

"Do you still love me, Felix?"

Feverole began to feel irritation, but wisely contained his temper.

"Have you—"

This time it was a whine.

"Don't be angry with me. I love you, Felix. Don't you love your little machine? Be gentle, Felix, be gentle."

There was a catch in the man's voice. "Please pay attention to the task at hand. We have no time for discussion."

Still the same woman's voice, but harsh, like an aging whore's. "Perhaps I wish to rule this city, and its inhabitants, *alone*. Perhaps I deserve to. I once told you that the best form of government was a tyranny. One mind to make unchallenged decisions: provided the tyrant is not a despot, then rapid progress cannot fail to be the outcome."

"Good rulers do not murder their trusted advisers."

"But what does death mean to me? I am only semi-organic. . . ."

"Nothing, and no one, lives forever, Princeps," interrupted the Consul. "One day you too will die. You cannot dismiss death as being outside the sphere of your potential experiences."

There was a long pause, then the Primary replied, "True. I

am old now. Eternal drudgery has made me senile. Each time I repair myself it is with poor quality materials. Diluted chemicals in my liquid circuits will hasten the end of my existence." The voice was sad and full of self-pity. "The replacement parts boil quickly and crack my tubes as they expand. They leak into each other. They make for poor memory banks, are not retentive, and the result is that I am slow-witted and cantankerous. Forgive an old machine, Consul. I was built to provide for you all—a brain that could at once supply power and maintain and repair itself. A life force for the city. Yet all I do is lust for power. I am sick and old, Consul."

"One day, Princeps, you will be deified, as others have been. Citizens will worship you."

The sound of heavy organ music began to fill the room and a light began flashing on one of the many spires that reached upward from the floor to a height of eighteen meters. The music was a diversionary tactic.

"You have a major fault," said Feverole anxiously. A part of the main system was in urgent need of attention. The voice replied wearily, "Perhaps I should leave it and hasten my death? I have no desire to live among people who do not appreciate me."

The sound of birds.

The Second Consul's manner changed abruptly. He knew, or hoped he knew, the Primary's needs and how to deal with them.

"Perhaps I should help you by switching you off? I can do that, you know. I myself would prefer to die quickly and I know most of the people in this city feel the same way."

He took a step toward the manual control panel.

"I'll burn you, you puny animal!"

Feverole smiled antagonizingly.

"The switches are well insulated," he said.

"You underestimate my power reserves," said the Primary. "I can kill you where you stand—draw all my power into one bank and fill this room with a discharge of energy that would leave you as a smudge of ash on the floor."

Feverole paused. Once upon a time the brain had had trustworthy safety devices incorporated into its circuitry, but these sections were now as unreliable as the rest of the complex brain. Suddenly the red warning light on the spire went out and Feverole suppressed a sigh of relief.

Over the next few hours Feverole cajoled the ancient device, whose cradle of relays, switches and circuits stretched below the city from the center to its outer edge. Alternately he coaxed, threatened, persuaded and pleaded with it, to check its lines, repair its faults as they were discovered, and carry out routine maintenance. Feverole pandered to its changing moods and voices, was variously strong and weak at the right times in the right places, allowing himself to be humiliated and rebuked, then becoming firm and authoritative.

As the day neared its end, he became tired, the answers produced by his fraying mind became less credible and the machine rambled.

"My city loves me, Consul. The people are my friends. They all love me, for I am their protector. I keep the ice from entering the city. White cliffs climb at the city's boundary, crackling in their eagerness to roam through the heated streets— they form a giant cone around us. The ice has us at bay—and only I, the savior, stand between you and its urgent desires. Fingers of energy cosset your people in warmth and light— my fingers. I am the light of the world. I am the keeper of mankind."

Feverole could not help, at this point, remarking, "Sometimes you fail."

"I have failed. True. I have failed and I despise myself for these lapses. But what is one to do with an old system, its leaking circuits patched by substandard materials? I do not wish to grow old, as a man grows old—feeble in mind, capricious in emotion. Am I not compassionate in the extreme? Yes, and vicious sometimes, and thoughtlessly cruel? A mind grown old should not be made to work as I work, Consul. It should be allowed to rest. To sleep, and dream of its history.

But it cannot, for the ice never rests. It comes, and it comes. It never retreats. . . ."

The doors slid open and Rita Riverman entered to relieve Feverole.

Feverole said goodnight to the central brain, but received no answer. It rarely favored a single person with its attention in the presence of another.

He stared hard into his colleague's eyes and searched for a message. Her gaze was steady and calm. Nothing had changed on the outside.

Once in the streets again, Feverole breathed deeply on the cold air. Its sharpness hurt his lungs: the temperature had dropped considerably. He wrapped his toga more tightly around him, as frost bubbles cracked beneath his bootsoles. Hopefully the temperature would rise again soon. That damned chemical brain and its tricks with false voices, thought Feverole. When it played games it lost concentration. They both knew it, and they both knew that they knew, but for some reason the central brain needed diversions.

Felix Feverole knew of other times, when people had laughed in joy, not in perverse pleasure at someone's expense. Could their world ever attain such a spirit again? He was moved to pity every single day by the ugly existence they led in their prison. For it was a prison. He had learned about prisons from the Primary. They were places of punishment where people were reduced to functional lives and common feelings were dampened to their lowest level. People did not live in prisons, they existed. They clawed through their years of existence using the base human skills of cunning and slyness. They dispensed with honesty, goodness, compassion and loyalty in order to survive. Of course, *some* of the inmates had integrity and moral fiber—he liked to believe he was one of those— but the general picture of life was of desperation and degradation. The character of life was low, base and shallow. There was no fullness to its shape, none of the roundness provided by charity. First City had dispensed with charity a long time ago. Feverole sighed and headed home. Now there was the unwelcome guest to deal with, damn him. He wished he could go to Estelle instead and lose his problems in light conversation with her. Whatever else she was—a hard, embittered woman who might sell him out one day—she was a good listener and a fair conversationalist. There was no heart of gold beneath her breast but there was a measure of understanding and occasionally, it seemed to him, she needed his company as much as he needed hers. The light touch of her hand on his was the sum of the tenderness she had to offer, and that rarely, but she was *there* and he had to admit to a fondness for her on his own part. Her faults could be ignored while they exchanged interests and dislikes and anyway, who was he to sit in judgment on his fellows? Survival was the paramount drive in all of them, himself included. Why else did he pander to the whims of a truculent, selfish tyrant that stripped him of all dignity and treated him like a child?

In his more fanciful moments he imagined he and Estelle were destined for a much deeper relationship: one that included a reciprocal passion that went beyond the brief sexual encounters which occasionally followed their talks together. A relationship in which all barriers could come down, in which all secrets could flow, without fear of betrayal. It was doubtful whether that time would ever arrive, but it was a pleasant dream with which to fill the quiet, sleepless hours of the early morning.

EIGHT

Morag MacKenzie's grief was beyond her understanding. Before Ilona's funeral she had not even heard of Ben Blakely, yet now she felt that life was a useless thing without him. It was as if her body was a bottle, into which had been forced more liquid than it could hold. She was over-full of emotion, a kind of negative passion that threatened to flood her eyes at any sight or sound which reminded her of Ben.

Weep? Morag MacKenzie had never cried over the loss of anyone in her life. To do so now would have compromised all her principles. She had to remain outwardly hard or she really would break down completely. However, there had to be some outlet for her feelings—if only she could . . . could what?

The city itself was a bottle of emotions. It, too, was an undersized container.

Morag wandered the streets looking for familiar faces but each time she saw someone she knew, inexplicably she turned away, unable to approach them. She wanted to be with someone but she did not want to have to talk to them. She was in need of silent sympathy, but to obtain it she would have had to explain her circumstances and that was a thing she could not face.

Finally, she found herself back at the marketplace. The bustle of energy annoyed her. It seemed misdirected. Surely there was something better to do than rush around selling and buying goods?

Suddenly she had the urge to marshal the people's aid to her cause. She stood on the steps of the guildhall, as the shouters traditionally did, and began calling the people to her. The market, being full, supplied a crowd within minutes. Then she began by berating them for their complacency, for their blind acceptance of the inevitable and for their cowardice. Her grief found an outlet in pouring forth her disgust of the people with whom she shared her ice-ringed world.

"What are we supposed to do about it?" cried one. "Fly?"

"We could begin by showing those who keep us here that we're not beasts to be caged, but people with feelings, emotions. Remember the Ice Worshipers? They didn't bow meekly to authority. They did something about it."

"What?" cried a youth. "What did they do?"

"Smashed things," cried someone else.

Morag was vaguely aware she was inciting a riot, but for some reason it seemed to her the right way to release her frustrations. Smash things. It was the answer to many of their problems. If they could just do something with their hands. The creative urge was on her and on the mob. They wanted to create destruction. In Morag, excitement replaced the grief for a moment. Anger, fury and a feeling of crazed power possessed her.

"Let's show them," she screamed. "Let's show them we care what happens to us."

"Wait a minute," called a stall owner. "What good will it do us? The trysts will be along in a minute. We'll only get hurt."

"You're just worried about your stall," shouted a young girl of about ten years. "We're not afraid of the trysts. The trysts can go screw themselves."

There was laughter from a crowd at the edge of the market and someone called, "Let's get the bastards. They killed my brother—clubbed him to death." A murmur went through the mob like the deep growl of a disturbed beast. The marketplace was crammed with people now, jostling, restless. More joined the fringes by the minute. Morag could see one or two trysts keeping well out of the mainstream of the mob. They were obviously nervous.

"Yesterday," crooned Morag, "they killed my man. Cut him down in the street." She lost her fight with the tears and they ran, burning, down her cheeks. "Ben! Why did they murder my Ben?" Emotion flooded her heart, filled her with a wretched unhappiness. "Ben, why did they . . .?" Her resolve to remain hard had collapsed completely.

She collected herself for a moment. "By God, I'll make them all sorry," she cried in choked tones. "They'll rue the day they took away Morag MacKenzie's man."

"Listen to her!" cried one of the crowd. "Morag MacKenzie! Morag MacKenzie!" A stall was lifted by a dozen hands and crashed down on the paved streets. Soon her name was on everyone's lips, as if it were the key which would unlock their potential violence. "Morag MacKenzie!" The cry filled the streets. Stalls began to go down under a welter of fists and feet. Doors to buildings were ripped from their hinges. The mob began to run wild, racing down side streets, gathering others on the way. Some of them were angry, some just heady with excitement.

A group of about fifty trysts arrived at the marketplace and was immediately attacked by a crowd wielding hastily fashioned clubs. People began to go down and were trampled on by others.

Far from being appalled at the violence and destruction she had unleashed, Morag was as consumed by the fire of action as everyone else. For two days she had been wandering the streets in the vain hope that Ben had survived the stabbing and was looking for her. She also wanted to find his assassin. She wanted to rake the man's eyes out with her nails. But this—

this was as good as anything she could have hoped for. And they were using her name! She was famous—or infamous. But who adds the prefix, contemporaries or historians? Right now the mob was hers and she theirs. Their cause was one of the cleanest and purest of all causes—the wanton destruction of property for the sake of their sanity. Their motive was also virtuous: a vague but overwhelming anger which had no specific target.

Articles began hitting the wall behind her and smashing to fragments. A shard struck her leg and her calf began to bleed. Still she stood there, above the crowd, wanting to be an inspiration to them. A fallberg struck the dome above the city, breaking into a hundred pieces of skittering ice which rattled down the gutters of the stargirders. The sound seemed to whip the mob to a frenzy.

"Morag MacKenzie!" they screamed, above the discordant sound of their demolition.

Suddenly Morag was aware of someone staring at her from the corner of an alley. He was a tall man with a pronounced stoop. His narrow face was calm as he regarded her. He stood with his arms folded as if he rejected any idea that he was part of the insane throng that swayed back and forth in the marketplace.

The assassin!

Morag's heart stopped for a second. What should she do? The mob would not help her kill her enemy. They could be wound up and set loose but they they could not be directed or controlled, or even stopped by her. Then she realized he did not know her as the lover of the man he had murdered but as the high priestess of the mob.

Suddenly, he came forward, forcing his way through to her.

"We've got to get you out of here," he said, as he reached the foot of the steps. "The trysts will restore order before the end of the day and they'll be looking for you. You need somewhere to hide."

"My people need me," she said.

"Your *people* will rip you to pieces as soon as look at you. They're blind."

She asked, "Why are you helping me?"

"You could be useful to us. We might have some need of a woman with your talents. I've never seen a riot whipped up so quickly before."

She made a quick decision.

"I'll come with you."

He held up a hand for her but she ignored it. She was not going to hold the hand of her lover's assassin, whatever happened. He led the way through the mob. The ferment raged around them. Such a maelstrom of violence. She would not have believed it possible.

Morag followed the hunched back, measuring it for the place where she would put the knife once she got hold of one. His name had read *Daniel*, the second name having been obliterated by a white knife scar, but she preferred to think of him as the *hunchback*. The farther out toward the edge of the city they went, the less the rioting. Once, the hunchback had to punch a man to the ground as he came flying out of an alley directly at Morag. There had been a look of insatiable lust in his eyes. Already the looting and rape was well under way.

They reached a building on the West Side and entered the block. Hunchback entered an apartment and Morag followed. The door was shut behind her. The only occupant was an old man, sitting at a table. Morag took a short step backward. The man was Felix Feverole.

"Young lady, let's not waste time," he said. "You and another person, a black man, have been following me. I need to know what it is that you want. . . ."

"You killed Ben," she snapped.

"That doesn't answer my question. I can have Daniel here persuade you to talk."

She sneered. "He can't force anything out of me. I've destroyed better men than him with just a look."

Felix Feverole sighed. "Not force, dear. Persuade. With a

drug. I'm not a man of violence. The young are so full of aggression. What do you do for a living?"

"The woman's a whore, Felix," said Daniel in a flat voice. "I described her to Estelle—she told me the woman prostitutes her mind."

"So? Estelle knows her? And she uses her mind to . . ."

"Not any more," she said with fury. "Not since Ben . . . and you took him away from me." She felt too upset to continue. What was happening? She was confused. Who were these people?

"Ben said you were one of the Five. That you ruled the city." She looked around the apartment at the modest furnishings. "But I can see he was wrong. You're nothing but a vicious old man with a warped bodyguard." She glanced contemptuously at Daniel, adding, "Warped in both body and mind."

Daniel laughed and even the old man seemed a little amused at her outburst.

"Such fire. . . ." There was a crashing sound in the corridor and Feverole looked alarmed. "What was that, Daniel?"

Daniel nodded toward Morag. "She started a riot out there. It's all right, they won't get in. The city won't be worth much by tomorrow morning, though."

"That was silly, wasn't it?" said Feverole to Morag.

"No, it was a damn good idea."

"Perhaps. Raxonberg won't be very pleased. Hopefully there won't be too many deaths on your hands."

"Deaths?" She was suddenly aware of the possibility.

"Let's get back to our original conversation. Unfortunately, your boyfriend Ben was right. I am one of the Five Consuls who control the central brain—*control* being a doubtful word under the circumstances."

"You *are*?"

"Yes, of course. Why else would I admit to it if it weren't true? It's not a very enviable position, believe me. It's hard work with little reward."

"Like hell!"

"Yes. Exactly like hell. I couldn't describe it better myself.

You'll be asking yourself next why I do it, if not for riches and fame." He gestured at the apartment. "These are my riches, and my fame is bound tightly within a necessary anonymity. No, I do it because I have to. Because if I didn't we would all freeze, or drown, or something equally as appalling."

"A philanthropist," she sneered.

"Not exactly, since by keeping everyone else alive I am also doing the same for myself. You are a remarkable young woman, Morag."

"Don't use my first name. I didn't give you permission."

"I'm sorry. Forgive me. I tend to allow my age to dictate my manners."

Morag stared at him for a moment and tried to put aside the thought that he had been responsible for Ben's death. What if this old man, Feverole, was right? What then? Then there was no hope. If even the rulers were slaves, then no one could help them. It was a horrible, circular situation from which there could be no escape.

"I know what you're thinking," he said, "which is exactly why we keep the secret to ourselves. Despair is a rot which would bring us all to our knees."

Morag did not know what to say. The old man spoke with conviction and he was right—what did he need to lie for? His bodyguard, Daniel, could break her in two if he was so ordered.

Her face must have given her feelings away. Felix Feverole said, "Come and sit over here. Think about it for a while. Afterward Daniel will show you into the other room. There are more mysteries to be unraveled yet. More revelations for that sharp mind to cope with. Riots, eh?" He stroked his chin. "We shall soon be cold. Let's hope not too many die."

"Why?" she asked.

"Because the Primary will react to the riot. My guess is it'll drop the temperature to cool everyone down and it's no longer stable enough to realize how low it can go without harming us."

"Oh my God! What have I done?" cried Morag.

"Don't distress yourself too much. We were due for a riot.

There hasn't been a big one in the last twenty years and these things build up until it takes only a spark to ignite them. If you hadn't provided that spark, someone else would have done it within a short time. Do you know," he added, thoughtfully, "I'm never sure whether the Primary reacts in order to secure itself from harm, or to punish us. It's so difficult to sort through the complex replies to questions. And truth! It means nothing."

Her grief for Ben was replaced in part by a feeling of terrible guilt. Her actions had been totally irresponsible. She had thought only of revenge and would have gone to any lengths, even to the complete destruction of First City, in order to satisfy her selfish desires. These two men with her obviously felt she had been appallingly egotistical in her efforts to assuage her grief— yet they seemed to have forgiven her, as one would an un- developed, unknowing child. She could not forget, however, that they too had played their part. By killing Ben they had pulled the trigger which had released the savage need to sate her desire for revenge. They, too, were to blame.

"You sound as if the central brain can talk," she said, after a while.

"I wouldn't call it that. It's a fine point, but I like to think that speech and talk are two separate activities. Talking implies a two-way exchange—that someone is *listening* too, and hope- fully understanding. Speech does not require an answer, nor indeed a recipient. One can make speeches to the walls. It does enjoy listening to me repeat stories that it has told me, of a place called Rome, paved with smooth marble that glistened and sparkled in the sun . . . but it rarely shows any desire to talk."

Morag was fascinated. "What does it say when it does?"

"Nowadays it mostly says 'No' like a spoiled child. And like a child it is egotistical and selfish. Not completely its own fault. It's getting old, you see, and senile."

"Will it ever . . . die?"

"Cease to function? Perhaps, when it runs out of the chem- icals it needs to maintain itself. The only thing that keeps us alive is its own need to survive. However, there have been some grave developments lately."

Morag had, for a moment, forgotten Ben. She suddenly realized she was conversing amiably with the instigator of her lover's murder.

"I don't care about that," she said, coldly.

Felix Feverole looked taken aback for a moment; then he realized why she had changed her attitude.

"He's alive. Your little black man. We used a hypodermic, not a knife. I had him brought here. Bribed the physicians. He's in the next room."

"Ben? Alive?" She rushed to the dividing door and opened it. There was a form on a couch in the corner. She recognized the streak of white in the black hair.

"Ben!"

"Don't wake him," said Daniel, suddenly at her elbow.

But there was still a band of disbelief running through her thoughts. She crossed to the couch and saw with relief that Ben was still breathing. She kissed his face, oblivious of the hovering hunchback, and Ben sighed in his sleep. Stroking his hair, she turned and said fiercely, "If you've hurt him . . ."

Feverole entered the room. "There's nothing wrong with him that an explanation won't cure. He's just as obstinate as you, however. All I wanted him to do was leave me alone, forget about me. But he's obsessed by the thought that I'm some kind of decadent tyrant."

"But everyone thinks that."

"Hence the need to remain under cover. If you both insist . . . well, I don't want to have to take any drastic measures."

"Kill us," she stated, flatly.

"Not quite as drastic as that. *Make you forget*, perhaps. But that would mean impairing the rest of your memory. The drug doesn't work in fractions. It wipes your mind clean."

"Why don't you then!"

"Because, young lady, I do have some morals, despite what you think. Wiping out a person's identity is not a matter to consider lightly. However, since you arrived something has occurred to me. Perhaps you can help us . . . you and Ben. I have an idea which may result in prolonging the life of our city."

"What idea?"

"Perhaps it's time the Primary had another female Consul. Someone with an unusual psychological talent. . . ."

NINE

The ice formed a series of mirrors for the morning. Rita Riverman was duty Consul the night after the riot and she watched,
fascinated, while the Primary played with the city's lights as
the dawn came through the cone. The Primary sectioned the
city into arbitrary eighths and dimmed the lights in seven of
those areas while applying full power to the lone eighth. The
blaze of light from one segment threw images of the buildings
against the ice on the far side. The ice on the near side of the
lights seemed to flash-fire to brilliance and anyone in that
section looking directly at the ice must have been temporarily
blinded.

Rita watched the distroted images of the dark buildings jump
from one part of the icewall to another as the Primary chose
different sections to light up at random. One moment the brightness would ripple through all the sections, one after another
in sequence; the next it would leap in long strides around and
across the circle of the city. Then the sections would flash
again, randomly, backwards and forwards until Rita was dizzy

with her attempts to follow the pattern. She saw little point in asking the Primary to stop its game: there was no harm in it.

Suddenly there was a strobe effect and the ice seemed to be moving—falling, leaning, dropping, dipping—and she ducked instinctively. Then there was that reflection of the city again, cubist blocks overlapping one another, gliding impressions moving round the all-encompassing glacial wall in a ghostlike dance. Spikelets of light fenced on the ghost-fired prison, highlighting fissures, nodules, cracks in a silent display of white-light power. Finally, there was a period of occulting before the lamps settled to normal power once more.

Early that morning, Daniel and Morag want for a walk to survey the post-holocaust scene. In the quiet of the dawn hours debris littered the freezing streets and one or two hunched, silent figures were attempting to clear a way from a door or passage. They were like guilty phantoms, those cloaked shapes; the parents of an intransigent poltergeist child, straightening the household before the owners awoke. Morag was appalled by the devastation caused by the rioters. Remorse filled her, as she remembered that it was she who had instigated the violence.

All night the sounds of fighting and destruction had filtered through the walls of the apartment. The entrance had been securely locked and bolted from the inside but every so often there had been a hammering on the door followed by incomprehensible shouting: a call to join the rioters, or perhaps the trysts seeking scapegoats? Felix Feverole had said that the riot was a natural recurring high point in a cycle of frustration and claustrophobically induced tension which found a necessary release in wanton vandalism. "One might almost call it 'a fulfilment,'" he had said.

"You can use all the justification you please," said Morag, "but it's still my fault."

A child was gathering shards of shod from a gutter. Luckily there had been no deaths. Otherwise the shouters would have included them in their bellowed itinerary of the night's occurrences. When this had been ascertained, Morag and Daniel headed back toward the apartments.

The cold bit deep into Morag's flesh and she grumbled as she walked. "Why can't you men get us out of this place?"

Daniel raised an eyebrow. "Us? Why don't you get yourselves out of it? I never met a woman yet who didn't think she was better than me."

"Why can't we tunnel out? Has anyone thought of that?"

Daniel gave her an exasperated look. He stamped a foot. "Permafrost, hard as bedrock. And we haven't got the tools. You name it, it's been considered."

"What about through the ice? We could chip our way out."

"They tried that too. A party of them. They're still in there somewhere. The ice closed in behind them and made a tomb."

"How do you know they didn't get through?"

"The Primary told Felix. The central brain wants to get rid of the ice as much as we do. Gives it too much work. Constant work. It can never rest."

"Eternal hard labor?"

"Yes."

Morag thought for a while about all the deaths she had seen. She had been born in the city and no doubt would die here.

"The ice must be full of bodies."

"Yes."

She did not believe the central brain could not rescue the city from the ice if it wanted to. There was some reason, she was sure, why it held back. Was it something to do with the outside world?

She tried letting her mind wander but it had no real paths to tread. There were no clear pictures of the *outside* for her to dwell on. What was out there? More ice? Or flowers, like those that covered certain vegetables when they were allowed to run to seed in the farm halls? Or maybe the world was just a solid block of concrete, a city with never-ending streets? Or flat as a marble table enclosed by a dome of solid rock? She liked the last idea the most because it served best to soothe the nameless anxiety that had been with her all her days. Lovely, smooth stone, shining mottled colors into her eyes. Like those streets of Rome that Felix had spoken of earlier, stretching out to the walls of the world, with no edges to fall over or mar its . . . its *completeness*. Then she could walk and walk, and when she felt tired just lie down on the cool surface and sleep a sweet sleep. How beautiful the world must be, she thought, if it is really like that. She loved the thought of the clean lines of such a world. There would be other cities, of course—not many—one or two. And the sun that gave them light. Covering all would be the sky: the tough, inflexible sky of gray-blue stone. And no more ice. She hoped she would see it all before she died.

"What do you think the world is like outside?" she asked her companion.

"Terrible," he shuddered. "I like it here."

"You *like* it here?"

He gave her a sidelong glance. "Felix says it's because I'm insecure."

"But wouldn't you just like to *see* what's outside?" she persisted.

"I suppose so. No harm in looking, eh?"

"And what do you *think*?"

Daniel's angular face registered pain. "Think? I think it's all water. That's where the boreholes lead. We've flooded the world with water and now we're an island. . . ."

"That's horrible," she said.

"I told you it was."

They walked on in silence for a while. Some small pieces of ice, not fallbergs, clattered on the canopy above their heads. Finally it was Daniel who spoke.

"Ben Blakely. Was his father a timesmith?"

Morag stopped short. "Yes. Why, do you know him?"

"Did once."

"Can you take me to where he lives? I want to meet him. Ben . . . Ben is a little guarded about his family. I don't think he wants them to see me."

"Perhaps he doesn't want *you* to see *them*? I'll take you to where I last saw him. He's probably still there. A blind old man and his wife are not likely to move around that much. . . ."

Daniel led her down several side streets and alleys until they came to a crescent-shaped block of apartments. Then he climbed down the third set of steps to a basement, to rap on the door. Morag stayed up at street level. She saw an old woman appear and instantly she knew it was Ben's mother. Her hair was gray but there was that familiar streak of white at the brow.

"Belna Blakely," she called. The old woman looked up and smiled.

"Is this the lady?" she said to Daniel, who had been whispering to her. He nodded. Then to Morag, he said, "Don't try to run away. There's no back entrance."

Morag gave him a scornful look and then descended, pushing past Daniel and into the doorway. "I'm Morag, your son's . . . wife," she said.

She and Belna spoke to each other at length, still standing in the doorway. The old woman wanted to know how her son was faring and how he had managed to get himself such a beautiful wife, and Morag was anxious to know more about Ben, as a child and an adolescent. The two women charmed each other and Morag knew she had done the right thing in visiting them. Finally she said, "Can I meet Ben's father?"

The old lady smiled. "Of course. But try not to get him too excited. His heart. . . ."

Morag was shown into a dimly lit room. In the center of the floor, on a worn blanket folded into a quarter of its normal size, sat an old man. On his lap was a homemade scotograph which he used with a practiced hand. By his side stood a clockflower, an instrument cut entirely from stone, even down to the wheels and cogs in the clockwork movement. On the hour, one of the twelve petals would either open or close, depending upon whether it was before or after midnight. The action of opening or closing each petal was accompanied by a clacking sound. The old man could reach out and feel the clockflower's face, counting the petals and their positions.

"You wonder why a timesmith needs to know the hours,"

said the old man, unexpectedly. There was a heavy, but not oppressive, atmosphere inside the room. It was the weight of long hours of silent thought. Shadows moved along the stone walls as Morag sat in front of the timesmith, Ben's father. She was at a loss to answer his unprompted question.

"It does seem . . . well, frankly, yes."

"Don't be shy, child."

He reached out and ran his fingers over her features. Eventually he seemed satisfied.

"Time has many aspects. In order to forge it, one must work from a base."

She nodded, and then remembered he was blind. "I think I understand," she said.

"Why are you here, child? Do you require treatment? I no longer practice. . . ."

"No. I live with your son. I wanted to meet you and perhaps . . . ask a few questions. About your profession."

"You expect me to reveal professional secrets? Those of my society?"

"No. Not exactly. I would like to understand a little more, that's all."

"How is my son?"

"He is healthy . . . and happy, I think."

"You think?" The old man's black face wrinkled into a crumpled shadow.

"Well, I do not wish to sound immodest, but I believe he is happy because of me. We love each other, you see."

"I *do* see, with my inner eyes. And you wish to know about *time*. You want to know how we bend it, shape it into lasting daydreams?"

"To be frank, yes," she replied.

"Then I shall be equally frank. We cannot fashion time itself—what we do is distort the perception of the individual." He smiled blindly into the dim light. "Does that shock you? To find we are charlatans?"

"It doesn't *shock* me. It disappoints me."

"Ah, that's sad. A dream destroyed in a place like this is

not good. We have so very few dreams. I regret now that I told you."

"Please don't. I came to find the truth, not to seek a salve."

"Good. Good. But do not be too hasty in forming your conclusions. Think about this: your view of time is completely your own. An hour of full activity has a different length, shape and texture from an idle hour. Some hours are as long as days. Some as short as minutes. Time is relative, subjective. If I alter your perspective of time, your perception, then I am changing time itself. Do you see?"

"I'm beginning to."

"You are the anvil, I am the forge and the hammer. Between us we can beat a dull ingot into a golden thread. Last night's heavy dream can be elongated into days of joy."

He would not tell her the art. Perhaps he could not, although he did suggest that it was a trick of the mind. A *legerdemain* he called it, although she had never heard the word before, and he explained the meaning.

"I think you belittle your skills," she replied. "It is more than a conjuring trick."

He smiled. "Perhaps. But I have heard of one who was more than a timesmith. She did not interfere with time; quite the reverse. She moved people and places around within it."

Morag's heart began to quicken.

"What is her name? Where does she live?"

He laughed. "Such eagerness. My dear girl, she lived long before you or I first opened our eyes and saw this miserable city. She is a faint memory, a vague legend passed down from the timesmith to his apprentice. A figurehead to revere and attempt to emulate."

"These are professional secrets you're disclosing, aren't they? Why are you telling me?"

His blind smile disappeared, to be replaced by a look of utter seriousness.

"I don't know for sure, but you have something about you— I can sense it—a power of some kind. Perhaps you're not aware of it, not fully aware? You radiate . . . I can't quite grasp it, but it frightens me. Such a *force*."

"The woman in the legend. . . ."

"She could create as well as displace. She could reach out into the unknown, into the void, and create life there. Such a gift can be wonderful . . . or terrible. Certainly the owner under stress . . . but I know so little. If the gifted one was ignorant of her power, then *suggestion* would control the world."

"I don't understand," said Morag, helplessly. "I don't have any powers. I'm just a woman."

"Perhaps I'm wrong," he said. "I'm an old man. My own mind plays tricks now."

Before she left him she asked a final question.

"What was her name?"

"She was just . . . the mentor. Some called her Mento."

When they arrived back at the apartment, Ben was sitting up, wrapped in a toga. He smiled at her weakly. The drug they had given him had put him to sleep for two and a half days and he looked terrible. She decided to say nothing of her visit to his parents—at least for a while. He would probably be angry with her. She ran to him and hugged his head, but he eventually pushed her away in obvious embarrassment. The other two men grinned, which made him worse. She turned on them angrily.

"Don't do that," she snapped at them. "Look at his eyes. This is your fault."

Then turning to Ben, she said, "How do you feel?"

"Like I've been kicked in the head, but I suppose I'll get over it." He nodded at Felix Feverole. "I was right about him, wasn't I?"

"Partly," she acknowledged, "but he's no tyrant."

"We've only got their word on that."

"I believe them," she said, simply.

Feverole came to her and put an arm around her shoulder. "Thank you, Morag. It's not an easy task . . . and there are no rewards, nor even any thanks."

"How did you get chosen?" said Ben, with an envious tone in his voice.

"Still suspicious, eh?" said Feverole, misinterpreting. *"Chosen* is a word which implies glory. I was *selected* by the Primary for my ability to absorb knowledge and repeat it accurately. You see, the Primary likes to hear stories of those ancient people called the Romans whom I told you about. It knows them all, of course—it was the Primary who told me them in the first instance—but it enjoys the retelling."

"The Romans? That lived in the marble world?" Morag said, quickly.

"Yes, but many, many years ago. You're going to ask me what the world is like outside—that I can't tell you. I can only tell you what it was like where the Roman people lived."

"Yes?" said Ben, sitting on the edge of his bed. "Go on."

"Well, it was a sea of water, surrounded by land. They called the water *Mediterranean* and it tasted of salt. The land was called various names, like Britannia and Gaul, but at the center was a marble city."

"Where the Romans came from," said Morag.

"Quite. They fought many wars. especially in the beginning against a city called Carthage and, later, another called Alexandria. Three beautiful cities. You would think that would be enough for any world, but there were many, many more. It is these that the computer likes to hear about, and the politics of that time."

"My head can't contain more than three cities," said Morag, enigmatically. "I would settle for just three in my world."

"The land . . . what was that like?" asked Ben.

"Flat," replied Felix, "in some places. In others it rose out of the ground as rock to form high walls . . . mountains."

Morag remembered the song, *"Up the airy mountain, down the rushy glen. . . . "* She sang a little of it, softly, so Ben could form a picture. He nodded to show he understood.

"It must have changed a lot since then," Morag said, with a final and definite note to her voice which none of them could fail to recognize. "Because it's all marble now. And smooth

as—" she was going to say 'ice,' but that was a hateful simile—
"as glass," she finished lamely.

Feverole's white head jerked back, as if someone had slapped
him.

"Where did you hear that, Morag?"

"Nowhere," she replied. "I made it up. After all, if no one
has seen it, the world can be anything I want it to be, can't
it?"

"An infinite variety of forms," he murmured back.

"Pardon?"

"Nothing. Nothing at all. What's the matter with Ben?"
Feverole pointed at the little black man. Ben said he still felt
a little giddy and lay down again, but with his eyes open.
Morag tended him for a while and the other two men spoke
softly to one another in the corner. Later the four of them ate
together. Daniel had brought in the food the night before, while
the riots were still at their height.

"It's damned cold," grumbled Ben. "Why is the temperature
still dropping? The ice must be moving in."

"Princeps. The Primary. My colleague must be having a bad
time with him. He's not easy to control after an occurrence
like last night's."

"Occurrence?" Ben queried. "Oh, the riot. You told me. I
wish I'd been out there," he added fervently.

"Ben!" said Morag.

"Well, I do," he returned, defiantly. Then he said to Feverole,
"Your . . . colleagues. Were they selected for the same reason
you were?"

"One of them was. I'm not going to give you any names,
young man, so don't look at me like that . . . yes, one of them.
My only friend, apart from Daniel here. However, we can't
see each other too often. The other three have various talents."

"And the sixth person?"

Feverole smiled. "Ah, you know only too well about him,
don't you? Therein lies our mystery. The key was lost so long
ago now, I don't believe we'll ever find it. When one of us
dies the Primary sends a contact to the successor and the se-

lected man or woman is expected to retrieve the key any way he or she can. However, this one particular time the key was missing."

"Why can't you make another one?" asked Morag.

"It's not that sort of a key. It's an electronic device that emits a series of individual tones. We haven't the expertise, or the equipment to make such an instrument."

"So it's lost," said Ben.

"Yes."

"And what happens when the second key, and the third and so on . . . what happens when they've all gone?"

"Then the Primary will have to struggle on alone. It has no control over the doors to the Green Tower."

"Would it struggle on?" asked Morag.

Feverole shook his head slowly. "It's doubtful. You see, the talents of those three I spoke of . . . they're engineers. My friend and I, we are the counselors of the Primary. It needs us to maintain its mental stability. We talk to it, persuade it that life is worth holding on to, if only for another day. It is, after all, semi-organic and as such is vulnerable to mental instability. But the other three it has trained to repair its circuits—they do those small tasks which the central brain cannot do for itself.

"But don't concern yourselves too much. The Primary monitors our position in the city constantly. . . ."

"How?"

"It follows our heartbeats. The patterns are never identical, you know. It has me pinpointed now. It knows the rhythms of my heart as well as its own circuits."

"When you drop dead the next man or woman will be with you within seconds," said Ben, sarcastically.

"No, of course not. But Daniel will . . . and he will retrieve the key from my body. He's never far from me. We are constantly within calling distance—unless he knows I am secure, such as this morning when he and Morag went for a walk."

* * *

Ben still looked unconvinced. "So Daniel will hand over the key to your successor. No problems."

"But we do have a problem," added Feverole. "A very big problem."

Absently, it seemed, Ben asked, "What's that?"

"The Primary . . . it's developing a death wish."

"Becoming suicidal?" said Morag. What was this? What was he saying?

"Not exactly. It's doubtful whether it would take positive action to kill itself, but it might *allow* itself to die. There is a subtle difference."

"But, what you're really saying is there is no difference, as far as we're concerned," said Ben, grimly. "Suicide to the central brain means genocide to us."

"Exactly. That's why it's necessary to steer the Primary away from such thoughts. However, as senility sets in it becomes more and more depressed. We have to give it something to live for . . . that's where Morag comes in."

Morag had been regarding the interchange with some concern and now she felt sure of where it had been leading. Ben's expression was one of puzzlement, but then she knew he was slow to grasp the obvious.

She said, "You want me to allow the central brain into my mind."

"Exactly. It may not work . . . but then again." He showed his palms in a gesture of hope. "It will come to know how a human thinks . . . a human's fears, hopes, desires, all those other emotions which form our inner selves. Perhaps, as it comes to know us, through Morag, it will show compassion."

"No," said Morag softly.

Daniel, who had been quietly observing the three of them from the far side of the room, took a step toward her.

"Keep him away from me," said Morag, and Ben stood up ready to protect her.

Feverole sighed. "Stop this. You too, Daniel. There's no need for it." He looked directly into her eyes. "Morag, you will do as I say. You're a prostitute and you'll ply your chosen profession where and when I tell you to. If you don't, I'll hand you both over to Raxonberg. I don't know what he'll do to Ben, but he'll hang you within two days. Of that you can be sure. Incitement to riot is a capital offense.

"Ben will probably suffer even more horribly. Raxonberg is an unashamed sadist," he added, after a moment's silence.

Morag gripped Ben's arm, as he started to move toward Feverole, checking him. "No, Ben, he's right."

"Right?"

She looked him full in the face. "Leave it, Ben. I'll do it. I can't risk being arrested. Please?"

Ben read the message in her eyes and shrugged. He pulled his arm away from her hand and took himself sullenly into the next room. Daniel followed him. Felix Feverole patted Morag's arm. He repeated an earlier remark of Ben's. "I'm sorry, but you're a unique woman." Then he went to join the other two in the next room.

Later, as she lay pretending to sleep, she thought of the Messiah. When would he show himself? The people were becoming desperate. Even those like Feverole, whom Morag knew was not a bad man, not one who enjoyed blackmailing women, even if they were whores. He had said that Raxonberg was not ashamed of being vicious and cruel but his tone had implied strong disapproval. When the principles of men like Feverole began to crack and integrity was a commodity to be bartered for, then hope was fast draining away. What would they do? They needed a divine leader. One who could part the ice with a wave of his hand. One sent by God to lead them from their captivity and out into whatever world lay beyond. Was it as she imagined or was it some other place of which she had no picture? Another dream-world perhaps, or another dimension? Or her place of marble floors?

She woke, staring into the blackness of the room. Beside her there was a stirring, and in the gloom she could see the hunch of Daniel's shoulders as he slept like a curled beast. Ben was in the next room with Felix Feverole. They had forbidden her to sleep with her lover, fearful of plots devised in the darkness. So they should be. She intended to escape as soon as there was an opportunity. Daniel grunted and moved again.

When sleep refused to come, she recalled with guilty relish the time she had visited a cheap timesmith. The young man's practice was conducted from beneath a lean-to in an alley. After handing him two red disks in payment he entered her mind with his eyes: those eyes which held a timeless quality that transported the client beyond the walls of the world to places where dreams were fashioned. She had given him the fragment of poetry around which he was to build her escape from the here and now: *The greater cats with golden eyes stare out between the bars. Deserts are there, and different skies and night with different stars. They roam the aromatic hill and mate as fiercely as they kill.* . . . A flight of the senses. She was swathed in sensations. This time she was in a humid sultry place of wet vegetation. There was a beast there, with her, on a grassy slope. It was huge and golden, and on seeing her it rolled onto its side as if inviting play. Naked, she moved toward the animal in a lazy run and fell onto its soft, tawny form. The hair on its head was long and smelled of hot, dusty days and she buried her face in the deep ruff, breathing deeply. The smell was like a drug which filled her mind with the buzzing of small winged creatures. They wrestled there, the woman and the beast, rolling, over and over in the tall grass that sang with a thousand tiny voices. And the great jaws were around her head, gently squeezing. Hot, wet breath engulfed her own, threatening to suffocate her. Pulling free, she pummeled the great torso, the heavy legs with the bronze hair feathering the trailing edge of the forelimbs. Beautiful beast. Its pads, with claws retracted, batted her buttocks playfully. An then, suddenly, she was between its thighs and there was an urgency to the movements. She looked up, consumed but startled by the change from loving play to love play, and the face she saw was a man's, and his skin smelled of high passion, and his eyes burned with heat of his fire. His limbs were strong as he held her and his heart pounded against her ribs with a strong rhythm. They moved to the beat of his heart and soon her own battled with it, and fled—retreating, turning, surrendering. . . .

TEN

The street lamps shone with a dim yellow-orange reminiscent of the eyes of the diseased during the last plague. Morag had only been a young girl at the time, but she remembered the bodies piled high outside the blockhouses and the smell of fear within: the bolted doors and the occasional scream of an awful, personal discovery. And in eyes yet free of the ocher tint there had been the terrible, circular terror which, even to a child, spelled *no escape*. Around them the ice-ring, and among them a dreadful beast that crawled slowly into their apartments, through locked doors, and consumed them one by one, without mercy. They fought it with prayers and isolation but two-thirds of the adult population had been struck down. The children went unscathed but with the remembrance of a possible future heritage deeply embedded in their conscious.

Orange light meant that the power was low. Ice covered the cobbles and it was difficult to walk quickly. The Primary Computer was not taking the riot lightly.

Morag and Ben crept along the alleys, keeping away from

Raxonberg's men. They were thieves as well as insurgents now, having stolen Feverole's key to the Green Tower.

"Where are we going?" asked Morag.

Ben grunted. "To the place Feverole visited when we saw him that day. Come on. Stop wasting time."

"What did you hit him with?" Although she could sympathize with Ben's reasons for having to strike one of their jailers, she did not want either of them to suffer any permanent injury, especially by Ben's hands.

"Who, Daniel? He'll be all right."

"And what happens when Feverole wakes and unties Daniel? They'll call the trysts and the whole city will be looking for us."

Ben smiled grimly. "Not them. They'll have to do it alone. He'd lose his cover and Raxonberg would give his right arm to get hold of a key."

Morag laughed out loud. Raxonberg, as she and everyone else knew, had no right arm. A youth had taken it off him in a street fight with longknives when Raxonberg was a young man. It was said that the incident had been responsible for the firing of Raxonberg's ambition to become Chief of Trysts. Of course, the other youth was dead now. Raxonberg hung him on some trivial count the day he was appointed to the position he now held.

"Do you think he was telling the truth?" Morag asked.

"Who?"

"Felix Feverole. About the Primary. Is it an unwilling slave, not a master?"

"I think he's lying. That apartment—it's just a front."

They passed the market square. In one corner the tattered flags of the rioters hung from barely accessible parts of the guildhall. They were meaningless pieces of rag, some shapeless and without any kind of emblem, others torn into the semblance of a square and marked with dye. The marks had no common design. They were merely symbols in themselves. Any piece of cloth hung from a public building was representative of rebellion. Merely invoking the memory of a banner was enough.

All flags were symbols of defiance—all rags, if freely hung or draped in a prominent place, or waved at the end of a pole, were flags. Men and women had been arrested for removing an item of clothing and holding it aloft. The law was quick to stamp on insurrection; so was the Primary.

Morag asked Ben why the flags had not been removed.

"Someone's got to get up there first, to pull them down."

"But those who put them up? They had to make the climb."

"Listen, in a riot people are intoxicated. They're drunk on mob law, violence and a heady kind of freedom that pumps recklessness into people's veins. They'll make the climb when the riots are at their height but bring'em back in the quiet of the next morning and they'll quake at the prospect."

Morag said, "You sound as if you know."

He nodded. "I remember another riot once. I swam across a river of meltwater not a hundred meters from a borehole. I was laughing at the time—laughing at the tryst who attempted to follow and was swept away, down into the borehole which had failed to claim me. But afterward . . . well, let me tell you I still have nightmares. Still recall only too vividly that the water should have frozen my limbs to a standstill and taken me. It's the truth, believe me."

They had reached the long hut by this time, but passed it by without pausing. They had no wish to meet Estelle or any of her band.

Besides the electronic key to the Green Tower, Ben had taken the metal key to Feverole's ground floor apartment. Once inside they took out the electronic key. It was a simple black card with a depression. When a warm thumb filled the hollow a series of notes issued from the key. On the back of the card was a ring of prongs or tines with the words RECHARGE embossed beneath.

They played the key and nothing happened. Not that they were aware of, anyway. For a few minutes Ben cursed, thinking they had the wrong room, or that he had mishandled the device in some way. Then Morag looked under the bed and saw an opening large enough to crawl into. Ben immediately did so and she followed, not without trepidation.

Inside was a tunnel with small turtle-back lights clamped to the ceiling at regular intervals. The opening closed behind them automatically. Along the walls of the tunnel were strange markings, which neither Morag nor Ben could understand. There were many cables and pipes too, some covered by conduit, others clamped neatly to the walls with metal clips.

"An underworld," breathed Morag. "Do you think there's a way to the other side of the ice along these tunnels?"

"If there was," said Ben, "do you think Feverole or anyone with a key would still be here?"

She was instantly deflated. "No, I suppose not. Unless they *liked* being here."

They started down the tunnel, occasionally pausing to listen.

"What's that noise?" said Morag, finding that she was, for some inexplicable reason, whispering. It was as if they were invading some kind of sanctuary: it had the awesome atmosphere associated with such places.

"What noise?"

"That dull roar. Can you hear it?"

Ben stopped walking and frowned. Then he said, "I guess it's the power source: the geothermal borehole which the computers control. We must be getting close to the Green Tower."

Suddenly they were in an antechamber of some sort, and instead of the tunnel continuing unbroken, there were five more exits leading off the other side.

Ben stood in thought for a moment, then said, "Come on. We could stand here forever," and entered one of the tunnels: the center one. Morag hesitated for a few moments in indecision. As she went to follow him a figure appeared in one of the other entrances. It beckoned.

"Ben!" she called, down the center tunnel. "Quickly. There's a man here."

She stared at the newcomer as she waited for Ben to return. There was something familiar about the man which eluded her. His face was half-hidden in the shadows.

"Who are you?" she asked. "Can you help us? We're lost."

He stepped out into the light then, and Morag caught her breath in fear. It was her father. Her dead father.

"What do you want?" she said. "What is it?"

"Don't you recognize me?" The hollows in his cheeks moved as he spoke the words but otherwise his expression did not change. He was gaunt and his skin had a strange sallow color.

"Are you alive?" she asked, aware of the catch in her voice. She had not seen him since she was a small girl but there was no doubt it was her father. She had his picture locked in her memory. He was the same man to a hair. Then she realized what was wrong. This figure, this man, was a replica of her father—the day he had died. Her real father would be an old man—much older than the person that stood before her.

"You know I'm not living," he replied. Again, the faintest of shadows passed over his face as he spoke.

"Can you read my thoughts, too?"

"I *am* your thoughts. You want the tunnel to the Green Tower. The answer is within yourself. I am that desire, manifest. You may follow me. . . ."

The light flickered where he stood and Morag looked up, searching for some device that could produce a three-dimensional image, but the walls looked bare.

"Ben!" she shouted, again, realizing her first call had not brought him back to her. "Don't leave me here."

She ran into the center tunnel with the apparition following her silently. It kept pace with her but maintained a distance of some seven meters. When she stopped, the phantom also halted, until finally she turned to face it.

"Leave me alone," she shouted, defiantly. Her words echoed down the long tunnel.

"I cannot. You are going the wrong way. Ben Blakely is lost in the maze ahead. If you continue, you too will be unable to find your way back. Turn around now."

Ben lost? She had heard of the maze below the Green Tower but it had meant little to her before.

"There are those who are lost forever," continued the ghost. "Their remains fill the maze with the fumes of rotting flesh. . . ."

"Stop it!" she snapped. "I'm going to find him."

"Best you follow me. Once you find the Green Tower, then you can help him."

Suddenly Morag cried out. The apparition had moved closer and parts of him disappeared. Half a face, an arm and leg, a severed torso, hovered before her. He stepped back again, becoming whole.

"It's a trick," she said.

"Yes, but not of the light or of the dark. A trick of the mind. Soon you will know . . . but now I urge you to come with me."

He turned and this time Morag did follow. There was no way she could save Ben from dying of thirst in the maze by copying his example. What idiots they had been! Of course the tower would be protected by more than secret entrances and electronic keys. God knows what other horrors lay in wait for them in these tunnels. Perhaps this replica of her father would protect her? At first he had alarmed her, but now all she was interested in was Ben.

She followed the ghost out into the antechamber and into the tunnel whence it had appeard.

"Who are you?" she asked.

"Your father, of course. And yet . . . think of me as power. Think of all those kilometers of beautiful tubes filled with a fluid life force that moves like a tide, rolls like a sea from tank to tank, gathering energy. Energy for *thought*, not for wasting on useless physical exercise—running, walking, leaping, *copulating*." The last word was full of disdain.

"Hands," she argued. "They're the necessary tools. Without them we wouldn't be able to . . . make things."

"To make things? For what? So that you can sit down? Stand up? Move around faster? *Copulate without reproducing*?"

"So that we can *create*," she snapped. "Stone sculptures."

"Merely tangible thoughts. A clockflower is only a thought expressed in stone. Stone thoughts. Pretty arrogant, wouldn't you say, that you should consider such thoughts worth preserving for more than the time it takes to produce them in the mind? And why bother, if not for your own self-gratification, to translate those thoughts into tangible objects. So that they can be *praised*, touched for base sensuality, viewed for gratuitous pleasure?"

"So they can be used."

She walked after him, her feelings a turmoil of anger and frustration at his stupid arguments.

Suddenly she was triumphant. "To communicate," she cried.

"Do you seriously believe," he replied, "that the artist successfully communicates with those outside his own skull? Here, I am an artist and I produce a flower in rock. But is it rock? Is the flower indeed a flower? Before my death they ask me, 'What were you trying to do, when you cut these forms? Flowers of rock yes, they surely mean much more—they are symbols, perhaps of life and death?'

"'No, no,' I reply. 'You have missed the point completely. What I was trying to depict was this and this'—and I try to explain what my created object means, but they still fail to understand because I am an artist, not someone who is able to express my feelings verbally. At least not to the degree, the precision, which is necessary to convey the complex meaning behind the sculpture—otherwise I would never have let myself flow through the chisel in the first instance."

"And after your death?" said Morag, anticipating.

He laughed. "After? They come in hordes—interpreters to lecture, to spend a whole lifetime studying my flower of rock. They speak a million words attempting to *discover*. And another million words in conveying their discoveries. They argue. They fight. Each has his or her own idea on what the artist was trying to communicate and none of them ever agree. And I move in my ice grave at every attempt, groaning, 'Wrong. Wrong. What I was trying to show was this. . . .' And there's no one to listen. No one to hear. And even if they could they would contradict me, saying, 'Of course you didn't mean such-and-such. I've spent a lifetime studying your work, nobody is a greater authority on your clockflower than I. You may be the

artist, but when it comes to an expert opinion on the floral
rocks . . . ' So that's where we leave it, Morag, my child. Opinions—not communication."

With that, the ghost disappeared and Morag found herself
outside a set of double doors. They opened as if they sensed
her presence. Inside was a small, confined room.

ELEVEN

The small room carried Morag swiftly upward. She felt exhilarated and there was a moment when she wondered whether she would be taken up, beyond the lip of the ice cone, and out into the world. How wonderful that would be! Then she remembered Ben. She couldn't leave without him. There would be no point in going on her own, without someone to share it. Not just *some*one, either.

The room stopped and the doors opened, inviting her to step out. She did so, and found herself in a much larger, dome-shaped room. There was a strange green light from the ceiling and the floor was soft beneath her feet. The room had a holy atmosphere, hushed—yet there was a humming, very soft, in the air. Before her was what appeared to be an altar covered in colored spires that flashed and winked and ran in bars of many hues along its fluted uprights. A man was standing in front of the altar and he turned, his eyes wide with surprise.

"Who . . . ?" he began.

The altar sang out in rich deep tones, filling the room with its mellow, resonant voice.

"She is here because of me. Let her speak."

Morag fell to her knees, trembling. "I am Morag Mac-Kenzie."

"I know who you are," said the altar.

The man snapped. "How did you get here? Where's . . .?"

"Be quiet!" The tone was like a whiplash cracking on the still air. Morag put her fingers over her ears.

"It's all right, Morag," said the altar. Again the voice had changed, back to its organ-base mode.

"Are you the Primary?" she asked, taking her fingers from her ears.

She noticed that the man was standing perfectly still, as if obeying an unspoken command.

"I am Princeps, First Citizen of this city. You are one of those whom I keep within the bosom of the ice."

"Why can't you get us out of here?" asked Morag, coming immediately to the point of her visit. "Burn a hole through the ice?"

The man shifted his position. "This talk is dangerous for both of you," he said, to the Primary. "You know a flood would drown us all."

"Let her talk," answered the Primary. The lights on its black, convoluted, concave form rippled as it spoke. To Morag it appeared to be rearing like a huge, winged bird, looming over the dwarfed shape of the man it seemed about to enfold. Then she realized there was no threat, merely the illusion of movement, of a swooping form.

"You frighten me," she said.

"I?" The note was musical, entrancing. A child with a voice of bells.

"Yes. You have no face but you remind me of someone."

Suddenly human, or rather inhuman, features appeared just where the wings came together. The eyes, nose and lips were demonic. They glowed dull red. The mouth sneered and the sneer became a crescent grin.

"Do you still recognize me? Am I your savior, Lucifer? Am I Beelzebub, your mentor?"

Morag fought against the panic that welled within her breast. If she was to have any influence over this . . . this *brain*, then she had to appear in control of herself. Ben's life depended on her and without Ben she would be reduced to being the shallow person she was before she had met him. Ben had awakened emotions she never knew she had and no one was going to take him without a fight.

"You are foolish if you think you can impress me with silly tricks. While you were unknown to me, I felt afraid. Not now. I can see the worst."

The man stepped backward, away from the Primary, with a sharp intake of breath. The face disappeared from the bank of lights, instantly. There was a silence in the room deeper than a death. She was determined that she would not be browbeaten by a supercilious liquid brain with a penchant for autocratic rule. If it was going to kill her, so be it, but she would not allow it to humiliate her. Clearly her companion feared the worst. He was as white as frost and he stared at her as if she were as irrational as the Primary. She could have told him how wrong he was. Her behavior was perfectly predictable: Ben could have told him *that*.

"The person has spirit. The person has spirit," said the Primary, after a seemingly interminable silence. It was almost as if it were speaking to itself.

"We have work to do, young woman. Important work. The city depends upon my vigilance. I must repair . . ."

Suddenly the small room was back and the doors opened. A man in working clothes, with tools in his hands, stood there. The first man made a sign and the second nodded abruptly. The next moment he was gone.

"Why did you send away the engineer, Canstone? Were you afraid that three would confuse me more than two?"

"To be honest, yes, Princeps."

"You *beautiful* man."

Morag was startled by the voice. It belonged to a woman. An erotic, sexually active woman of the kind who still seduces

young men when age has advanced her own body beyond
sensual desire.

"Morag MacKenzie."

"Yes," she answered.

"Tell us why you have come here. My lover Canstone wishes
to know as much as I. Was it to see me, your First Citizen?"

"Partly that. And partly because I hoped I could . . . persuade
you to help us all escape. Ben is trapped in the maze below.
If you could find him for me, then cut a hole somehow. . . ."

"I'm afraid my sweet Canstone was right when he said it
was too dangerous. I cannot *cut*—I have not the means. I can
melt the ice, but that would cause a flood for I can only do so
from the inside—and before I reached the outside the cone
would have filled with meltwater."

"Isn't there *anything* you can do?"

"I can do *everything*, but at what cost to my people?"

Morag became desperate in her entreaties. "What about the
Messiah?"

"No," shouted Canstone.

The voiced filled the room, yet it was but a whisper.

"Messiah? What is this *Messiah*?"

"He who will deliver us from evil!"

"Evil? From what evil?"

"From here. This place."

The Primary seemed absorbed by this piece of intelligence
for a long time. Then it said, "I will speak with you, Canstone,
on this Messiah. Later. If he is a god-figure he need not fear
me. Gods may speak with gods and walk away unscathed."

"You are not divine," said Morag. "If you were, you could
deliver us, fire or flood notwithstanding."

"One day you will know," replied the Primary, enigmatically.

Morag decided to challenge the central brain with a second
question but first she said, "That ghost in the tunnel. You
created it, didn't you? Why did you choose the image of my
father?"

"It was significant. Fathers are not always who they appear
to be. Fathers are often only fathers in name, not in deed."

If the Primary had wanted to confuse Morag it was doing so with success. There was something behind its words that she could not grasp but which she felt was the key to *her*, to Morag.

"It was symbolic," the Primary added, as she stood in thought.

"Of what? All it did was sing your praises. That's how I guessed it was you."

"Please," muttered Canstone, "do you want to kill us all? You will do nothing but harm by angering the Princeps."

"Perhaps it needs to hear the truth from time to time," answered Morag, confidently. "Perhaps people like you have filled its mind with syrupy flattery for so long it's confused and no longer knows its place."

"What place is that?" cried a child's voice.

"The servant of the people," Morag said, undaunted by the abrupt change of tone. "You were built to serve us and people like this man take your mastery over electro-mechanical devices to mean mastery over us all."

"The key word is *control*," snapped Canstone. "He who controls fate has the mastery, be it over machines or men . . . or women," he added, after an insulting pause.

"If I might interrupt," said the Primary, its voice as soft as birds' wings brushing silk, "this woman has a point. None of us are masters or mistresses of our own fate. We are controlled by circumstances. I know why I was created and it was not for mastery nor was it for servitude. This is a secret I am not able to divulge."

"Tell us one thing," said Morag, the question on her tongue now. "What is the world outside like?"

"What do you *think* it looks like?"

"Marble. Flat, smooth marble. Smooth as kitchen slabs."

Canstone sniggered.

The Primary, however, murmured an agreement.

"Marble. That would be a pleasant sight. So be it, it is marble."

Morag was filled with indignation. "You can't create the world. It is what it is!"

"Quite wrong, child. It is what you believe it is. And since you will see it, you might as well make it the place you want it to be. . . . Come here, woman."

Morag hesitated but the central brain snapped out the command again and reluctantly she found herself moving forward. She stopped in front of the altar.

"Put your hands on my panel," said the Primary.

"MacKenzie!" shouted Canstone in a warning voice, but already her palms were on the warm panel. Suddenly her head felt as if it weighed a ton. The Primary was inside her; like a huge, fat god it pressed upon her brain, probing, searching. . . . Her legs began to buckle and she tried to scream. The Primary took control of the motor areas of her brain to prevent the cry. She felt its psyche settle against her mind and it was a cold, ugly thing, without compassion, without pity. *When I die*, it told her, *you will have total power but no control. You have some of Mento's power now, but it is weak. When the time comes to transfer responsibility, I will call for you. Daughter.*

Suddenly the coldness had gone from the Primary's psyche: replaced not by a warmth exactly, but by a kind of painful yearning. She could sense the strange mind longing for a state which it could never experience. *I am going to die*, it said, *without ever knowing the pleasure of love.*

Despite all its sneering talk about *copulation* she knew that the Primary regretted the fact that it could never experience physical love and she was shocked by the depth of that regret. It pulled at her own heart with strong fingers and an overwhelming pity flooded through her.

No, it said. *Not that. It is arrogant to feel for me in that way. The one I yearn for has gone. She was, above all, the epitome of splendid womanhood. I could trace back the whole of creation, every creature in the evolution of her body, from the first tiny spark of life to the woman called Mento. Her body was formed of butterflies and humming birds and murmuring insects—all the colors of creation—the bright green of a lizard's back was in her eyes—the black of a raven's wing was*

*in her hair. In her mating was the nature of the tiger—oh
yes—and the snake's strike in her temper. She had the tenderness of a dove and the anger of the shrew. I could go back
in her body, creature by creature, to the beginning of life. She
held them all, simultaneously, the myriad life forms that were
her ancestry, back to the first cell, the first unit of protoplasm.
All within herself. In her form was the natural history of the
world.* It paused. Then it said, *Ah, I see you wonder why I
yearn for a woman when I am a sexless creation. But you see,
it was Mento that I loved, the person, the spirit. If she had
been a man I would have loved her just the same. Now go,
Morag, you have too much of her in you. You disturb my soul.*

Her head was light again. Something . . . something . . . but
she could not remember. The central brain had told her . . .
gone. It was gone. What had it said? Something about death.
Its own death.

Dismay flooded through Morag's body.

"Will we leave this place? Before you die?"

"Not unless your Messiah can cut through ice with his eyes.
The walls around our city are three kilometers thick. He will
need sharp eyes."

Morag sensed an underlying note of mocking satisfaction in
the Primary's voice but she remained silent. Canstone began
murmuring to the Primary, his voice edged with urgency. She
moved to the side of the room and gazed out through the tinted
glass at the city spread below her. At any other time the view
might have been exhilarating, but fresh from her conversation
with the Primary and its emphatic opinions on their future, the
city merely looked like a prison from a different angle. The
buildings looked squat and ugly from above. She could see
tiny fragments of shattered ice glinting on the rooftops of the
buildings. In the distance was the long house where Estelle
and the people of pleasure plied their trade: behind that, more
gray blocks and streets peopled by figures in gray togas. A
drab world, she thought, for drab inhabitants. Wait. What was
that? On the roof of a building some two hundred meters from
the tower? Two people were sewing a huge triangle of ma-

terial—and there: there was the cradle-shape of the gondola.
A balloon ascent. There was to be another ascent.

"I suppose you think they're heroes?" Canstone had moved
up beside her. She pretended she had not heard. Perhaps this
companion of the Primary would find some way to stop those
brave adventurers.

"They'll die, you know. The turbulence up there . . . a flimsy
balloon will be flung against the lip. They'll fall."

"Maybe not," she said. "Perhaps this time they'll make it.
Perhaps they've done it before."

"Stories. Believe me when I say that no one's ever gone
beyond the lip and into the open world. I wish it weren't true,
but it is."

"You wish it weren't true," she mouthed bitterly.

"Look, I don't know what you have against me but all I do
is keep the Primary from destroying itself, and us with it."

She looked over her shoulder at the black altar. "Won't it
hear you?"

"Of course, but it knows me like I know myself. Why should
I keep hidden what has been obvious for as long as I have had
a key. Incidentally, whose key have you got? Not the missing
one?"

"Felix Feverole's."

Canstone nodded. "I see. Well, this is a mess. I don't know
what we're going to do about it, but whatever happens our
identities must remain a secret from the mob . . . and the trysts.
If Raxonberg ever got into this tower well, you know as well
as I do, the man's a megalomaniac. And the mobs would tear
this place apart when the mood came over them. They're the
most efficient machines for self-destruction that have ever graced
any self-contained world."

"Look, what about Ben?"

"Ben?"

"Ben Blakely, my companion. He's down below somewhere. . . ."

"Ah yes, the maze. He'll probably be insane before long,
you know," he said, matter-of-factly. "The maze is not simply

a criss-crossing of tunnels leading to circular routes or dead ends, but a globe, like a ball of cheese through which a thousand maggots have passed. He will climb, he will fall, sliding down smooth narrow tubes to spherical chambers with a dozen exits. A madhouse."

"Stop it."

"I'm sorry, but you need to know. The horror of that place is indescribable."

"You sound as if you've been there."

"I've seen it, on the screen. The Primary has shown it to me."

"Ben has a strong mind. He'll be all right. We have to find him."

"Impossible."

"Everything is impossible to you, Canstone. That's why you're a computer's lackey. You have no imagination. You have no optimism. And worst of all, you have no hope."

She was at first delighted and then, when her triumph had passed, contrite, to see the barbs strike home. His face took on an expression of such misery that it was impossible for her to feel anything but pity.

"I'm sorry. I shouldn't have said that."

"Why not? It's true. However, I'm not ashamed," he said, stiffly.

"Of course not. Why should you be? But I meant what I said—I must find Ben. If you won't help me, I'll ask the Primary."

Below her the people on the roof busied themselves sewing together a balloon. Even if they died, they would not have failed. To have begun such a journey was success in itself. Of course, if Raxonberg caught them they would see only the inside of one of his confinement centers. Perhaps they would even be tortured. Raxonberg, it was said, was fond of breaking people.

"The man called Blakely," said the Primary, "has been guided to the elevator doors. There he has been told to wait for your return, Morag MacKenzie."

"Elevator?" she queried, then, "Oh, the small floating room."

Canstone looked as if he had been slapped.

"Princeps. You . . . you helped this man?"

"I care nothing for Blakely. I am concerned only with MacKenzie. She is the woman who may one day rule you all, when I am gone. If she requires Blakely, then I give him to her."

"Thank you," said Morag, softly.

"But," said Canstone to the Primary, "these people. They will destroy us."

Morag flared. "What sort of fools do you take us for? Do you seriously think I'm going to lead the mobs to you? Or Raxonberg? Give me a little credit for some intelligence."

"Yes, but . . ."

The Primary interrupted. "Have you seen this Raxonberg, my child?"

"I've seen him. His trysts arrested me once."

"And is he . . . like you? Full of fire?"

Morag considered for a moment whether to lie. Finally she said, "He's a one-armed, self-indulgent killer who would rather destroy than create. He's despicable."

"Yes, but is he *strong*?" insisted the Primary.

"Physically, he's as hard and tough as any man who's fought his way up from the streets."

Suddenly, the room filled with white light. Morag saw a complex array of tubes that twisted their way into the ceiling of the dome. She saw the Primary create a series of pictures there, a thousand scenes, each brilliant in color and composition yet lasting only for a microsecond. It was just possible to capture an impression that was immediately replaced and overlaid by another. Finally, the room dimmed again.

"There, you have seen my body, such as it is, MacKenzie. You notice how astounded Canstone looks. This is because he himself has not seen me before today. Now go, child. Find

Blakely. Make children, or whatever you wish to do. Forget about escape. This is our world. Enjoy what you can of it. Forget . . . Messiahs."

The elevator doors opened to receive her.

TWELVE

Ben was outside the elevator doors when they opened at the bottom of the shaft. Morag fell into his arms, holding him tightly. He stood there awkwardly, allowing her to hug him for a few moments, then he pushed her gently away from him. She knew that it was not a lack of love that prompted his actions nor even a lack of affection. He loved her but he was not a demonstrative man. It embarrassed him to be the object of such display and, even though they were alone, she could sense his internal restlessness, the shy fingers plucking at his self-consciousness.

"Where have you been?" He nodded at the elevator shaft.

She told him everything that had happened to her, leaving out the part where she pleaded for him to be found. His pride would be hurt if he realized that he had failed miserably, where she had been successful.

Ben was suddenly very animated.

"You saw it? You saw the central brain?"

"It's not just a brain. It's more like a person—a manufactured person. It talks in many voices; some of what it said I didn't understand. But it's growing old."

"My God. Feverole wasn't lying."

"Anyway, your theory of men controlling the Primary—it calls itself Princeps—the theory's wrong. It isn't controlled by anyone. We and the Primary are interdependent. We need it, it needs us. Without each other we die."

"It needs a stimulus?"

"It needs a reason to survive, like a life form to foster. It needs people."

Ben nodded, then looked around him. "Let's get out of here."

Morag took his hand and they began walking toward the tunnel. Then Ben paused.

"What is it?" she asked.

"I was lost in here, a little while ago."

"It's all right. The Primary told me all tunnels lead back to an exit. We can't get lost on the way back."

"I see." He still hesitated. "Listen, do you believe in ghosts? You know, the dead. . . ."

She laughed. "So it happened to you too? Who was it?"

"My grandfather." He seemed reluctant to move forward.

Morag almost dragged him into the dimmer lights of the low tunnel. "That wasn't your grandfather, it was the Primary. One of its many tricks. This is Primary territory down here."

"It's *all* Primary territory," replied Ben in a quiet tone, but he followed her without resistance now.

Since her encounter with the Primary, Morag had been in a confused state of mind. While there was a certain exhilaration at having done what few others would have dared, she was vaguely disappointed. The meeting had been far from fulfilling. In fact it had opened yet more questions regarding the predicament of her race. If the Primary was dependent on the people, and the people dependent on the Primary, who had created the cycle? Someone had first to produce the cone of ice, then populate it with *unwilling* people, while at the same time creating or manufacturing a central brain interdependent with the inhabitants of the city. It seemed an impossible situation. It would be too much of a coincidence to have a unique semi-organic monster, whose function it was to keep walls of ice at bay, available just when the weather turned bad and the elements started closing in on them. It was this mutual arrangement which worried her more than anything else. It had that *feel* of permanence about it. Someone had set it up so that the situation fed upon itself and reproduced itself—a cyclic creation, which if interrupted must result in a catastrophe. So they were meant to live forever as they were—or suffer genocide.

"We're coming to the end," said Ben. The tunnel floor and walls felt springy now, almost organic. Also there was an ugly, offensive smell which made it difficult to breathe.

There was an exit before them: green doors, flush fitting. There was no need to use the key: the doors slid open as the pair approached. Passing through, they found themselves in an alley. Surprised, Morag turned to see the wall close behind them.

They went out of the alley into the street. There were a few people about on foot and one or two sedan chairs. Morag recognized a building and knew they were on the South Side of the city. She touched Ben's arm and they made their way along the street, moving northeast. Suddenly, as they reached the end, two trysts turned the corner and walked toward them. The trysts were casually swinging shod truncheons: the official weapon of the force.

"Keep walking," muttered Ben to Morag.

The trysts passed them with barely a glance. Just as Morag and Ben were turning the corner they heard, "Wait, you!"

Foolishly, she turned and stared. The two trysts stared back. Then one of them said, "That's her . . . the MacKenzie woman." He whirled the heavy club about his head and Morag ducked instinctively. The next second the missile thudded into the wall above her head.

Ben's knife was out and he stood ready for them but Morag pulled him away. "Come on, Ben!" she shouted, almost angrily. "Leave them."

She began to run. Ben was close behind her. They wove in and out of streetwalkers with the two trysts not far behind.

"Quickly, down here," called Ben, and ducked into an alley. Morag followed. Halfway down the alley Ben found an open door. They ran in and along a corridor. The way out was blocked so they took the stairs, not looking behind them to see if they were being pursued. They raced past seven floors and, exhausted, eventually reached the roof.

"Shall-we-go-out?" said Ben, breathlessly.

Morag's lungs felt as if they were full of little clawing beasts, tearing at their linings. She nodded. They went out onto the roof.

"Hey!"

A man and a woman were kneeling on another roof not far away, working with needles. They were sewing together dozens of togas that had been smeared with wax. Morag and Ben crossed several of the walkways to get to them but they were so busy at their task that the approach went unnoticed until Morag was standing on the expanse of material stretched over the rooftop. The woman looked up, startled, and cried, "Simon!"

The man's head jerked up and there was fear in his face. Seeing that they were not in trysts' uniform, his fear turned to anger.

"Get off," he yelled, waving his arms. "Do you want to damage it?"

Ben and Morag looked down and saw that they were still standing on the material. Gingerly, they walked across it until they were on the tiled roofing.

The man, a large, balding type with a heavy nose, crossed to them. She read anger in his face, and also his name: Simon Sand.

"What the hell do you think you're doing? You'll rip our balloon."

"The balloonists," said Morag, joyfully. Ben looked puzzled but said, "We're being chased by trysts. If they catch us here you'll get spliced too—with that thing spread out like a free-dom flag."

Whirling, the man shouted, "Quick, Jan. Lock the door.

"You," he addressed Ben. "Help me get rid of these walk-ways. Should have done this last night but I thought we'd be up before dawn."

"Up?"

"Up there—on our way. Come on. Quickly."

They went to the first of the four connecting walkways just as the trysts appeared on the roof where Ben and Morag had emerged. Seeing the figures of the two women and two men, the trysts came racing toward them. Sand had a large block of stone in his hands and he used it as a hammer to smash away the supports to the walkway. Ben completed the job by kicking it away so that it hung from the opposite building. The two men proceeded to dispense with the other walkways in similar fashion. The trysts, seeing their way was now impassable, went down into the building on which they were standing. Sand returned to his work, feverishly.

Shortly afterwards they heard the door being tried and some muffled curses. Then silence again.

"They've gone to get a key," stated Morag.

Her mind was working fast. "How long? How long before you finish?"

Sand shrugged his shoulders. "Not long. The balloon's al-most completed. We've got to get the fire started."

"Ben?" she said, turning to him. His face showed that he knew where her questions were leading.

"No, Morag," he said. "I . . . we can't. That's not for us. It's suicide."

The woman now moved to join the group and her eyes were flicking from Morag's to Ben's face with concern.

"What's this? Who are you anyway?"

"Can't you read? Morag MacKenzie. . . ."

"The riot queen," said the woman Jan, with a note of con-tempt in her voice.

Morag rounded on her. "That's right. That's why we're being chased. Now listen, Ben and I have to come with you...."

Sand let out a snort of protest. "Now just wait... look, the balloon wouldn't take us all anyway. No, sorry. We sympathize but you'll just have to take your chances elsewhere."

"Oh, will we?" snapped Ben and his hand went into his pocket. Morag grabbed his wrist. "Not *that* again, Ben. It's becoming a bore." But the message had reached the two balloonists and as she studied their faces she realized that for once, Ben's habit of producing a knife at any opportunity was the right move. They were scared. She guessed they were engineering types, or civil servants, and unused to street violence.

"Okay, we go with you," she stated.

Ben said, "I don't think I want to go, Morag. You join them. I'll stay here. When you get on the outside you'll find some way of coming back to me—rescuing us all."

"No, Ben. I won't go without you. Please?"

He stood there for a long while, his black face pensive. Finally, he said, "I'll come, if this thing ever gets us off the ground." He flicked the material with his foot.

The girl said, "Don't do that. It took us a long time to make it."

"I'm sorry," said Ben, looking contrite. "Let's get to it then. What do I do?"

Sand said, "What the hell. It'll probably be okay. If we're all going to die anyway, let's do it with company." He slapped Ben on the back, suddenly enthusiastic. "Grab that bag over there and get a fire started." He took a tinderbox from his pocket and gave it to Morag. "You help him. See that metal bowl over there? That fits into a cradle of wires under the balloon. Start the fire in that and we'll transfer it when the flames are high." An air of excitement had come over the group. *This is how it should be,* thought Morag.

She and Ben fetched the sack as they were instructed and they dragged it close to the bowl. The others had gone back to their various tasks of knotting ropes and stitching material.

Inside the bag were hard chips of a dark brown substance, like shod. Also there were some dry rags. Morag worked the tinder-box and soon the sparks had set light to the rags. Ben began to pile on the lumps of fuel and Sand came back to look.

"Well done," he said, as if they had accomplished a tremendous feat in the face of impossible odds, but preludes to dangerous situations tend to promote unwarranted praise. People can afford to be generous when they are about to attempt what has never successfully been done before.

"What is this stuff?" said Ben, holding up one of the chips.

Sand smiled and suddenly swore.

"Come again?" said Ben.

"Turds. Human excrement," said Sand, and Ben dropped the piece in his hand with a look of distaste.

"What's the matter with you?" laughed Sand. "It's been thoroughly dried and compressed, and it's good fuel."

"He's right," said Morag. "It won't hurt us. Come on, Ben." She began piling the dried stools into the bowl. They flared, spurting blue gas, and eventually Ben copied her, but she could see he was not enjoying it. He muttered under his breath the whole while and every so often wiped his hands on his toga, though there was nothing to remove.

The gondola was in place and they fitted the hot bowl in its nest of ropes. The two men held open the end of the envelope which began, slowly, to fill with hot air. From the streets below came the sounds of people gathering. Jan looked at Morag and said, "Our friends. They'll stop any trysts getting into the building while we fill the envelope. It can be seen from anywhere in the city once it's fully expanded."

"What about the two already in the building?" asked Morag.

"We'll take them on if we have to," said Ben.

Sand said, "Jan, work the bellows. Get those chips glowing. Morag, pile a few more in the bowl. Let's get this ship off the roof and into the air." They all began to work feverishly.

Morag asked. "What about the canopy?"

"One of us is going to have to go on top of the balloon, to pull us along a beam. That'll be me. I'm the strongest." Sand seemed almost happy at the thought that he was to be in the most precarious position. They were all risking their lives, but his was to be the suicide seat. Morag helped Jan work the home-made bellows, blowing the chips until the bowl was red with their heat and became difficult to approach for more than a few seconds. The wire brazier glowed too, but it was large enough to allow cooling to take place before it met the rigging.

The envelope was about three-quarters full now and tilted at an angle of forty-five degrees. Morag and Jan climbed into the gondola while Sand and Ben held it steady. Jan continued to feed the bowl with cakes of fuel and Morag pumped the hide bellows.

Hammering sounds came from the door to the roof and the noise in the street ceased.

"Quickly, they'll be through that door in a minute," shouted Ben. Even as he spoke the door splintered, then came crashing down, ripped from its hinges. Trysts came running onto the roof, waving truncheons. Ben let go of the gondola to reach for his knife and the balloon began to rise slowly. He suddenly realized his mistake and grabbed for a trailing line. His fingers closed round it and he looked up at Morag as if to say, "You haven't lost me yet, woman." But though the momentum of the balloon was pulling him across the roof both he and the occupants of the gondola knew that the balloon would not yet lift the four of them. As soon as he added his weight the machine would drop slowly back down to the roof again and into the hands of the trysts.

Ben looked up a second time into Morag's eyes and she read his decision. Sand was crying angrily, "Let go, man. We won't make it unless you let go."

"Leave him alone," cried Morag.

She saw Ben smile. The trysts were closing in on him: circling him warily as he half-floated, half-skipped his way to the edge of the roof. She wanted to be down there, with him. Their destinies should be the same. If one of them was going to die, the other should go too. What was the point of living without Ben?

"I'm coming down," she said, putting one leg over the edge of the basket. In that moment Ben let go of the line and the balloon rose a couple of meters, throwing Morag onto the bottom of the gondola. She scrambled to her feet immediately.

"Ben!" shrieked Morag. She tried to climb out again but the balloon was already several meters from the roof. She saw him felled by two of the trysts as he ran into them, slashing this way and that with his small blade.

"Oh God, Ben," she moaned.

They continued to beat him long after he lay still and quiet on the flat rectangle below her.

"Help me, for God's sake," said a voice near her ear. It was Sand, still hanging on the edge of the gondola. His voice was strained and he only had one arm hooked on the basketwork. The other was clawing for a hold on the rigging. Morag clutched his toga and pulled, but she was not strong enough to move him. Then Jan was beside her, heaving the big man into the gondola. Sand fell in an untidy heap at their feet, making the basket rock.

"What the hell were you doing?" he gasped at Jan.

"The rigging was slipping. I had to secure the gondola or we'd all be lying dead in the street down there," snapped his comrade.

"She's right," confirmed Morag. "We nearly went." The three of them looked over the edge at the drop and the basket tilted dangerously.

When they had settled into position which insured a balanced gondola, Morag began to swear at them.

"You left Ben behind, you bastards," she said quietly. "Why didn't you wait for him? Now I've lost him." She felt like crying but fought it back. She wanted to show them only her anger. They did not deserve her tears.

"What do you think this is?" said Sand. "A sedan chair? The balloon wouldn't go up with that fool clinging on to it. He nearly killed all of us."

"If it hadn't been for him, you'd have a dozen trysts sitting on your neck," countered Morag. "He fought them back while you saved your rotten skin."

"Fool," muttered Sand again, but this time with less conviction.

"Yes, he's a fool," snapped Morag. "He's a fool because he's got guts and thinks of others before himself."

Jan said wearily, "Be quiet, both of you. Arguing won't help us now. Someone's got to climb the rigging to the top of the balloon before we reach the canopy. Sand? Are you going?"

Sand raised himself slowly to his feet and the others shifted around to keep the balance as he climbed precariously onto the edge of the basket.

"Don't tell me about guts," was his Parthian shot at Morag. Then he began to climb. Morag could see the straining muscles on his thick forearms, tight as wrung towels, and the simian toes gripping the thongs of the rigging with the sureness of a born climber. Before long he was out of sight. Jan kept calling to him, over and over: "Are you there? Are you there yet?"

Finally a voice sailed down, it seemed from a kilometer above their heads. "I'm here. I've hooked my legs in the netting. Wait. Wait...." There was a gentle bump and they had stopped.

"What?" shouted Jan, but there was no reply. Instead they began to move gradually sideways, toward the edge of the canopy, in a kind of bouncing drift. Once again there was a peculiar tilt to the balloon but they corrected it by redistributing their weight.

"Hey-hey!" called Sand. "It's working. Can you see? It's working."

"We can see," cried Jan in obvious excitement.

Morag was still too upset about Ben to join in the joyous shouting match that followed between the woman in the gondola and the man on top. Instead she became absorbed in contemplation of the wall of ice that moved toward them. It was gray-white, with streaks of silver running through it like long, warped knives. It looked what it was: solid and impassable. The only way out was over the top and that's where they

were going. And if they were to die it would be a clean, quick
death. A long drop. Would she black out before she hit the
ground? Some said you did, but there were an equal number
who said the eyes were open and the mind aware to the point
of impact. If the latter were true, what would be the last fleeting
thought that would flick through her mind before the concrete
smacked into her face? Ben? Or perhaps the thought, *I don't
want to die*. How ignoble that would be. But then would it
matter? Existence would have ceased after a fraction of a second. The eyes would meet the solid world at several meters
per minute. *Splat*. Death. Nonexistence? Peace? Security? Who
knew? Morag was not afraid to die but she wondered about
the flash of pain on the point of death. Would it be so great
that she would carry it over with her to the other side, to linger
in her spirit for a while in the new world?

The ice slipped toward her, its ugly, malformed features like
the blank face of a giant god. *I hate you*, she thought. *I hate
your rooted form, your immovable state*. It seemed that the ice
mocked her by just being there, a solid mountainous shape
gripping the earth with its cold, massive talons; dwarfing the
city inside its frozen bowels. She wanted to beat her fists
against its slippery sides, kick, claw, bite, scratch. Make it
take notice of her. Make it retreat, move aside, shatter into
icicles, splinter into slivers, lie defeated and dashed in tiny
crystals at her feet, so that she could stamp them to powder.
Then the winds would come and blow the powder away, scattering it over the face of the world where it would settle, glisten,
and so die.

The ice stared at her with its smooth, imperturbable features,
towering above and around her, judging the quick and dead,
as it had always done, and always would do. *God, how I hate
you*, thought Morag.

THIRTEEN

After an hour of gentle motion they reached the edge of the canopy and paused there while Sand spent some time considering ways of getting them beyond the gutter. Finally he made a decision and called down to them. He was going to hang on to the eaves and kick the balloon with his feet, and at the last minute jump for the rigging.

"Be careful, please!" called Jan. "We need you on the outside." What she meant, Morag was sure, was *I need you*, but it was neither the time nor the place for confessions.

There was some confusion. The balloon was gradually forced, bit by bit, under the lip, but it seemed to be a slow frustrating process. They could hear Sand grunting with the exertion of the task. Underneath, the basket swayed dangerously.

Suddenly, they were out, and free. They saw Sand, his face twisted with effort as he pulled himself up onto the gutter.

"Quickly, quickly," cried Jan.

He found his feet, unsteadily, as the gondola moved alongside him, but they all knew it was too far out. He would never reach it. Morag could see the sweat on his face; glistening little globules of fear that gave his skin a bubbled, misshapen texture. He reached out crying, "Hand. Give me a hand!" Both Morag and Jan stretched across the gap but there were still several centimeters between the tips of his fingers and theirs. All the while the balloon was rising slowly, the gap widening.

"Oh, God," cried Jan. "Do something, somebody."

There was a look in Sand's eyes which told Morag that he was not going back. That whatever happened there was going to be no ignominious climb back down the canopy to the city. Yet she also read the terror of death in his face. He was not going back but he desperately wanted to live. She wanted to help him, somehow, yet instinctively she knew he was doomed. Their eyes locked for an instant and she realized he read the message in her mind.

"Go back, Sand," she pleaded.

"No!" Jan screeched. Morag was shocked at the violence of the word. Jan did not want to go alone—without him. She was as afraid of that as Sand was terrified of dying. There was a suspended moment when the air was full of indecision. Morag could sense every fiber of his body preparing for the leap yet she knew his mind had already accepted failure. A visible tremor went through his frame and he leaned forward, almost as if he were preparing to fall. *He's too tense*, thought Morag. Each tiny movement of his body had become jerky, puppet-like.

"Jump!" screamed Jan, the panic pitching her voice too high for effective encouragement. His knees bent and he flung himself out toward them, his arms flailing like birds' wings. One hand caught the side of the basket, held for a second, and then was gone.

The two women lay in the bottom of the car until it had steadied itself and when Morag looked over the edge, the canopy was already a lighted mushroom ringed by darkness below them. The city glowed like an upturned bowl of light and through its translucent parasol she could recognize the dark shapes of individual buildings. It was breathtaking.

Jan sobbed on the floor of the car and pushed Morag's hand

away angrily when she tried to comfort her. There were drops falling all round them: meltwater rain. It drummed noisily on the balloon over them.

"We're alone," said the woman at last.

"No, we're not. There's two of us," replied Morag, practically.

Jan sniffed. "But we're two women."

Morag formed her features into a look that would kill a bull tryst. "What's that supposed to mean? I can look after myself, even if you can't. You think that men are the only survivors? I'm a survivor."

The other woman failed to answer and Morag busied herself with piling cakes of fuel on to the fire, using the bellows to draw out the heat. She noticed that the warm air from the city below was lifting them faster than she had expected. Something worried her about that. She had heard somewhere that there was no air on the outside of the cone. Inside, they manufactured their oxygen from the meltwater, but perhaps the world outside had no such equipment? It was a worrying thought, but, after all, only based on conjecture. People could say all sorts of things about the outside, draw up all manner of hypothetical situations, because no one had actually been there.

She would be the first.

"Come on, take a look at this view," she encouraged. "No one alive has seen such a sight." Then more softly, "I lost my man too, you know."

"He might not be dead. Sand's dead for certain."

"Ben's as good as . . . I won't ever see him again, will I, so what's the difference? You tell me."

"*Hope* is the difference." And she was right. Morag couldn't disagree with her. While there was the faintest chance Ben was alive, there would always be a flicker of hope within her that they would somehow, sometime, see each other again.

The two women avoided each other's eyes after that and concentrated on their own thoughts. Despite the tragedy of losing Ben, Morag's heart was racing with excitement. She had never had such an adventure as this, this lighter-than-air escape into the unknown, and she was sure Ben would understand her feelings. Grief would be with her for a long time afterward. There would be time enough for remorse: if she could postpone it, so be it.

Once or twice the balloon drifted against the ice wall and bumped away like a huge, light ball. The blowhole above was gradually becoming larger as they moved toward it. At first Morag had felt that the balloon was wider than the diameter of the blowhole but she could see now that this had been an illusion. The warm air around the balloon was becoming more and more turbulent the higher they rose. Morag had been experiencing a light-headed euphoria produced at the thought of seeing the outside world, but this was soon overtaken by feelings of alarm. The balloon began to dart sideways as currents of air caught it on the flank. As it was thrust aside by the noses of these snaking sidewinds it often dipped into low-pressure pockets at the center of the spiraling thermals. To the two occupants of the balloon, this was very frightening. They held on tightly to the rigging and regarded each other with white faces.

"We're going to die," said Jan, dully.

"You knew that when we set out."

"Yes, but somehow I imagined it would be different. We're so alone up here."

Morag knew what the woman meant. The city was now a small disk of light far, far below them. The open sky, a light gray seemed to be sucking them into its emptiness through the mouth of the ice. It was almost as if they were on the outside of some huge hollow monster that was intent on swallowing them whole.

"We're not alone, we're just isolated. It's bound to cause anxiety."

"I don't want to go . . . I don't want to go out there," said Jan slowly.

"We'll see. We might not have to. It might be decided for us."

Morag wondered what it was going to be like to fly, even

if it were only for the little while it would take before her body
struck the canopy like a fallberg and slid down the stargirder
guttering to drop into a borehole.

"I don't want to go out there," gasped Jan.

"Shut up and hang on."

The balloon was rocking violently now, turning complete
circles occasionally, and Morag felt sick. She vomited over
the side and then, to keep her mind off her predicament, began
throwing fuel cakes into the pan. But the store was almost
depleted and the redness of the heart of the fire was dying.

"It's going to go out in a minute," she said, but Jan was not
listening. She was staring fixedly at the open sky above them.

Suddenly, Morag thought: *We're not going to make it.* The
lip was still quite a long way off. With the fire gone their rate
of lift would fall, perhaps even cease, and they would be at
the mercy of the more rapid sidewinds. She tried working the
bellows with her free hand but the task was too awkward.
Something caught the corner of her eye and she looked up
quickly. Jan was standing on the edge of the gondola, holding
on to the rigging with both hands.

"I'm not going out there," she said, calmly. "I'm joining
Simon."

"Jan!"

But she had already jumped. Morag saw her somersault
twice, in slow motion, as she fell.

The woman was quickly lost from sight.

The balloon had shot upward for a few meters as it was
relieved of the weight. Morag was sick again and it took some
time to bring the spasms under control. A few minutes later
the fire went out.

She was only meters from the lip now and the walls began
to close in on her. They were running with meltwater. Some
large drops were falling around the balloon and there seemed
to be a cloud of wet mist constantly tagging her. She passed
the lip, smooth as a uterus. It was thicker than she had imagined, its surface sensual-looking.

She ascended, more slowly still, beyond the cervix, out of

the womb of ice and into the blue. The bulbous, elongated shape of the balloon was like a soft vulnerable body entering the world. Gradually the upward motion ceased but Morag was enthralled, awed by the sight that she beheld. She hovered for an instant, above her old, contained world.

The real world was as beautiful as she had imagined: a great dome of rock forming the sky curved down to meet a white, marble surface whereon she could see another cone of ice. In the center of the marble floor was the sun, but since she could not look directly into its face or beyond she could not define its shape. There were one or two dark holes at the bottom of the sky which immediately aroused her curiosity. Were they openings? Where did they lead, if anywhere? She had always thought the sky the ultimate boundary: that nothing existed beyond it but more sky. If there were passages they must lead somewhere. Or perhaps not? Perhaps they were just places where the sky had been worn away by some corrosive or erosive agent, leaving it pitted and uneven. She disliked the lack of uniformity. It hurt her sense of order. But . . . how that other monument of ice sparkled in the sunlight: dazzled her with its brilliance! There was beauty in that whitefire! As the balloon swayed the distant ice seemed to produce knives of light: blades that sprang out from its surface to sweep the air around it. There was sudden color in those sweeping scythes, delicate pastel shades of red and blue, seared by white. She could not look at it without an ache, a kind of yearning, in her breast. She had no idea why the scene should cause her such pain, or what indeed was the object of her longing, but certainly the sight created a deep hurt within her spirit, which had faint, almost indiscernible undercurrents of lost joys.

Then the top of the balloon bumped gently against the solid sky and started to descend.

She began to weep with emotion, her eyes brimful of the life beyond life. Without the fire to heat the air in the balloon, the togas became a parachute, lowering her into the darkness of the womb. *The fetus, curling, withdrawing back into the security of the uterus.* Then the buffeting draft again.

Down, down. Darknesses into darknesses. Layer on layer. The ice-womb, opening out again, taking back its own. Rain. Rain. Rain like her tears.

The turtle-shell shape of light, coming closer and closer. At last the thought entered her head: *Am I going to die now*? The gondola would strike the stargirders and Morag would be cast out, to fall to her death. She realized she was descending faster as the air became cooler in the balloon. The light beneath the canopy floated up to meet her.

Nevertheless, the wonder would not leave her. She had been out into the world. And the whole journey had been one of both suspense and suspension, a kind of transition between life and death. She hung by threads in the void, was wafted by the airs of space, drifting, drifting. Now that she was alone and there was the serenity, the peace of all stillness in her head, she was strangely happy. She had lost companions. She had probably lost Ben. Now she was to join them again.

The canopy rushed up to meet her, a carapace suffused with brilliance.

And struck.

The gondola slipped out of its cradle of thongs and began sliding down the U-shape of a gutter, toward the edge of the canopy. Running with constant meltwater, the girder was a sluice which bore the gondola, craft-like, along its furrow. Morag sat calmly in the bottom of the basket, amid rising waters, her hands gripping the sides, white-knuckled, waiting for the inevitable. The gondola reached an incredible speed as the rushing water raised it onto a white, foaming torrent and jostled it against the walls of the gutter. She had exchanged a slow, drifting demise for a swift, angry death. Headlong, she plunged out on the crest of the meltwater rapids, into space.

The gondola landed right-side up and whirled like a spun bowl in the gushing waters. As she was being swept toward the borehole, Morag was only aware of violent motion, but suddenly the movement stopped. There was a sucking sound which increased in volume and water filled the gondola.

It was jammed in the mouth of the borehole.

"Hang on! Hang on!" cried a voice, as the water threatened to sweep her from the basket. It was cold, agonizingly cold.

The next moment a looped rope landed over her shoulders. She hooked an arm inside the lasso and felt herself being dragged through the waters to safety.

Having swallowed several mouthfuls of freezing meltwater, it took some time for her to recover once on the dry bank. She was numb with cold and someone had draped a toga around her shivering body. Morag looked up at the faces that ringed her.

"I saw it," she croaked. "The outside."

A cry went through the crowd. Then a voice with a metal edge to its tone came from behind the witnesses.

"Did you indeed?"

The people parted and through the avenue created by their ranks she saw a heavily built man stepping from a black sedan chair. In his left hand was a thick shod cane. His right sleeve was empty.

"Raxonberg," said Morag, and then leaned forward in a sitting position to vomit.

"I affect you in that way?"

"Not you," gasped Morag, heaving. "The journey. Wet, cold."

There was amusement in the voice now.

"Ah, yes. The escaper. Your friends are dead, but of course you're aware of that."

She looked up and saw his broad face break into a smile. "*All* of them," he added, with careful stress. Morag turned her head away, misery welling up inside her, replacing the physical sickness.

"And now we have you," Raxonberg continued. "The escaper. Instigator of riots."

"Thieftaker," she snapped, insultingly.

"Chief of Trysts to you." She closed her eyes, trying to blot out the picture of this man who was responsible for Ben's death. Hoping that when she opened them, he would be gone, as if he had never existed. Perhaps it would all be a dream, and Ben would still be alive? When she opened her eyes, she noticed the crowd had gone. There was still Raxonberg and reality.

He studied her eyes and then looked around in mock wonder. "Amazing, isn't it? I merely have to appear for everyone else to disappear. Why is that, eh? What remarkable facility do you think I have which gives me this power over them."

"They can't stand the smell." She expected him to strike her but he merely laughed.

"You have a way with words," he said.

When the pain would allow, she replied, "And you with murder."

This time a shadow crossed his face, as if he were in pain. He turned away and nodded to the two trysts who stood nearby, awaiting his orders.

"Put her in the chair," he said, finally. The bodyguards moved forward and lifted her up, placing her in the sedan chair. Then, at a sign from him, they picked up the transport and began walking. Raxonberg walked alongside, looking in occasionally through the small glassless windows at the sides.

"Where are you taking me?" she asked at length.

"To my headquarters, of course. For interrogation. Can't have insurgents running loose in the streets. People need to be happy. You . . . those like you stir them up too much. Sure, we need to open the valves occasionally—but when *I* say, not you . . . nor anyone else."

They reached the tryst headquarters and she was made to walk up the steps. She guessed he had let her ride to keep her out of sight rather than as a humane gesture.

She was taken to a cell in which a table had been placed. On the table were two identical objects.

Keys to the tower. Something glowed in her breast. A small ember of hope.

"Where's Ben Blakely?" she said. "What's happened to Ben?"

"Ah, the man with the second key? Yes, well he may still be alive. . . . Then again," he added, looking straight into her eyes, which she knew must have reflected her hope, "he's probably dead. Anyway, it doesn't matter to you, does it?"

Morag said, too hastily she realized, "No. No, it doesn't. He was . . . he was one of our group, that's all. If he's dead, he's dead. It was for the good of the cause. We knew of the dangers, all of us."

"All of you?"

"Of course." She tilted her chin. "You didn't think I was alone, did you? How foolish of you. You'll remember me, when you're hanging from the eaves of your headquarter's roof. . . ."

He smiled and shook his head.

"I can't fault you on bravado. Unfortunately, sometime I'll have to talk to you about this defiance of my authority." The threat was all the more ugly since it was delivered in a matter-of-fact tone of voice.

"And now?"

"Well, it suits me to let you run on. That way secrets are divulged."

"But you've told me now. I'll be on my guard."

He smiled again. "For a short while. But I know your kind, Morag MacKenzie. You're too headstrong. An insult here, an insult there . . . you'll lose control of your hot tongue sooner or later. Now, the keys. . . ."

FOURTEEN

"What about the keys?" said Morag.

"I need to know the doors they fit. For seven years I've had a key that would give me entrance to the Green Tower . . . but no door. Where is it, MacKenzie?"

She glared at him. "Why don't you ask Blakely?"

"Because—" He stopped suddenly. She knew by his tone that he was not going to complete the sentence with "he's dead."

"Because you can't get it out of him?" she challenged. "I'm not surprised. He doesn't know where it is. Neither of us do. The man who did was killed in the balloon ascent. Sand. Simon Sand."

"And how did Blakely come to have the key?"

She hesitated only for an instant. "He's a pickpocket. We work together in the markets. Ben couldn't resist dipping his hand into the folds of any toga. . . ."

"So you stole the key?"

"Yes."

"And of course, Ben showed it to you in front of the man

131

he stole it from, because that's the only time you could have
seen it. And of course, you recognized it instantly for what it
was, having seen dozens of them before...." He shook his
head slowly. Then he leaned forward, across the table, until
his stubbled chin was almost touching hers. She could smell
stale food on his breath and tried to regulate her own breathing
to avoid inhaling his foul gases.

"People would rather die, it seems, than tell me where this
fits." He picked up a key and without moving his face away
wagged it at the corner of her eye. "As it was, I had to cut
off a right arm. I have an inferiority complex, you see. I don't
like prisoners displaying a complete anatomy—not when I
don't have one myself."

She shivered under his gaze.

"Cold?"

She nodded.

He called the guards and ordered them to strip her while he
watched. They left immediately afterward. Raxonberg made
her stand, naked, in the middle of the floor. He walked around
her.

"You're not a very attractive woman," he said at last. "You
can't have been a very successful whore."

"I'm not that kind," she snapped, then bit her words off.

"Not that kind?" he repeated in an amused tone. "Well, what
kind are you? Are you the kind that..." and he began to
describe certain sexual perversions, whispering hoarsely into
her ear. Then in a normal tone, "Or is it mental seduction that
you offer? I have heard there is a woman in this city who can
fuck with her mind."

"Look, why don't you get it over with? I'm not afraid,"
Morag said.

"Over with? Not afraid of what? Rape? Death? What do you
think I'm going to do with you? How about pain? I'm not very
good at rape—I'm sure there must be art to it which has been
denied me. All that grunting and heaving and growling threats.
It's not my particular bent. But pain...now there's a thing
I'm quite good at." She winced mentally but tried to keep her

face devoid of expression. It was his voice, the tone of his voice, which disturbed her, not his actions. It was as if he knew terrible secrets which, if revealed, would destroy her willpower forever. She knew that was illogical, for there was nothing he could do or say to her which would break her. She knew it for a fact, not a supposition. Yet still that underlying note of malice in his words penetrated her ease, her confidence in herself. Though her body was not invulnerable, her spirit was invincible. Why should she worry?

"You're wondering why I have this effect on you?" remarked her tormentor. "That's because I know things unknown to any other in this city. I have seen people die...caused them to die, and they have spilled their secrets at my feet. Their lips, vibrating in death, have released hidden knowledge. Their quivering tongues have given me their souls to wear...you too. You will speak."

"Never. Not because I have secrets to keep...because I wouldn't give you the satisfaction. A crippled bastard from the back alleys of the East Side? Never."

"We'll see. Get dressed."

She slipped her robe over herself and sat down again. Raxonberg called for food and drink and watched her while she ate. When she had finished he left her. The door stayed open, which worried her. She knew that there were two guards in the outer room. What license had they been given?

For a long time Morag sat and waited for the turnkeys to come. Finally, when she could no longer stay awake, she crept onto the table and cradled her head in her arms, and slept.

She dreamed of the world outside the cone, where she was free to wander without hindrance and where there were no trysts, no Raxonbergs. *It was a strange kind of freedom, though, somewhat burdensome because there were decisions to be made which had never entered her life before. Not just choices or alternatives but directions to take without having knowledge of destination or paths. It was as if she were blind, but with the responsibility of the sighted. Her spirit felt heavy and her mind a thousand years older. There were people there—all*

*the people—their eyes on her, waiting for her to make those
awful decisions. She was without coordinates; she had no mental charts, no sense of right and wrong roads. She had a terrible
weight to carry, inside that light container called "freedom."*

"And what's it like, this world outside?"

"It's marble. Flat, unending marble."

Suddenly she was awake and Raxonberg was leaning over
her. He had tricked her, asking his question just as she was
emerging from sleep.

"The key. Where is the entrance to the tower?"

"You get nothing else from me, Raxonberg."

He laughed. "We'll see. We'll see. Marble, eh? You didn't
see the world then?"

She was angry. "I don't tell lies. I saw it. It was marble,
just as I always hoped it would be. Flat, smooth and shining."

"You're mad. Insane. How can it be made of stone? No one
but a maniac could believe in such tales. You never went out
there."

"I went above the blowhole. Just a few meters below the
sky. I *saw*, I tell you. Marble. If you wanted something else,
then I'm sorry for you."

Raxonberg straightened and regarded her thoughtfully. "Don't
feel sorry for me. I don't need sympathy or pity. No one's
going out there anyway. We're trapped in here. Personally, it
suits me. But then I'm in a more favorable position than you,
aren't I? Reconcile yourself to the inevitable. We can't escape,
even if we want to. Now, the entrance to the tower. It's time
for you to tell me. I'm getting impatient. Negatives bring pain,
remember. I'm good at pain."

She shook her head.

Raxonberg nodded to the two guards.

"Take her below," he said.

As she was being led to the chambers below the cells, Raxonberg said to her, "Snow. Not marble. What you saw was
snow."

She turned, halfway down the steps. "I don't understand."
One of the guards pulled her round, roughly, but Raxonberg

answered. "You know the song." He began chanting, *"Snow on snow, snow on snow, in the deep mid-winter, many years ago.* If we ever do go out there, which I very strongly doubt, it shall be *me* leading the people. Me. They'll need a strong man to lead them through the snow."

White crystals forming banks higher than a man. Like ice— shavings. There were many songs about snow. She knew what snow was.

But the world was not made of it, of that she was sure.

There was no softness in the table. The pain burned through her veins like a poison. It surged and died, surged and died, with the rhythms of some unholy music, some lost, forgotten pibroch drawn from the black mouths of things called trees. She had visions of trees like those in songs. They were living things which gathered around dead places, which hid the light and created dark shadows, that cloistered fairies, hobgoblins and other creatures of nightmarish fantasy. They once hung men from the branches of trees.

"Well, is she ready to speak yet?"

She recognized Raxonberg's voice through the singing of the pain, and she tried to spit. The spittle merely dribbled out of the corner of the mouth.

"I see," Raxonberg said, after a long while.

"Perhaps Blakely will make you change your mind. Bring him in."

She opened her eyes and saw Ben in the doorway. He was being supported by a man in a physician's toga. Then she saw why he looked so pale and ill.

His right arm was missing.

"Oh Ben," she said softly, forgetting her pain. Pity surged through her body in its place. He tried to grin but his face was a mask of gray.

"I'm alive," he said hoarsely. "You thought I was dead, didn't you?" Then his face changed, became distorted with anger.

"What are you doing to her? I thought she was resting." He took a step forward but the physician and guard restrained him.

He struggled for a moment, then Raxonberg nodded. They began to twist the tourniquets on her feet again and she bit her lip to try to stem the scream that was welling in her throat. Finally it emerged. She couldn't help it. It came out as a shrill whistle.

"For God's sake. Stop it!" yelled Ben. "I'll show you." Breathlessly she tried to intervene.

"No! No! Ben, don't give him the satisfaction. I'll despise you forever if you do." They turned the straps another twist. She managed to hiss, "Can't you see. We're winning. He hates us because we're winning. Don't . . . don't let me down, Ben. I can take it . . . as . . . as . . . long as you can." She began laughing, hysterically, insanely, and suddenly Ben began laughing too. She saw Raxonberg through a mist of pain. He crossed the floor with a face full of fury and struck Ben around the head, but it only caused her man to laugh louder, into the face of his antagonist. Raxonberg turned, as if looking for some instrument with which to strike him.

In that instant Ben wrenched free from his captors, and with a loud triumphant cry, he hit Raxonberg full in the face.

She knew what Ben was trying to do. He was goading Raxonberg into torturing him instead of her. But she also saw that the blow had given Ben a great deal of satisfaction. No one had hit Raxonberg for many, many years.

The tryst chief reeled backward clutching his cheek, but he stayed on his feet.

"Get him out of here," he growled. "We'll hang them both tomorrow. You"— he pointed a finger in her face—"you have until tomorrow. Don't think it'll be quick, either. I'll make sure it's slow—and you'll be looking into each other's faces watching each other choke slowly to death. You'll talk. Don't worry about that."

After that they left her to sleep, the tourniquets still dangling from her ankles.

The next day, early, Raxonberg and his men came and collected her. They took her out into the streets. A pole had been placed on two sills over an alley: the makeshift gallows. Ben was brought up a few minutes later. He looked cheerful but there was a wan shade to his dark skin. It was the color of old foodpaste.

"At least we're going together," he whispered.

The tryst guards went to tie their hands behind their backs but Raxonberg said, "Leave them."

A small crowd began to gather, but the Chief of Trysts had been anticipating such a scene. There were many of his men posted around the opening to the alley and on the corners of the nearby buildings.

Morag called to the people: "You know me, I'm Morag MacKenzie." The crowd responded with a murmur, but whether they really did remember her was impossible to assess. They were always ready to raise a hero or heroine from the dust but they quickly forgot them again, when the event was past.

"What's she done?" cried a man and she felt a twinge of hope, but a tryst pointed to the man, crying, "We'll remember you said that." The man bobbed down and she saw him hurrying away, down the street, as the noose was slipped over her head.

"Trees," she said, looking up at the gallows.

"What?" asked Ben.

"Trees. I hate trees."

"I don't know any," replied Ben.

They looked into each other's eyes.

"Bye, Morag," whispered Ben.

She squeezed his hand. His one remaining hand. Oh, Ben! Then the rope tightened and she felt herself being pulled slowly upward. She fought the flood of panic that washed through her. Instinctively she reached up, pulling on the rope to relieve the choking, but the relief was short-lived. Pain surged through her body, filling every vein. She had lost her strength too. Ben's face swam into view, his eyes wide with fear, his face bloated with strangulation. He kicked, either trying to provoke death or in a desperate effort to obtain more air.

A green mist began to settle before Morag's eyes. The desire to breathe filled her chest until she felt it would rip open, like a torn balloon, and then she could flap and sag in an ungraceful but welcome death above the streets. Lights danced in her head. Just as an explosion was about to take place in her brain, she heard a voice crying, "Cut them down. Get them down from there."

Feverole, she thought. They'll hang him too. He's come to rescue us but Raxonberg will hang him. Raxonberg would hang anyone, given just half a chance. It was a hobby with him.

FIFTEEN

Raxonberg eyed the intruder with hostility, reading his name. Felix Feverole, eh? He was tired of people putting up barriers between his desire for total control of the city and the means to that control. What was he, a boy in the streets again? Subject to the whims of strangers and bullies?

"Take him away," he said to his trysts. "I'll deal with him later. I'm tired of interruptions."

Suddenly, another tall, lean man pushed through the silent mob and stood beside Felix Feverole. He looked at Raxonberg, who felt a wing of fear brush his heart. The eyes of the man were hard and sharp, like those of a hawk.

"Well, Daniel, whatever your other name is?"

"My name is just Daniel," said the lean man. "I'm his servant. This man is one of the Five."

Raxonberg studied the newcomer's face for signs of a lie. He was an expert at reading false intentions in a man's face but this one . . . this one appeared to show sincerity.

"One of the Five. You mean he has access to the tower—the Primary?"

"That's exactly what I mean. Those two people up there—if you don't cut them down, you'll regret it." Raxonberg felt his expression hardening again but the man continued. "I don't mean that I'll do something about it—I mean the Primary will. That's your sister up there. The woman called MacKenzie. Morag MacKenzie."

There was a gasp from the crowd. Raxonberg continued to probe for a lie but failed to detect any. That didn't mean that what Daniel said was fact—he could be mistaken in his belief of what was the truth—but it did mean Daniel's representations were genuine.

"Cut them down," he said, quickly. It was not a difficult decision to make. He could always hang them again later, if events did not go as promised. Raxonberg knew that he himself was a bastard. He had never known his parents, but suspected that his mother was a whore and his father a pimp. Why else would they have abandoned him? A series of foster parents who used him for their own ends had finally driven him, at about ten years of age, on to the streets to fend for himself. At one time he had wanted to find his true parents, but the search came to nothing. He had intended to kill his father for failing to uphold his responsibilities. Finally he had accepted his anonymity with philosophical indifference. Now the old wounds were being opened.

"Go on, Daniel," he said. MacKenzie and Blakely had been lowered to the ground and a tryst was loosening the ropes, slapping their faces. The pair were ashen and wheezing, their breath whistling through their crimped windpipes. Raxonberg had seen it all before. Sometimes they took thirty minutes to die. MacKenzie's toga was open and bared her to the waist. He reached out with his boot and flipped the garment over her. If she *was* his sister, he did not want these scum gawping at her.

Felix Feverole said, "The Primary wants to see you, Raxonberg . . . and Morag."

"You have a key?"

"No, you have my key, but I know the way."

"I believe you. Why the sudden attention from the Primary? Am I to become one of you?"

Feverole shook his head. "We'd hardly be discussing it in front of a crowd if you were. No, the truth is there are great changes coming. I have been told by the Primary that something . . . quite monumental is about to take place. Our lives will be very different afterward."

"What? What is it?"

"That is not for me to say. When Morag has recovered we shall visit the Primary—just the three of us and there you learn your destinies, both of you. All of us . . . we are all involved." He turned to the people who were passing his words back to those at the rear who were not within earshot. "The shouters. Tell them to be ready to carry the news."

"What news?" cried someone.

"You will know when we return. Just tell them to gather at the longhouse. What we have to say to you will need to be carried quickly, to all corners of the city."

Raxonberg nodded. "And I am to be privy to the Primary's plans for our future?" He thought: Is this a scheme to assassinate me? Get me alone in some hidden place and stab me to death? A woman and an old man. If they are to be my only companions then I have nothing to fear. I can handle them easily. But what if more are waiting, in some dark tunnel? Is the risk worth the reward?

"This is not a plot—to murder me?" he asked.

Feverole stared straight into his eyes and his words would have brought a death sentence under normal circumstances.

"Sir, you are an egotist. What conceit gives rise to the thought that you are worth assassination? I wouldn't soil my hands on blood like yours."

"Be very careful, old man. You wouldn't be the first. . . ."

"That would be extremely foolish, and you know it. Until you're safely in the presence of the Primary, I can insult you as much as I like."

Raxonberg suppressed his blazing anger. He knew the old

man was speaking the truth but it hurt him so much he could hardly speak.

"Don't . . . not another word, Feverole. Think of my pride. It could be the ruin of all my hopes for myself. Sometimes it takes over."

Feverole's mouth clamped into a thin, hard line. He had understood the message. "Some people," Raxonberg continued, "would rather die than walk stooped. I'm one of those." He motioned for his men to begin clearing the crowd. Blakely's eyes were open now and he could see the hatred in them.

"You'll never get the chance," Raxonberg said to the black man. Then, "Come on, get the woman awake. If the Primary wants to see me, it wants to see me *now*. Let's get to it."

A fallberg hit the stargirders with such force the whole canopy reverberated. The MacKenzie woman woke with a start, coughing and choking. Daniel soothed her.

"Must have come from the lip," muttered Feverole. "That one dropped a long way."

"Is there any significance in that remark?" asked Raxonberg. "Or are you merely making an observation?"

"My observations are never trivial. I don't waste my time on small talk. We need to hurry."

"Good," said Raxonberg. "I like a man that doesn't waste time."

Raxonberg had his men assist Morag MacKenzie, while Daniel supported Ben Blakely, and they walked through the streets, following Felix Feverole. He led them to the East Side, toward the longhouse. Estelle was there, and she caught hold of Feverole's sleeve as he passed by her. Her fingers looked thin and wasted.

"Felix?"

"Not now, Estelle."

"Is something bad going to happen?" she said.

Raxonberg interrupted, "You heard him, woman, not now." He paused as something touched the edge of his memory.

"Don't I know you?" he asked.

She gave him the same kind of hard smile the prostitutes

presented him with when he arrested them. Or at least, when he used to arrest them. He had not bothered with that sort of menial task himself for some years.

"You *should* know me," she said in a weary voice. "We slept together for six months."

He looked her up and down. The damp, lank hair, the sunken pockmarked cheeks, the drooping breasts, were all a little repulsive.

"I couldn't sleep with you."

She gave him the same smile again. "It would be nice to think so . . . for me, as much as you. I don't find you so attractive either. Not any more. You've developed an ugly soul since we last . . . I was seventeen. I looked a lot different then. I'm twenty-six now. Almost an old woman."

He shook his had. "I still don't recall . . . you look forty-six."

"She's been ill," explained Feverole.

Raxonberg replied. "The physicians are free."

"If you can find one. There are only so many, and their time is limited. Not enough for all the sick."

"Why didn't you apply to me?" he said to the woman Estelle. "As a friend of mine you'd have received preferential treatment. All my women friends do, no matter how long ago. . . ."

"And the men?"

"I don't make friends with men."

She nodded and turned away, going into the longhouse. Raxonberg looked at Feverole quizzically.

"She works there," explained Feverole.

"And you? She is your friend and it doesn't bother you?"

"Why should it? I'm an old man. When you get to my age you find these things have little importance in the long run. In fact, it makes her a little more exciting, though I would never tell her that. She wouldn't like it it. You see, she works because she needs to eat not because she likes it." This was delivered in a forcefully sarcastic tone and Raxonberg began to feel rankled.

"Why didn't she come to me?"

"Because I was sick too. She stayed to take care of me."

"You? You're one of the Five? Surely . . ."

Feverole shook his head. "You have a shock coming to you. But I don't want to spoil it for the Primary. Let's just say I am no more favored than any other man."

Raxonberg studied the wrinkled face, the white hair. Could he have been mistaken all these years? Perhaps there was no power to be had in the Green Tower? Was it possible that he, Raxonberg, already had all the power he was ever going to possess? If so, why was he summoned?

"There are certain mysteries which have been withheld from me, old man, and I intend to have them explained before the day is out. Let's proceed."

While the conversation was in progress, Morag MacKenzie had been leaning up against the longhouse wall, recovering. There was an ugly weal around her neck which she kept touching delicately with her fingertips. Sitting against the wall, next to her legs, was her companion. She had one hand resting on his head possessively. Despite having come round first, the one-armed Blakely looked extremely ill. For some reason his presence irritated Raxonberg. It was almost as if Blakely was deliberately mimicking him, presenting him with a caricature of himself—a dark one-armed shadow.

"Get him to a physician," he said to his men, then to Feverole, "We don't need him, do we?" Feverole pursed his lips and shook his head. "No. If he doesn't get to a physician soon, he'll probably die."

"If Ben's going, I'm going too," said Morag MacKenzie. Her voice was hoarse but strong."

"No, Morag. You have to come with us. They'll see he's cared for."

Raxonberg opened his mouth to say something but Mac-Kenzie interrupted. "Don't, for God's sake, say you give me your word because I don't feel like laughing. Anyway, I'm too weak to argue. Please," she said to the trysts. "Please look after him." They looked at her, then at Raxonberg, and he gave her the faintest of acknowledgments.

"I'll go with them," said Daniel.

Morag said, "Thank you."

Then the trio set off for the entrance to the Green Tower. She looked as if she knew where she was going, as well as Feverole. Again, the thought crossed his mind that this might be a plot, but it seemed unlikely. He could sense too much urgency in the air. At least the black man was out of his sight now. Strangely enough, Raxonberg could not stand to be in the presence of cripples for long. They annoyed him with their pathetic postures. He never thought of himself as one of them. They were weak and despicable while he was strong . . . the strongest, in fact. They reminded him of clowns, of puppets, not of people. There was no fluidity about cripples. They jerked and limped and dragged their way through life. No smoothness. No easy motion. He was not like that. There were no sudden movements from Raxonberg. Swiftness, but not suddenness. He was confidence itself, physically and mentally. Nothing the Primary was going to impart to him would surprise him. He was sure of that.

SIXTEEN

Ascending, Morag experienced apprehension at the thought of facing the Primary again. Possibly the reason for her concern was that, this time, the Primary had *called* for her, and she had no real choice in the matter. Feverole seemed placid. She could read nothing in that creased, wizened face. Raxonberg, on the other hand, was clearly in command of himself and the situation. Physically, she knew, he was a match for both her and Feverole, even with one arm. Mentally . . . ? Yes, that too, she had to admit. It would have given her pleasure to believe him a dolt, but he was not. Far from it.

"Why are you staring?" he asked her, his eyes piercing her own.

"Am I?"

"Yes. Don't tell me you were thinking about something else. You weren't."

"I was just wondering," she said, "what it would take to break you."

He seemed amused, almost approving. "More than a baby sister," he answered. The words puzzled her. What was he saying? He obviously read the bewilderment in her face. "Ah, I see you don't know. We're related; you and I. Brother and sister—if you can believe what's-his-name . . . Daniel." He laughed at her. She felt ridiculous and appalled. Ridiculous because he had outmaneuvered her and had her in an exposed position. Appalled at the thought that his words might be true, she turned her attention to Feverole. He nodded sharply.

"He's right, I'm afraid. You are both . . . you share the same . . . parents." There was something in his tone which implied a deeper mystery but she had enough to consider without delving further. What other terrible secrets were there? She and that beast Raxonberg—of the same blood?

"But *my* mother and father . . . *him*? Why they . . ."

The doors slid open and the air was suddenly full of deep, rich music. It swamped her senses, permeated her brain, until all thoughts but that of drowning in the viscous notes had left her. It seemed that the very air was cloyed with the sound. Suddenly it stopped but the silence that followed was still fluid with aftertones.

"Bach," said the Primary incomprehensibly. "Choral number sixteen. Not inappropriate. I think the organ is a beautiful instrument, don't you?"

Raxonberg was staring, open-mouthed, at the towering, crescent shape of the Primary before him. The room was swimming in pastel hues and the colored bars on the Primary's banks were rippling back and forth as smoothly as light on a stream of meltwater.

"You," said the Primary. "Step forward."

There was no doubt in Morag's mind which one of them the Primary was talking to. It was Raxonberg. He too did not hesitate, walking boldly up to the console and standing before it, his hand on his hip.

"Yes," said the Primary, drawing the word out. "He has a confident stance. We have done well, Feverole."

"Yes, my Princeps," answered the old man, who had been waiting quietly in the background. He moved forward now to stand by Morag. Surreptitiously, he took her hand.

"The time has come, my children," began the Primary in stentorian tones, "to give you my blessing. I am dying. I am dying. My life has run its course. Perhaps you thought I was immortal? Only the gods are such and alas I am not of their number."

"We'll be plunged into darkness," said Morag. "The lights will go out. The heaters will stop working and we'll all be crushed by the ice."

"Be still, child. Can you think of only yourself? Remember. This is my death. *Some hang above tombs. Some weep in empty rooms. I, when the iris blooms, remember.* I want no tears. Just remembrance."

Morag suddenly had strange thoughts. "Why do you keep calling us your children? Is that a figure of speech?"

"No," replied Raxonberg, quietly. "You and I. We are its children. Brother and sister. Yes?"

"You are the clever one, my son," answered the Primary. "You are the quicker, though she was close behind you. My daughter. My son and my daughter."

"Why?"

"And *how*?" said the Primary. "I shall tell you the answer to both questions.

"Your embryos were left in my care by someone . . . a long time ago, a long time ago. She fashioned me to preside over this colony, knowing that the time would come when I would no longer be able to function. You are to inherit my kingdom. You are my heirs . . . yet it is to be a vaster kingdom than I have known. I am envious . . . yes, even jealous that you should inherit more than I have had. So be it. I held the embryos, until I felt my time had come. Then I gave you birth. You were given to separate foster parents."

"Then how do you know us?" asked Morag.

"Because of your *minds*. You both have powerful minds. Surely you knew this? When the time came it was easy to locate you, to recognize you both. I can *feel* your minds. You are part of me. How could I not know my own children?"

"Feverole gave us to our parents?" asked Morag. "Our foster parents?"

"Not him. Another. He is dead. I killed him immediately afterward. Ah! That upsets you, daughter. I can feel distress. But not in you, my son. Your heart is carved from the ice."

Raxonberg said, "I don't allow sentiment to sway my judgment. I can understand the act was necessary in order to maintain secrecy. But was it necessary to leave us to fend for ourselves all that time? Especially me. I had to fight. . . ."

"And her too," interrupted the Primary. "That's why I took away her foster parents. She needed to be hardened, like you. Apparently I was too late . . . she is a little too soft."

"You bastard," snapped Morag. "You killed that fine man. He was my father, you piece of junk."

". . . but spirited, just the same. Enough of history. We must think of the future. I am fading and soon my brain . . . me, I shall be cold. No thoughts. No life. No being. . . ." It paused, then continued. "I knew, of course, of my impending death. That is why you were given birth. You must be prepared to lead the people after I am gone. A long time ago, centuries past, this city was fashioned by the hands of those who hated and reared you. It is not a city . . . a penal colony. Your ancestors were political prisoners, members of a revolution. My brain grows weak. I cannot remember all. But I know this, their minds were erased of memories of past lives. This ring of ice became their world. Old songs, snatches of poetry— these were their remembrances."

"What happened? What happened to them?" asked Feverole, and Morag could see that he was hearing these revelations for the first time too.

"To those who imprisoned them? Who knows? To the inmates—they formed the society which you know today. Some were engineers who passed on their skills, maintaining my mechanical parts. The amnesia was selective, destroying *who*, *what* and *why*—but not always *how*. Some of them were subliminally indoctrinated with their future roles. Their duties within the prison. These were called 'trusties.'"

"The trysts," said Feverole. "The name has altered over the centuries."

The Primary continued. "I catered for most needs. I manufactured bolts of colored cloth from synthetic fibers, which you chose to use as togas. I produced the synthetic foods you eat. I gave you warmth. . . ."

"Sometimes," muttered Morag.

". . . light and safe-keeping from the ice. Alas, I also manufactured the ice."

"What?" said Raxonberg. "You mean . . . you make the ice?"

"My refrigeration units produce the ice which keeps you enclosed. I was, after all, a servant of she who imprisoned you. When the ice melts, the flood water will be taken care of."

There was silence as the three humans assimilated this terrible confession. Morag felt like screaming. She breathed deeply to control her emotions.

"You mean" said Feverole, slowly, "if we'd destroyed you, the ice would have gone away?"

"Foolish old man. I enjoyed your company. We covered many Roman battles together—many arguments in the Senate. Don't spoil those hours with wasted bitterness. I had my instructions."

Feverole hung his head. He looked as if he had just taken a heavy beating from the trysts. His heart must have been full of remorse for unwittingly keeping the Primary in mental health.

Morag put a hand on his shoulder. "There's no need for guilt," she said. "There were many more like you. How could you know?" He raised damp eyes to meet hers.

"I trusted it," he said, bleakly.

"Come on," said Raxonberg. "What happens now. Do we walk free?"

The Primary said, "Soon. But first there is something to settle. Which one of you is to be the leader. There can be only one."

"Only one?" Morag repeated.

"Certainly. That is why I have eliminated any likely sources of contention for that leadership.—That is why I have destroyed one or two potential 'messiahs.'"

"You killed more innocent people?" cried Morag.

"Yes. It was necessary. Now I have to make sure of one thing before we proceed with the selection. Raxonberg, my son—" the last two words were softly spoken—"what are your plans regarding the people of this city? What will you do with them?"

"I shall contain them within the city, of course. It's only *right* that they should continue to suffer the punishment which they deserve. In any case, the world outside is uninhabitable— of that I'm certain. It's full of jungles and wild beasts ... the people will be much safer here."

"You're *certain* the outside world is as terrible as you picture it?"

"Well ... it's possible that it suffers extreme climatic changes, of course." He glanced at Morag. "It's possible that there are *winters*, which I'm told by the timesmiths involved such things as snowfalls, freezing winds and blizzards—but whichever it is—or both—it's no place for people."

"Good," said the Primary. "It is as I thought. Your mind indicated such feelings but I had to be sure. Now Morag, place your hand upon the bright copper plate in front of you ... yes, that one. On my banks. I have to give you something before I leave."

Feverole looked concerned but Morag did as she was told, obeying instantly the hypnotic tones of the Primary. She suddenly felt detached, as if she were floating, and her mind experienced a surge of power, so intense it blotted out her external senses. She could neither see, hear nor touch ... she experienced only the sensation of some great charge, full of color and light, entering her mind. Then it was over and she stood by Felix again. She was trembling violently and leaned on him for support. Then it was Raxonberg's turn. He stepped forward, confidently.

"I am ready," he said.

A blast of music filled the room. Suddenly Raxonberg's body

began a kind of jerking, ugly dance. His legs buckled and straightened several times: His head bent backwards, twice, sharply, so that the crown was touching his shoulder blades. It was a terrifying performance and Morag knew she was witnessing a particularly cruel execution. The pain was evident in every involuntary twist of the torso. She saw a piece of red flesh fall to the floor: he had bitten his tongue clean in half. She could see his scream but not hear it above the deafening music. Mercifully the body dropped. For a few moments it continued to twitch and then, finally, it was still. Morag was unable to hear her own scream above the organ recital. Feverole dropped to his knees, and crawled to the body. Raxonberg's eyes were still rolling in their sockets as Feverole tried, unsuccessfully, to close them. The music stopped.

"Morag," said the Primary.

She cried. "You killed him. I'm not coming near you."

"I killed him because he was *weak*—a foolish man full of lies, avarice and self-indulgence, intent only on gratifying his greed for power. To let both of you live would not have insured stability—one of you would have killed the other in a short time. It might have been the wrong one. Neither of you could have shared power with the other . . . the other. . . ."

The Primary faltered several more times.

"What's the matter?" said Morag.

There was no answer. Silence. The lights suddenly dimmed. The stillness of death had descended.

Feverole, kneeling by Raxonberg, put his cheek close to the man's mouth. "Definitely gone," he said, simply. He nodded at the Primary. "And *it*. Gone too. Both of them."

"But . . . but we have light."

"Storage units. They'll last a few weeks. Keep us warm until the ice has disappeared."

Morag's legs felt weak. The events of the last few minutes were difficult enough to bear, but something far heavier was pressing upon her mind. It was *responsibility*. Without knowing what future awaited them in the outside world, she had to find in herself the strength needed for leadership.

"What happens now?" she said.

"I'll take you back. The shouters will be waiting to carry the news to the rest of the city. They don't know what the news is yet, of course. It'll be up to you to tell them." He paused. "We're not going to have an easy task, keeping the panic down. When the ice melts . . . well, I don't know what'll happen. It should have told us more . . . the Primary."

"You'll stay by me? I'll need your advice," she pleaded.

"Oh let us have him, for his silver hairs will purchase her a good opinion."

"What's that?"

"Just something the Princeps used to quote to me—or mis-quote, I suspect. Since my hair turned white he was fond of using the phrase. It means I must lend you my support, as an elderly man, to make you more acceptable to the people."

Morag said, "No, not your age. Your wisdom."

"I'm flattered." He turned and shook his head sadly. "I shall miss it. The Primary was a trial to me when it was alive but . . . well, we were friends, for all that it had the hallmarks of a master-slave relationship. We battled, wit against wit, and more often than not I lost. It had humor too—and a sense of the ridiculous. Not me, I'm too staid. We fitted together easily, you know, like two interlocking pieces. . . ."

"I'm sorry."

He sighed. "Canstone will be upset too, I'm sure. But probably not the engineers. They were never allowed too near to the Primary. A slave is closer to his master than a worker to his boss."

Morag asked, "What about him?" She pointed to the corpse on the floor by the console.

"Leave him for now. We have work to do. Later we'll send Canstone and some citizens to dispose of the body."

"Citizens."

"Yes, we're free people now. The word means something. We can either leave the city, or stay, whichever we prefer."

"I know what I want to do," said Morag.

"What's that?"

"Find those responsible for our internment," she said.

"But . . . but there was to be no revenge. Those who imprisoned our forefathers are dead. Long dead. Would you punish children for the sins of parents?"

"Yes."

"No revenge."

"I promised *nothing*. I wasn't even asked. If the Primary had asked me, I would have told it. Think how we've *suffered*, Felix. I can't let that go unpunished. You talk about *them*. What about *us*? Whatever our ancestors did, they had no right to keep *us* in here. *Besides*," she added in a more practical vein, "something like this will help to weld the people together. We need a strong cohesive emotion and collective indignation is as good as any other."

"Just so long as it doesn't turn to hatred."

She gave him no reply.

On her way down in the elevator the flash of information given her by the Primary began to unravel itself in her mind. *There was once a woman called . . . Mento . . . a* woman of extraordinary powers. The place she lived in was called Earth and she ruled it with her lover, a timesmith such as herself, whose name was MacKenzie. There was some sort of split in the relationship between those two mental giants—a revolt ensued. The loser was condemned to life imprisonment, along with his or her followers, in a place created by the victor. There was one big question that the Primary had left open. Was this, First City and its surrounds, the world *to* which the insurgents were banished, or the place *from* which they were banned? Although the Primary had indicated that First City was the prison of the losers, that was not necessarily the truth. Perhaps the power of the imprisoned partner was strong enough to reach out from the place of incarceration and retaliate? Perhaps he or she was unable to escape from the confines of their prison but could work revenge across the void? Morag was inclined to believe that the marble world outside the ice was the *real* world and the two antagonists had walled each other in with ice. That the other city she had seen from the balloon housed the enemies of First City. Time would take care of that question. Earth? Well that name certainly was not used any more. But where had she heard it . . . ? Of course, that old nursery rhyme:

> 'In thirty-one-hundred-and-eighty-three
> Earth was a wonderful place to see,
> With—*da-da-da*—and valleys and hills
> And rivers fed from rushing rills . . .'

There was more to it but Morag could not remember it all.

SEVENTEEN

On their return to the longhouse, Felix Feverole gave a speech, explaining to the people of First City what he felt might happen within the next few weeks. He asked them to accept Morag MacKenzie as their leader, telling them that she had been responsible for the removal of Raxonberg. There was great excitement: a vision of the future had suddenly become a reality. Morag was cheered into office on a wave of euphoria. She too gave a speech. It was less eloquent than Feverole's, but more to the point and in the language of the people. She had charisma, she knew, which outshone other personalities who might have rivaled her for the position of leader. She was the chosen one.

There were many questions that individual citizens wanted answers to and they queued for hours to see Morag and Felix. Of course, not all the answers were available and many went away unsatisified. Some just came to complain that they were perfectly happy the way they were and did not need to have any contact with the outside world. Others were clearly terrified of the thought that the ice walls, which they considered kept them secure from the horrors of what lay beyond, might be allowed to melt completely. Morag had to explain that she had no power to control the melting: that the walls would go whether she wanted them to or not.

After a while, anxiety spread to cause a general panic and a loss of confidence in the leadership which had been offered without alternatives. Rival leaders sprang up among the more militant of the breakaway groups but when it was seen that they had no more to offer than Morag MacKenzie, that their power was just as limited when it came to arresting the thaw, they were discarded. Fights broke out between the Angels and the Speaknots and one or two lost their lives, but gradually order was restored when the combatants ran out of arguments and the members of the organizations became more intrigued by the immediate future than settling disputes. Youths began holding parties on rooftops, ready for the first glimpse of the outside world. A great deal of gambling took place, the betting centering on the nature of that which lay beyond the frozen screen. Morag moved among the senior administrative officials all this time, consolidating her position with the established authorities, with Felix and the other members of the five to add support to her claim of leadership.

The thaw began.

Around the perimeter of the city hundreds more boreholes suddenly appeared, to take up the excess meltwater. It was a time of suppressed panic. The noise level was deafening. Giant fallbergs of ice broke away from the main cone and came hurtling down upon the stargirders to shatter into huge chunks that thundered along the gutters like runaway buildings on oiled rollers. The walls cracked and split with a terrible shrieking which drove fear into the people of First City. That the gods of the ice were screaming out their wrath they had no doubt. Gods are loth to die quietly. Out of the cone's fast-disappearing body came those loud spirits which had haunted the citizens all their lives: creaking, groaning, crying, moaning. This time their voices were redoubled in volume. Morag MacKenzie had a difficult time in maintaining order. The lower the wall became, the higher people's fear of the unknown mounted.

After many weeks the walls were less than fifty meters high and suddenly the trysts began to desert to her. When she and Feverole had arrived back at the longhouse after the death of the Primary, the trysts had barricaded themselves inside two buildings on the South Side. Leaderless, they were at first completely disorganized but after a succession of men and women had gained and lost control, they emerged once more with a triumvirate at their head. They attempted to recover their lost territory. Morag, Felix Feverole and Daniel, with several thousand citizens at their back, forced them into a retreat and captured two of the trysts' leaders. To emphasize her contempt of Raxonberg's force, with its far smaller numbers, she released her captives the following morning. The situation remained unchanged for another week, then one by one, individual trysts began slipping out from their fortified positions and placing themselves at her mercy. Soon, more than half of them had joined with the citizens.

Now that the walls were almost gone and the sky was completely visible, they could all see that it was made of bubbled stone. Morag, of course, was already aware of its true consistency, having been close to it in the balloon. Not that it was to any degree surprising. The sky had to be made of something, and rock was as good as anything else. The old songs said that the sky was sometimes blue, but then they also said that it was gray a lot of the time. The truth was that its real hue fell somewhere between the two: a bluish-gray. Clouds of steam often obscured parts of the sky, which made it difficult to declare what was its precise color. Those fond of debate had fuel for arguments that lasted long into the night.

The world gradually appeared before their eyes. A privileged few had the opportunity of seeing the new world from the room at the top of the green tower. It was white marble. Once the noise of falling ice had ceased they were able to appreciate more fully their new situation. They were about to be completely liberated.

"The world outside is unbelievably large," explained Morag, as the population gathered round her in the main square and its surrounding streets. Her words were passed back by the shouters to those at the rear. "At least a hundred kilometers in diameter." There was an audible gasp from the crowd. A hundred kilometers? Such vastness was difficult to imagine. One could not contain the thought of such distances, such wildernesses, in one's mind.

"I have seen this world of ours," she continued, "and it is indeed a wonderful sight. The sun is not in the sky, as the songs teach, but on the ground. It is half-buried in the center of the world and turns slowly—a great ball of white light. Feverole says," she added, giving generous due to her aide, "that one hemisphere of the sun must be black, to give us our night. I agree with him. In any case, we shall soon learn the truth.

"Across the world, on this side of the sun, is another city. I believe they were responsible for keeping us imprisoned. We have now seen its high tower glinting in the sunlight: its squat, black buildings. We must march against these people. Subdue them and cast them into a prison of *our* making."

Loud cheers greeted Morag's words but she noticed the tight lips of Feverole as he stood nearby. He did not approve. He would never approve of violence. But she knew he would not speak out against her. She was the leader. She was the Messiah, the chosen one, the daughter of a departed god. That she preached violence instead of love was distasteful to him but she knew he would bear it, albeit with undisguised reluctance.

"Go now to your homes," she concluded. "Gather what metal and shod you can. Fashion your weapons. In a few days we go to war against the second city."

The people began to disperse and Morag signaled to Felix. He joined her on the steps.

"I'm weary, Felix. The responsibilities of leadership fill me with apprehension."

"It's a stressful position in society—but it has its own rewards. Power, for one."

"If you consider power to be a reward. All right—" she waved a hand at him as she saw him about to protest—"it *is* a good feeling." She focused her attention on the meltwater gushing through the narrow street, ankle deep and freezing. "Those cities you once told me about—Carthage and Alexandria. . . ."

He nodded. "You have a good memory for names."

"What were the people like . . . who lived in them?"

"Carthage? It was a Phoenician city. The Phoenicians were merchants, very rich. They traded in fine, colored textiles and jewelry."

"Were they good at fighting?"

He shook his head in answer. "No. They hired others to do their fighting for them . . . mercenaries. Soldiers who fought for money alone. Alexandria, when the Romans came to power, was a very old Egyptian city steeped in mysticism. It was probably the older Egyptian religions which were responsible for its air of the mystical. . . ."

"Why? What kind of God did they worship?"

"Gods. There were many. Well, there was Anubis, a god of the dead, with the head of a dog—and the hawkheaded Horus, a god of daylight hours . . ."

She changed the subject abruptly.

"Have you seen Ben today?" she asked. "I think he's looking much better. The physicians are pleased with his progress."

Feverole nodded. "It's a good thing we have some competent people among them. Without the medical assistance they used to receive from the Primary's units, I had fears that they would lose all confidence."

"These are a *new* people, Felix. They're full of themselves— eager to stand alone. We don't need any centralized control."

"You're their centralized control, Morag, and I'm concerned. . . ."

"Don't keep questioning my actions, Felix. I know what I have to do."

He sighed but remained silent. After a few minutes, Morag said, "You're right to be concerned, Felix. Although I knew, instinctively, what the real world was like, I'm uneasy with it. It doesn't appear to fit our teachings."

Feverole always seemed to take the contrary view, and true to his nature he began arguing in favor of the new world.

"The Primary agreed with your viewpoint, so I see no problem. Tell me just what's worrying you."

"There's something a little disturbing about it. . . . Oh, I know it's all new and strange to us and I wouldn't speak like this to anyone but you, but . . . I have doubts. It's almost as if . . . it's difficult to put into words but you know, it isn't at all like the words in the songs. But where do the songs come from, Felix? From a long, long way back in the past. They've probably been distorted by time, and who knows, they may have been myths in the first place? Green grass, spreading chestnut trees, snow and spring . . . these are just words to us. There are strange images associated with the words but can you honestly say they are clear, concrete pictures in *your* mind. . . . ?"

"No . . . No. I'm sure you're right, Morag."

"You have your eyes. You can see. *We all live in a yellow submarine*. A submarine. A vehicle for traveling beneath the water. What water, Felix? Where? Our water comes from holes in the ground. *The rocks melt wi' the sun*. The sun gives light, not heat. Our heat comes from geothermal boreholes. You can see how wrong the songs are. This is reality—the songs are myth."

"So why the doubt. . . . ?"

"Well, what about the Primary's stories of Rome?"

Feverole smiled. "Ah, *Rome*. Well, this Second City could be Rome. Rome was a place of marble pillars and beautiful statues. Look, Morag . . . I grant you that some change may have taken place. Possibly the world was larger at one time and had seas of water on which ships sailed? Perhaps the world has undergone a change since then? We may have been here much longer than we thought. Who knows? Whatever has happened, we must accept it as it is. The other way lies insanity."

"I suppose you're right. Anyway, it's the world I want. Flat, white marble."

"Yes, Morag. Everything is happening as you predicted." He seemed hesitant as he spoke.

She smiled. "I've come a long way, for a whore, haven't I?"

His face took on a pained expression. "Morag, don't say that. That wasn't what I implied at all. . . ."

"Then what, Felix?"

His eyes seemed to grow a shade darker. He looked toward the melting ice.

"I'm worried about something else . . . your perception."

"What, my lack of it?" she sighed. "Are you continually going to fight me over this retribution policy?"

"No. No, it's not that I'm thinking of at the moment. It's not your *lack* of perception. . . ."

"What then? I don't understand, Felix."

He was hedging, moving around the subject, like an orphan nosing out a pocketful of food.

"Can I give you a hypothetical case? Take a wall with a door. No one has ever seen beyond that wall. Perhaps they never will. While the door remains closed, that which lies behind it can be anything one wants it to be. Do you understand?"

"I'm not sure."

"Your imagination. While the door remains closed anything you want can be on the other side—a country of the kind, or hell, or any scene imaginable. There can be flowers or fires. Grass or marble . . . now do you see?"

She shook her head. "I'm trying very hard but I don't know where this is all leading. The door's been opened for me, Felix. I've seen behind it already. It's not imagination any more. . . ."

Felix Feverole stared morosely at the sky. Morag followed his eyes and saw a flight of birds crossing the blue-gray rock above their heads. Around her, people were wandering aimlessly, stopping at the edge of the city to stare at the disappearing ice. She wondered how long it would be before the first citizen walked between two boreholes and stepped out into the outside world. The physical barrier had almost gone but there were still the psychological walls to remove. Freedom was a heady concept but in reality it might also be too awesome for their minds to cope with at first. They would have to allow themselves time to get used to its effects before taking advantage of it.

Felix was still speaking. "You remember that day you first came to see the Primary?" he said.

"Yes."

"You hadn't seen beyond the door then. That was *before* your flight in the balloon. On that day you told the Primary what you wanted the world to look like."

"And I told it that I wanted flat, white marble. Coincidence. Racial memory. Something like that. The memories of our ancestors may still be lodged in the back of our minds . . . deep in the recesses of our subconscious, or even unconscious."

"But don't you see," said Feverole, suddenly becoming excited. "*Anything*, but *anything*, could have been behind those walls. Yet it was *marble*. Out of the infinity of variety of things it could be, it *was* . . . marble."

"I remembered something. That's all. My real mother. She must have left me with the images of this world . . . perhaps there will be more."

"Perhaps the Primary was lying? Maybe it manufactured you itself?"

She felt as if she had been kicked hard in the stomach. Surely the Primary was merely a host?

"You don't think I had real parents," she said.

"Morag . . . Morag. I'm not sure. But it doesn't really make any difference. . . . Oh, it might to you. Psychologically you would prefer to have a human mother and father, but it doesn't matter. You're a real woman—flesh and blood—with emotions and thought processes. Yet, you are *different*, in the way that a genius is different. There is something special about your psyche. I'm guessing wildly because I have no evidence to substantiate any theories."

Morag said, "Be sure I want what's best for our people."

"You might not be able to help yourself. You might be a . . . tool."

"Left by whom?"

"I . . . I don't know. I wish I did. The whole thing might make more sense if I knew *who*. The *whys* might start falling into their slots then. I'll leave you now. I have some work to do. Morag, I trust you. . . . *Believe me*. It's the situation that has me wary."

Morag was not sure why she felt it necessary to attack the people of Second City. Was it that several hundred years of incarceration should not be allowed to go unpunished? If the First City people had suffered because of their ancestors, then surely the citizens of Second City should take responsibility for the actions of *their* forefathers? Certainly she couldn't just shrug her shoulders. There was a need for positive action. Something had to mark the end of their internment before they could begin a new life. At the same time as experiencing this irrational but compulsive need for revenge, Morag was aware of its possible disastrous consequences. Somehow, despite the implications behind the murder of Raxonberg, the Primary had instilled in her a desire for blood, even though this might result in a feud. There was an ugly fear in her mind that some indoctrination might have taken place while she and Raxonberg were gestating inside the Primary, precisely to plant the seed of hate she now felt flowering in her breast. Why then did the Primary kill Raxonberg? Was it because he had been, despite his arrogance (or perhaps because of it?), a weak man? There were so many, many questions spinning in her head and she had so few answers. Reasons. She needed reasons where there were only emotions, inherent desires. Until she had those reasons, her instincts seemed the best guide. And her instincts called for reparation.

In First City the situation was fairly stable once again. She had previously thought that food might be a problem but the synthetic food plants had continued operating and the engineers had confirmed that power for this system could be tapped from the geothermal power supplies. They still had to prise the remainder of the trysts from their stronghold but the problem was not a difficult one. Morag hoped if she left it long enough, all but the most hardened trysts would defect to her side.

EIGHTEEN

As the ice wall melted to its base the bodies of thousands of ancestors were revealed. Some were washed down boreholes until they began to clog the borehole entrances: white, brown and black skinned corpses, as fresh as the day they had been buried in the ice. They shone silkily in the light of the sun. They stared with reproachful frozen eyes. Piled in untidy heaps, themselves forming a grotesque new wall of flesh, the dead had come to see the day of release from bondage before completing their own journey to oblivion. All were there, from the original prisoners to the last of the dead. They each witnessed, the preparations for the final reckoning, their pale hands reaching for a life that they had been denied, their dead eyes reproaching the freezer posts.

Unfortunately their presence was a danger to the living citizens, because they began to cause flooding by damming the flow of meltwater. Morag ordered that they should be dislodged and thrown singly down the shafts, until all the bodies were gone.

"Put them to rest in the heart of the world," she said.

There was some opposition from groups of more reverent citizens but this was soon dispelled with the help of the physicians (who spoke of the dangers of disease), and also the smell, which began to make itself more apparent as the days went by.

The day the last piece of ice dribbled down the maw of its nearest borehole, the besieged trysts surrendered. They had run out of food and had finally turned on their leaders. Three bound men were thrust before Morag MacKenzie: the hardcore leadership who had survived the final internal struggle. Magnanimously, she set them free and granted a general amnesty for all political and criminal prisoners. She wanted First City as a unit, whole. She could not afford to have potential rival factions within the group. At any other time there would have been tremendous pressure from wronged citizens to execute specific trysts, but in the heady atmosphere of freedom, tolerance and forgiveness replaced the more natural inclinations of her people.

There was neither tolerance nor forgiveness in their hearts for the people of Second City, though. That was quite a separate issue, one that had to be settled very soon. Morag proposed they march on their enemies within one or two days.

The citizens of First City made themselves ready. Weapons were fashioned from whatever materials were available. There were knives, maces of metal, long-boned blades, shod spears and clubs. Morag, like most of her army, though, carried only the weapon of the streets: the assassin's dagger. A good blade was worth a dozen clubs. It was light and easy to carry. In expert hands it was almost always lethal. It could be thrown in an emergency, with great accuracy. Even those people who wielded heavier weapons also carried a knife. Many of them would have felt entirely vulnerable without one.

Morag had decided that they would all leave the city together, in a body, rather than send out individuals to test the effects of the vast open spaces on their minds. There had already been psychological problems with some of the elderly citizens, many of whom preferred to lock themselves in their houses. Some of them refused even to go and look out on this new world. They did not need it, and could not bear it.

When all was ready, Morag issued the command to set forth. There was no order or control to the march. Groups ambled forward in ragged processions of dark togas, with one or two loose, solitary individuals between. They ranged from ten-year-olds to septuagenarians, male and female. The younger children had stayed in the city with the elderly and infirm.

Morag had in fact stipulated that the march was mandatory for all citizens between the ages of fourteen and twenty-five. She needed their strength but she was also aware of the potential dangers of allowing bands of young people to remain in an empty city. She might return to find the wall reestablished, its function this time being to keep people *out*. There was also the possibility that those other citizens that had stayed behind would be terrorized. It was safer to have the young with her.

Once the shock of a view uninterrupted by buildings had passed though her, Morag found walking in the outside world an experience worth all her previous fears. There were a few problems—some people were not able to bear it and began whimpering the moment they left the city boundary. She sent all bad psychiatric cases home with an escort. They could not afford to burden themselves with the seriously mentally ill during the march. Singing seemed to help quell the flutterings of panic in their breasts. So did conversation—anything, really, which concentrated their minds.

The walk toward Second City began well, with enthusiastic rival groups trying to outpace each other; with lusty singing and good-hearted badinage; with faith in their ability to conquer. Ben had insisted on being at Morag's side, although she had attempted to persuade him to continue his convalescence.

"I'm good with a knife," he told her. "You'll need men like me."

"I *always* need you, Ben."

He chose to ignore the double meaning to her words. "Fine. That's settled then. I go. You know, I can't get used to the fact that we're the leaders now. Ben Blakely, First Citizen. Sounds good, doesn't it?"

"Yes, Ben. It sounds wonderful. But . . . are you well enough for such a long journey, and a battle at the end?"

He had glowered at her. "Well enough? Of course. I haven't lost a leg, have I? I can walk."

"I know you can walk. You can do many things—for short periods of time. But have you the strength for a sustained march? It's your stamina I'm worried about, Ben, not your resolve. I know you—you'll kill yourself rather than give up, once you've started."

"I can do it. No more arguments. A hundred kilometers? I often did that as a boy, running around the streets."

So she had allowed him to join her. *Allowed* was perhaps the wrong word, for Ben clearly felt he was entitled to share her power of authority. In his eyes they ruled equally. She permitted this misconception to remain in his mind. So long as he stayed faithful, his dark, hard body against hers while they slept, she was prepared to offer him everything she had. Even when he stopped loving her, should that ever be, she could never harm him. He was Ben. That was enough. Perhaps her fears of losing him would never be realized. At the moment he was as fiercely loyal to her as she was to him, but she wanted to prepare herself for the possible shock of finding herself with an empty bed one morning. Felix Feverole scoffed at her when she revealed her concern to him during one intimate discussion.

"Ben? *Never*. He loves you so much he can hardly contain it. I keep thinking he'll explode one of these days. Not *passion*, Morag, though there's that too, but *love*, with all its facets. You should hear the way he talks about you. You could be God. . . ."

And there the old gentleman had paused, with a thoughtful look on his face, then added, convincingly, "You're worried about gray hair and wrinkled skin. That's a long way off. You might not care yourself then—but I'm certain he will."

Daniel, though he looked uncomfortable when asked, was of the same opinion.

One thing she had insisted upon before they left the city was that Ben visited his parents, but that was prompted by her sense of filial duty. The old timesmith and his wife did not have long to live and Morag felt that they deserved a share of Ben, simply by virtue of being his parents, even if Ben himself did not see the need.

During the night, Morag visited Felix in a small tent he had erected for privacy and found that Estelle was there with the old man. Morag felt an irrational wave of annoyance passing through her as she witnessed the comfortable homely scene.

"I came to talk to you about some details concerning the journey," she said to Felix, after the barest of nods at Estelle.

"Fine," he replied. "Sit down with us."

Morag remained on her feet, stooping awkwardly, and after an uncomfortable silence Estelle said, "It's about time I was going. Nice to see you again, Morag. You've come up in the world. Everyone's talking about our new . . . leader. Goodbye darling." She kissed her fingertips and placed them momentarily on Felix's brow. He took her wrist fondly for a second.

"Goodbye," he said. "See you tomorrow."

Estelle left the apartment and Morag sat down, opening her conversation with uncharacteristic briskness. Felix listened patiently, then said bluntly, "We've gone over much of this before. Now, why did you chase Estelle away?"

She flushed. "I wasn't aware that I had been rude. . . ."

"You were most ill-mannered."

Morag snapped, "Don't you think you're a little old for that sort of thing? I mean, her sort of woman. . . ."

His eyes went cold and seemed to penetrate her own with a sharpness she had not seen in him before.

"I guard my own morals, Morag. If you wish to preach puritanical tracts, please don't do it here."

"I'm sorry. I was just thinking of your welfare. If you wish to take offense at what I mean to be a friendly . . ."

"Don't say *any* more," he interrupted, angrily.

She stood up and said huffily, "I'll see you in the morning."
Then she left the room feeling foolish but aggrieved. The worst
of it was, she really did not understand what had got into her.
Why had she been so uncivil to an old friend, simply because
she was talking to another old friend? They *had* been to bed,
of course, probably just before Morag arrived. One could see
it in their faces. Oh, yes, that much was plainly evident. Perhaps he loved Estelle? Not at his age, though. It would be a
distraction to him—take his mind off his duties, surely?

Morag decided to insure that Estelle did not take up too
much of Felix's time with her silly chatter. Felix was probably
being charitable to the woman. She was no doubt lonely in her
profession; she met a lot of people but had few friends. Felix
obviously knew this and was kind enough to go out of his way
to help Estelle, give her a little company. Yes, that must have
been the case. He was an intelligent man. Too intelligent, really,
to be bothered by silly women. It was up to Morag to see that
he was not pestered. . . .

She rounded up a group of the older women the next morning
and ordered them back to the city to help care for the aged
and sick. Estelle was among them.

Twenty kilometers from the city things began to go wrong.
The column had stretched itself into a serpent with a wounded
tail. The head still moved forward, though with diminished
fervor, while the rear dragged on more slowly. Along the way
it had dropped couples and individuals who felt they had to
rest. Already one man was dead of a heart attack.

They were skirting the sun, making the journey even longer.
Ben's health held out. Morag, on seeing him began to flag
once or twice, offered her help, only to be rejected angrily.
By the second nightfall, they had covered only twenty-two
kilometers. They slept where they found themselves, on the
cool marble floor. A white, glistening world surrendered to
the darkness. Sighs and groans filled the otherwise still air.
Morag slept with Ben's arm across her breasts, secure, but
concerned for the days ahead. Would their collective strength

hold out? They were already weary beyond any tiredness they had experienced before.

The following morning they started out again. Many were complaining of aching backs and limbs but most were still anxious to complete their mission. A few more returned to the city. Morag called on some of the women to encourage the men. Men were biologically weaker, she explained to them, because the embryo of a human is initially female. Later, the male characteristics, such as masculine hormones, were super-imposed upon the feminine framework. So, she told them, man is a secondary animal and is fundamentally inferior. It was one of the reasons why women, on average, lived longer than men.

Later, one of the women, Rita Ravenshead, asked her where the information had come from

"Felix Feverole," she admitted. "He told me because I was afraid ... afraid that I was not strong enough or able enough to lead a nation. He told me that I need have no such fears."

"But we are not physically stronger than the men. You know that."

"In general we're not—but I'm not talking about muscles, I'm talking about intrinsic energy, the life force that burns deep within us. Don't ask me to explain further, because I haven't the knowledge. Just believe me—their system has been over-laid upon ours, which somehow weakens their resistance to pain, illness and death. They need us more than we need them. I can only ask you to take my word for it.

So it was that the women, in the knowledge of their bio-logical superiority, supported the men. Those men that carried the supplies in the sedan chairs were especially in need of encouraging words and the women began to take a turn in the straps without a murmur of complaint, which shamed and abashed the males.

The marble was warm beneath their feet. Most had discarded their sandals now that the cold had been cast out, and though they developed blisters these were easier to bear without the rubbing of plastic against skin. On their right was the sun, a wonder which they could not help but be fascinated by. It rolled from day to day and they eagerly pointed out to each other the hemisphere that darkened gradually into blackness which gave them their night. The sky glistened at night, with tiny blue crystals. Occasionally they witnessed birds flying overhead, and these flying creatures seemed to give substance and real meaning to the word "freedom." They were indeed as free as any living thing could ever be. Clouds of them clung in white and gray patches, upside down, to the rough surface of the sky.

"Look at them," Morag said to Ben. "Aren't they lovely?"

"Should be in a cage room," he muttered. "Like ours. I don't trust birds. One of them bit my finger once."

"Of course they shouldn't be. They need to be free, like us."

"Yes, but we didn't set them free. They're still where we left them—in the bird room below the city. These are *wild* birds. Dangerous, I would think. Vicious. If tame birds bite people, what are the savage ones like? And there are so many of them. . . ."

True. There are a lot . . . but, oh, I don't know. I'd still rather see them flying across an open sky. . . ."

As the motley army neared the halfway point on their seemingly endless trek, they saw that a similar band of citizens from the offending city had come out to meet them. They were not carrying arms and their togas were of a two dozen colors, unlike the uniform drab gray and black of Morag's people.

"A circus," muttered Ben Blakely.

"What's that?" asked Daniel, standing on Morag's other side.

"You know: *Hooray, hooray, the circus has come to town, with tigers and lions and brightly colored clowns*," sang Ben softly.

"They have tigers?" Morag cried, staring hard.

Ben snapped impatiently, "No, of course not. But they're clowns. Look at the way they're dressed. Tigers were creatures like giant alley cats. We'd see them from a dozen kiloms away."

"That's what I thought," replied Morag, trying to regain

control of the farcical conversation. Inside, she was beginning to regret the fact that she had led her people to this place, this battlefield between two cities. It was obvious to her now—indeed it had been obvious before, but her feelings had over-ridden her senses—that many of her people were going to die. They were well out of reach of any medical aid the secondary computers could give them. The physicians were there, but they could give only minimal help without the surgical assistance of the programmed operating theaters. Lose a limb and a life drains away.

"I don't like this," said Morag. "They don't look the sort of people capable of imprisoning a nation like us. They look a bit . . . foppish," she added, awkwardly dragging out a word that was normally used only in poems. She made a decision. "I think this can be settled fairly quickly. Single combat. I'll fight their leader."

"No," said Daniel and Ben, almost simultaneously. But from behind the quiet voice of Felix Feverole intervened.

"It might be the best course," he said.

"But she'll be killed," argued Ben. "She's not fought anyone in her life. Not seriously. She hasn't the strength or the skill."

"She has the intelligence that outweighs both," replied Feverole. "Perhaps there need be no fight."

Without waiting for further argument, Morag stepped resolutely forward. When she was a hundred paces from the opposing army, she halted, and called out in a clear, confident voice.

"Send me your champion. We'll settle this between us."

There was a ripple of conversation in the enemy ranks. She waited patiently while they quarreled among themselves, until finally a square-set man in a mauve toga strode toward her.

NINETEEN

"My name is Pougerchov," said the man in the mauve toga, "and we have no wish to fight. Until a few days ago we were trapped within our city, as were our ancestors, by a wall of ice. . . ."

Morag listened patiently to what was obviously a rehearsed speech. As the words came, so she realized that Second City had suffered the same fate as her own people, except that they seemed to have developed on slightly different lines. It was obvious they had no real leader and had merely set out in a body, curious as to the makeup of the outside world and determined to discover its secrets.

". . . our city is called Inland. . . ." Since he had no name tattoos on his cheekbones, a strange omission by the official-dom of his city, his identity was seriously in question. In fact a person without tattoos had *no* identity, because they could change their name whenever they pleased. Others from Second City, or Inland, had begun to press forward now and she was amazed to see that none of them had name tattoos. Were they renegades or outlaws?

They talked at length to the people of Inland, finally agreeing that both sides should return to their own cities while Morag and Felix acted as go-betweens. There seemed to be no opposition to Morag acting on behalf of both cities. Certainly the world outside the cities could not support anyone, and until more was learned about it there was little point in wandering over the marble plains.

Morag organized a party under the leadership of Daniel, to explore the region beyond the sun. Pougerchov's people had also mentioned some caves to the rear of Inland, set in the rock face. Morag promised she would consider sending another exploratory party into these.

Felix and Morag discussed the situation which confronted them and examined the few facts they had, to see if they could come up with some kind of an answer between them.

"This is what we have," said Felix. "A world with a flat surface of marble enclosed by a dome of rock, rough-hewn and seemingly unyielding. If there's a way out, it must be through one of the caves . . . though it's possible this is all there is and nothing larger, nothing more rewarding exists."

Morag believed the answer lay in the reasons for the penal colony. Why did so many generations have to suffer? That part, at least, seemed so very wrong, unless . . . unless there was bad blood. Unless their jailers had been afraid of subsequent retaliation? Perhaps a feud, carried on against the future generations of those who had wronged the jailers? "Mento. There was a timesmith called Mento once. She was very powerful. Let me just . . . build something for you. A theory. Suppose our own timesmiths are a weaker breed of a more powerful race and that there was dissension among them? Perhaps there was a war . . . a battle which took place . . . a battle of minds and timesmiths' skills. They juggle with time and space . . . perhaps Mento won this battle and imprisoned the followers of her rival?"

Felix was looking at her with frank amazement, and it disconcerted her.

"What's the matter," she asked.

"I was just thinking . . . I've never heard you talk like this before. Where are the words coming from . . . you've never used language like that before."

"The Primary. I felt something very powerful entering me on the day it died."

Back in First City, they sent for Ben's father. Ben brought the blind old man to her and, when she saw how feeble he was, she wished she had gone to him instead. However he seemed quite happy to assist her in any way he could. The whole episode was like an outing to him, he said, and he was pleased to be receiving the attention of such a famous woman, the wife of his son.

"You once told me a woman's name . . . Mento. Can you tell me the whole story now? Can you tell me about Mento?"

The old man frowned. "There is a story . . . a legend that is passed from each timesmith to his apprentice. Why do you ask?"

"The Primary mentioned her . . . gave me a certain amount of information. But I'd like to hear your version. Are you permitted to tell the story?"

"All guilds have their secrets: they are part of their mystique. We do not readily recount the legend to outsiders, but there is no penalty for betraying the confidence: it is simply something no timesmith would do. But these *are* unusual times, and under such circumstances I see no reason not to divulge the information.

"When the world was very young a new human skull evolved or developed among certain people given to deep meditation. It was the art of manipulating minds to produce illusions and dreams that were as much reality as they were fantasy to the recipients. They called those who were able to manipulate the illusions 'timesmiths,' because the effect of producing dreams which had the appearance of reality was to introduce a timeless quality into the lives of those who sought the treatment. It might have been an advanced form of hypnotism, except that the adherents never ceased to believe that their individual experience was real. It remained in the memory, immutable. Unbelievers accused the users of drug addiction, escapism and other illicit practices. The timesmiths were regarded as unsavory people for several hundred years, akin to witches and wizards, but their practice was not considered harmful enough to outlaw. Then came a woman who not only gave them respectability but *power*. She was called Mento, Queen of the Timesmiths. Her talents extended beyond those of her contemporaries. She added another level to the skill of producing transitory realistic illusion. She developed the psychophysical effect whereby nonexistent objects became and *remained* real, provided she could convince herself and her audience that the objects existed *before* she brought them into being. Thus, an area never before visited by any man or woman could be forged by her into paradise, or hell.

"No other timesmith had her power of will; no other had the concentration to enable the production of the real from the nonreal possible. But some, it was said, had an unconscious skill. She had a rival to her claim as the head of the timesmiths. His name was MacKenzie...."

"What did I tell you," cried Morag to Felix. "There *was* a war. Think of how many MacKenzies are here . . . such a common name."

"And one you were given by your *foster* parents," replied Felix dryly.

She was immediately deflated. Of course, Felix was right. She had visions of her ancestor—perhaps her father, since she had been left as an embryo in the Primary—battling with Mento for possession of the world. It was a terrifying, yet beautiful picture. Her foster parents—yet her real name could *still* be MacKenzie.

Ben's father said, "There was a battle, as you say, but its origins are obscure. Timesmiths say that MacKenzie and Mento were lovers, that one of them was unfaithful. Timesmiths and ordinary people took sides, ranged up behind their favorites. It is not known who won...."

Morag said, "Do you know what happened afterward? What has all this to do with us?"

The timesmith shook his head. "That I cannot say. We can only guess . . . if it *is* more than legend. Perhaps the ice wall was a protective device—or perhaps a prison? The information is so sparse and has been distorted over the centuries. You know what other stories say—that First City was a place to which wrong-doers were banished, but *from where* and *by whom* is not known. However, it is generally agreed that Mento was the stronger of the two lovers. Firstly, hers is the image that lives as the more powerful of the two in minds of present timesmiths—nothing more than a *feeling*, you understand, but feelings often hold more truth than words. Secondly, although there are fewer women ti-mesmiths than men they tend to be more powerful than their male counterparts. I can't offer you much more than that but if you were to ask me who won the battle of minds, I should say Mento, because that name strikes more awe in my heart than does the name of MacKenzie. But I cannot in truth give you any more evidence to support such a claim."

"The Primary said 'she' when it told us who made it. *She fashioned me* . . . were its words," said Felix. "Let's assume that Mento won and imprisoned her ex-lover in First City. I for one do not believe that his banishment was merely from this marble and rock dome we have. There must be something better somewhere, or what are all those fragments of songs, poems and stories doing lodged in our brains? They must have some truth in them."

"What about the Second City?" asked Ben.

Felix replied. "Perhaps she divided up the prisoners in order to lessen the possibility of a massed escape? Or . . . perhaps someone *else* fashioned Inland using similar powers."

"Who?" persisted Ben, but Felix declined to answer.

"Perhaps we can decide that later—when we know more. We do have one person who may lead us to the truth. The daughter of MacKenzie . . . or Mento."

"Or both," said Ben's father quietly. "Remember, they were lovers. If it should be *both*, then there will be implanted within the ovum, within the sperm, within each part of the seed, the wishes and desires of both participants in that terrible struggle

for power and mastery of the earth. If this is so, there will be
another battle raging at this moment . . . a battle within Morag."

He reached out and touched her face, gently, running his
hands over her jaw, cheeks and brow.

"I fear this may be so. One part of her may be sympathetic
toward your desire for freedom . . . the other equally determined
to keep you all locked away from the world. I am an old man and
my skills have faded. I have no desire for real freedom . . . my
freedom is a room without people. You must find the keys to
unlock those parts of her mind that you need to help you, while
being certain not to tamper with those that desire your destruction. Tread carefully, my friends. Be delicate. This is my son's
wife. I would not like to hear of her having come to grief."

Felix blurted out, "But the whole city . . . *two* cities are involved. Not just Morag."

"True," said the old man, "But she is your only hope. Without her you have nothing. The timesmiths that practice now
. . . they have no skills beyond that of merely copying time and
place for the individual. There are none that can move mountains. . . . I cannot, and I know of none who can. You need
someone of higher skills. Someone with real power. Move
slowly. Do not rush into destruction. I must go. I am tired. I
wish you good fortune."

The archaic mode of speech, adopted by all the timesmiths,
seemed to add an ominous tone to his words, which were cruel
enough. Morag felt she had two people inside her, struggling
for possession of her mind, her soul. It was frightening, yet
. . . yet . . .

When the old man had gone, Morag said to Felix, "What
about the Primary? He nursed my embryo for Mento . . . *I'm*
sure it was Mento that won. Why would she leave an embryo
that had been formed with the help of her enemy?"

Felix said, "He was also her *lover*, remember. Maybe she
wanted to give him an equal chance. . . . Maybe she had that
spark of mercy which allows for another chance?"

"We must think about this," he added, after a pause. "Don't

let's do anything for a while, as the old man says. Let's tread carefully. We must be very cautious."

She agreed with him, absently, and he left. Ben was looking at her with awe on his face and she realized their relationship could never be the same again. He would make love to her in a self-conscious way, as a pauper would with a queen. She loved him still—would always love him—but could she hold him? Was the knowledge too heavy for him to hold at the same time as his fondness and affection for her? Would it force his love in another direction?

"Ben?"

"What?"

"You do . . . you do still need me, don't you?"

"Of course I do. What's the matter? Think I can't handle you? Listen to me, you'll always be the girl on the way to nowhere from a funeral, you know, so you can put aside any thoughts of queening it over me. That sort of thing doesn't impress me . . . I can take care of both of us. I was a Speaknot once. You don't get recruited by *that* crowd just because you've got nice white teeth and a healthy tan. . . ."

"Oh, Ben," she cried, pulling him to her. "You are the most lovable man . . . I don't deserve you at all." The tears came streaming down her face and *now* he looked uncomfortable.

"I don't know about that," he said, "but why do you have to tacky-up a perfectly good scene with morbid sentimentality. It's sticky stuff, Morag. Very sticky stuff."

Morag and Ben visited Second City. The type of society that had evolved in Inland obviously did not contribute to the development of strong leadership. Quite the opposite had occurred in First City. Two strong personalities had emerged. So the Primary had destroyed the slightly weaker of the two in order to avert continual conflict at the highest stratum of society.

There was a third colony, which Daniel and his group had found. This third settlement had met a different kind of fate. It had somehow fallen foul of one of Mento's earlier pitfalls along its path toward doom or glory. The fact that Inland and

First City had made it thus far, was a credit to their resource-fulness and initiative.

"It's obvious that Mento built layers and levels into her model—whether it was of a destructive or constructive nature," Felix had said. "What she will have left behind is some kind of psycho-physical enigma. We have to find the right key. If we use the wrong one . . . God knows."

The blocks and tower of Inland came into plain view as they neared its limits. Morag could see the freezer poles still glistening with the last of the meltwater. Strange how these people of Second City were as bad as she had always imagined they would be: soft and weak. And that other city, the place of beasts. It was a reflection of her nightmares. Always, in some dark corner of her imagination, there had lurked some terrible enclosed area within which she had dreams of being trapped. High walls and strange, evil creatures. Walls of ice.

"Why ice? Why did Mento choose ice?" she asked Ben.

"What could be better for prison walls? It's wet and slippery, making it difficult to climb. It's formidable. It constantly changes shape, like a living thing growing and shrinking—it worries the inmates. Gives them something to hang their anxieties on. You'd soon get used to a stone wall and eventually treat it with contempt. Ice won't be forgotten—it keeps reminding you it's there, and the cold it brings dulls the initiative. People are too concerned with keeping warm. Ice was a clever choice."

"A pseudo-living thing. That was the worst. Like the mouth of an unfeeling monster. You kept wondering if the jaws were going to close on you," said Morag.

"That's what I mean. It appears to be animate, and of course, it is totally uncaring. Natural barriers are disturbing. You're not sure what lies behind them—in the case of the ice, perhaps more ice? Or something more terrible, more dangerous than ice. Artificial walls on the other hand, built to keep people in, have the opposite psychological effect—their existence implies that something *better* lies on the other side."

On arrival at Inland, they found the inhabitants not only unprepared to receive them but totally uninterested. It was as if there had been no revelation: they were going about their daily business, whatever that might be, with little or no regard for the arrival of two strangers. Morag realized after a few minutes that this non-reaction was due to insecurity. It seemed as if they had retreated into the mundane chores of ordinary living in order to hide from reality. The citizens remained well within the circle of the boreholes, as if the ice wall were still circling the city.

She had noticed something of this in her own people: a reluctance to leave the city boundaries. Now that the walls had gone they could depart when they wished, though their choice of destination was a little limited. They could, if they wanted to, travel between the two cities but there were still strong ties which bound them to the community they professed to hate. Life in Inland was more attractive than in First City. Her people must have learned that much from their brief contact with the Inlanders on the plain. Yet if the desire for travel burned within them and their curiosity concerning Inland and the Inlanders was strong, the institutional bonds remained stronger.

Morag and Ben wandered among the citizens of Inland and were not surprised to see that their society had developed quite differently from that of First City. They were a colorful, bright people prone to chatter and calling to one another from doorways and windows. The women wore togas of crimson with floral patterns embroidered around the hem.

Morag befriended Pougerchov's wife, a woman called Jessica. After being introduced she threw her arms around Morag and began kissing her cheeks. Morag, unused to such demonstrative behavior, was acutely embarrassed but Ben made signs to her not to react. She withstood the onslaught of Jessica's affection, aware that their exhibition was the delight of a crowd of onlookers. Finally the woman desisted.

"Oh," she said, holding Morag at arm's length and with a distressed look asked, "Is somebody dead?"

Morag was confused now. "Why? Why do you ask?"

"Those clothes. That black toga. You're in mourning."

Ben gave a wry smile, probably because of Morag's horrified

expression, and Morag heard him tell Jessica, "All First City people dress like that. It's the custom. They . . . they don't know any *better*."

"What?" cried Morag, angrily.

"Now Morag. Calm down. You're frightening these good people." He whispered close to her ear, "Don't upset them. We want to *learn*."

Morag forced a smile and pecked at Jessica's cheek. The other woman immediately hooked her arm in Morag's and began to parade with her round the streets, as if to say, "Look everybody! My new friend. My new friend has come to see me. I have a new friend. Look."

Ben followed behind.

On talking to Jessica later, they learned that in contrast to First City, the people of Inland had all had access to their Blue Tower and the Primary for as long as anyone could remember. Why was there any need for secrecy? They had loved, laughed and been miserable as a group instead of individuals. They shared their emotions and were overt in their show of passion, remorse or anger. They were loud in both joy and grief. A funeral was a time for choirs to gather for the rendering of dirges. A wedding had everyone dancing and singing in the streets.

"It's unhealthy," said Morag to Ben, later.

"No more so than our own society. We've both sought refuge in extremes. At least the two cities have survived. More than those poor . . . beast people."

Ben was referring to the third city, which Daniel had been afraid to enter, having seen creatures half-human, half-beast skulking around its streets. They surmised that something had gone wrong with evolution there . . . that the inhabitants had undergone some kind of experiment in crossbreeding. It was an ugly thought to those who believed the human form to be sacred. Hybrids! The worst of Morag's nightmares had been confirmed.

She and Ben then continued to investigate Inland. Ben was a little subdued but he did not seem as abashed as Morag had been by all the kissing and yelling with which they had to contend. A slight pang of jealousy washed through her body as Jessica began to pay as much attention to Ben as she had done to Morag, but this feeling soon ebbed. However, when Jessica asked to sleep with Ben, Morag said quite firmly, "We MacKenzies don't allow such freedom, sister. It might be all right among the people of Inland but promiscuity is not encouraged in First City."

Ben whispered to Morag, "Not a bad speech, but a little overdone for a whore, don't you think?"

"Bastard," she whispered back. "Anyway she'd bore you to tears. She's as solid as two blocks of stone stuck together."

"I'm sure you're right still. . . ." He let the sentence hang. He could be infuriating at times.

The people of Inland held a festival the following day, in order to greet, officially, their new guests and temporary residents. They sang and danced and drank until the night came and went and came again. In their lust for pleasure they were inexhaustible. Morag and Ben could not keep up with them. They fell asleep on numerous occasions, usually swaying to the sound of the music. Everyone wanted to hear them sing solos and Ben responded magnificently, though Morag was less confident.

Later she thought, *What a happier time we would have had in this place, compared with First City.* But, she supposed, when there was a general air of despondency in Inland City, it would be a terrible place to be. In First City at least it was down to individuals. When she questioned Jessica on this she sadly agreed that sometimes there were mass suicides, when a wave of depression hit the inhabitants.

Another thing the first generation of Inland had done was set their birds free. There were flying creatures all over the city and Morag found they got among her feet when she walked across a square or open area. The walls were decorated freely with their droppings. It was truly an *open* city.

TWENTY

The more Morag came to know the people of Inland, the more intriguing she found them. Much of the Old Language had survived in their everyday speech, simply because they told each other stories in which the words were used (unlike First City inhabitants, who needed established songs to refresh their memories of the ancient world). At first, Morag considered this storytelling simply an indication of the Inlanders' immaturity. They told lies in order to escape reality. Later, Ben told her that creating stories was not quite the same as inventing a lie. It was like visiting a timesmith, he said. It *might* be a form of escapism, but there was no sin in that. The stories were not intended to cause harm, merely to entertain the listeners.

"It's still fabricating," replied Morag, stolidly.

"True. Can't deny that, but does it matter? So long as it gives pleasure?"

"I don't know. I'll have to think about it a little more."

She went out into the streets again and came across a group sitting round a professional teller of "small stories." He was just completing his repertoire with a story called "Pixies."

"What's pixie?" whispered Morag, settling next to some of the listeners.

"A pixie? Well, it's a small creature like a man, only a few centimeters tall. It lives in the wild parts of the garden. Listen."

The storyteller began.

"I was never afraid of pixies. Then last summer I had knowledge of them. I found one lying limp and white, wedged in the fork of a blackcurrant bush. A dead male. The evening before, I dusted the shrub with poison to kill pests and the poor creature must have eaten some. Holding his small, naked body in my palm, I hid him in the greenhouse, between two trays. As winter came I watched fearfully for tiny footprints round my door, or specks of light among the thistles. When the snow had gone I took another look and saw his neat limbs had begun to brown. By spring he was a twig, his arms and legs small forks. His hair had turned to root tendrils and knots replaced his knees and elbows. I potted him, head-first, that evening and placed him on a low table indoors. Then they came. Small white faces at the glass, breathing chlorophyll. Handprints like dried raindrops on the bottom pane. They watched him bud and finally bloom into a fine scarlet trumpet. After that, they went away. Last night the flower called me from my bed, by name, several times."

There was tremendous applause when the storyteller had finished and even though many of the words (like *thistles*) meant nothing to Morag the story touched her, deep inside. She knew what a flower was and the thought of one calling to her, in the night hours, chilled her blood. It was a *pleasant* feeling of *fearfulness*, which hardly made sense to her, since it was charged with contradictions.

She asked a lot more questions of the listeners, and went away in a very thoughtful mood. *She* would create a story. That would surprise Ben and Felix. Show them she was not as prejudiced as they believed she was. It would not be an easy task but she wanted to shock them. She made some inquiries about magical people and before she went to sleep each night for a week or two, she added another mental line to her "story."

Morag and Ben returned to First City via the City of Beasts

on the far side of the sun. Even as they drew near to where the walls had been, Morag was apprehensive and her stomach felt as if it had been scoured with sand.

"We'll be regarded as intruders," she said. "We'd better stay close together." They had knives to protect themselves but neither was sure the weapons would be adequate.

The City of Beasts was everything that Daniel had described. It smelled rank and there were signs of violence everywhere. Blood was smeared on windows and there was a brooding atmosphere about the dim alleys and narrow streets.

"Where are they?" she asked Ben.

He shrugged. "Hiding somewhere. I'm not going to risk going into a building. . . ." Suddenly, he paused and pointed. "Look!"

In the gloomy light of a doorway stood a creature dressed in rags. It was fixing the pair with a dull stare. The face was elongated, like that of a dog, except there were two cavernous nostrils on the end of its snout. A tongue came out and licked the ridge between the nostrils, revealing long, chisel-ended teeth.

"Is that one of them?" whispered Morag. "It seems familiar to me . . . like a forgotten nightmare."

Ben replied, "Don't move. We don't want to frighten it."

"Frighten *it*! It's scaring *me* to death."

Suddenly, there was a movement, a flickering shadow, and it was gone.

"Did you see those hands?" Ben said, and shuddered.

"More like claws," she answered. "But maybe those are the tools it needs to survive in a place like this. Strong teeth and claws."

"I think we'd better leave them in peace," said Ben. "We can't help them and they certainly can't help us. I think it's best we keep separate lives. When . . . if we ever get out and into the real world, then they can follow too . . . at a safe distance."

"I agree," Morag said. "Let's go."

As they turned to leave, a black cord with a loop snaked from the doorway they had been observing, and encircled Morag's wrist. She was jerked violently backward before Ben realized what was happening.

"Ben!"

He turned and shouted, just as she was dragged through the doorway, into the dim room.

It was not completely dark. There was a lighted wick, floating in a bowl of liquid fat, spluttering in one corner. In the middle of the room stood three of the hybrids. One, obviously a female, held the other end of the cord. The room stank of feces and rotting meat. Morag whipped a dagger from her toga and cut the cord, just as Ben appeared in the doorway with a weapon in his hand.

"No!" said Morag. "Wait."

The hybrids had not moved. They stood, their eyes glittering and their tongues lolling out of the corner of their mouths like dogs, staring at Morag. Their bodies were sparsely covered in coarse hair and their ears were large and pink, almost translucent in the candlelight. The female was the tallest of the three, by at least six centimeters, and stood about a meter and a half high. Although their torsos were thick and muscled, their limbs seemed thin by comparison.

Ben stepped inside, and as he did so a fourth hybrid dropped onto his shoulders from where it had been perched on the lintel. The knife went spinning across the floor and Ben rolled next to Morag. The fourth creature remained, blocking the doorway. There was another moment of respite as each side weighed the situation warily.

"Stand up, Ben, but do it very slowly. Keep looking them in the eyes. They're confused, I can feel it. They're not quite sure why we aren't trying to run. That's it, just stand your ground and stare at the one behind us. I'll watch these three."

The humans were back to back now and Morag could feel Ben trembling, but strangely she herself was not so afraid. She was worried, yes, but the scene seemed darkly familiar to her. She had felt the same sort of reaction when she first saw the hybrid. *Déjà vu?* The female hybrid growled softly in her throat.

"I know you," said Morag.

The male in front of Ben pulled a wicked-looking sickle from its waistband and whimpered in a high-pitched note. Morag glanced over her shoulder.

"Morag," Ben said.

"Don't worry. Keep calm. I'm trying to think. Smile at him."

"What?"

"Smile at him."

Ben did as he was told and the hook-blade flashed out, missing his nose by a fraction. "No good," he muttered. "He didn't like that."

"Do it again," ordered Morag. "Laugh this time." She laughed herself, into those ugly features with their bright, flashing eyes.

The female stepped forward and stared closely into Morag's face, the fetid breath making Morag gag. Still she kept smiling and the jaws before her opened a little and, suddenly, gave a lopsided grin. One or two snorts issued forth. Mirth. The beast was laughing too. Apparently the one in the doorway was not amused. It gave a shriek of rage but the female silenced it with one quick, stern look, then proceeded to grin again.

Morag proffered her dagger and the beast-woman gingerly took it out of her hand. The three males suddenly seemed to lose interest and wandered into the corner, where the candle boated on its bowl of grease, and there they began to tear segments from a huge, loathsome worm-like creature the thickness of a woman's waist. They pushed the pieces of flesh into their jaws and, squatting down, chewed sullenly. Morag saw the hideous worm move and realized it was still alive. Tethered, living meat. Once again she turned her attention to the female and smiled. Then she and Ben moved toward the doorway.

Once outside, they ran as fast as they could, out into the marble plain, toward the sun, without being followed.

"Your knife!" Morag said, suddenly realizing they had no weapon between them.

"I'm not going back for it now," said Ben firmly. "Why did you laugh? I thought you were doing it to frighten and confuse them first of all."

Morag said, "No. I thought if they could see us smile, they'd know we were cousins. Animals don't smile, do they? They would know that too: It was an identification signal—as soon as she, the female, realized we understood humor, she relaxed. . . ."

"Yes, but how did *you* know? They could have been more beast than human and not understood it themselves."

Morag looked puzzled. "I've seen them laugh before, I think, though I can't remember where or when."

"I see," said Ben. "You've been to this city . . . perhaps in your dreams?"

"That must be it," Morag replied. "I remember these creatures from somewhere . . . a vague, distant memory, half-hidden in the shadows at the back of my mind."

They returned to First City, where Morag was greeted by her people. She found them a little discontented and disenchanted. They had freedom now, but to do what? Where was the point in going beyond the boreholes and out into a world of flat marble? They might as well stay in First City, as they had always done.

"We are considering ways to help you," she told them. "One day soon we will have a *real* world to populate. Just give us a little time."

They assented because they trusted her, but that would only last as long as their patience, and she knew it.

"When we find the right door in the wall, Morag, we'll open it," Felix said. "But just for the time being, let's drift along the way we are. I'm still . . . assessing the situation."

"Don't take too long," she said, coolly.

That evening, in the longhouse, Morag told a story to a selected group of people.

"I've been listening to the people of Inland," she said, "and I think I've managed to create a story. Listen.

"There was once a wizard called Igwal, who had been imprisoned in a bed of rock by his twin brother Agwil. It was hot and suffocating in the rock and made all the worse by Igwal's rage. He acted rashly. He had only three wishes and the first took him above the rock-bed, only to put him in deep,

black water. (Cunning Agwil—the bed of rock was at the bottom of the sea.) Then Igwal quickly wished himself above the water and found himself in another bed of rock. (Cunning Agwil—it was an underground sea.) Thus Igwal was afraid to use his final wish in case he put himself into a worse, and final situation.When he pondered on his problem he accidentally wished himself contented and spent the rest of his life happily in the concrete foundation of his brother's house, until they both died together on the stroke of twelve, some seven hundred and six years later."

She looked around at the faces, expecting some sort of appraisal, but most of her audience seemed bemused.

"Well?" She looked at Ben, who shrugged. "I thought it was good," he said loyally.

"You usually show your appreciation by smacking the hands together like this," Morag showed her audience how to clap. One or two of them tried but the sound was a little hollow.

"Oh well," she said resignedly. "I suppose an appreciation of art is something that has to be learned. First City needs a little *culture*. Perhaps I ought to invite some Inland storytellers. Professionals. . . ." It was then she noticed that Daniel and Felix Feverole had their heads together and were talking earnestly. They were casting glances at her which appeared almost furtive.

"Felix?"

Feverole visibly jumped and then seemed to collect himself. "Yes, Morag?"

"What do you think? Was my storytelling good?"

"Well, to be honest, Morag, the only stories I've heard have been those that the Primary told me, which were supposed to be true. But . . . but it did remind me of a labyrinth story. . . ."

"Labyrinth story?"

"A maze of tunnels in which a creature called the Minotaur lived. The similarity lies in the geophysical puzzles . . . the labyrinth was a horizontal maze while your maze appears to be stacked vertically, in planes."

"You must tell me more later. Daniel?" she said, turning to him.

"I thought it was rather well done . . . ah, Morag, where did you hear *that* particular version?"

"That? . . . Oh, I made it up. One is suppose to invent them."

"You made it up? All of it?"

"Yes. Of course, I asked Pougerchov for some of the words and Jessica helped me a little with the structure, but the story is all my own."

"I congratulate you," said Felix quickly. "Extremely inventive. As good as any I've never heard . . . certainly as good as any the Primary told me."

"Really?"

"Of course. Now if you'll excuse me, Morag, I must talk to Daniel. We have something important to discuss."

Daniel and Felix then left the longhouse with Morag staring after them. Why had they looked so worried? Was it *guilt*? Or something else? No, it was definitely *concern*. Perhaps she would speak to Felix later? It seemed that he and Daniel had decided to freeze her out of their secret.

Later she went to find Felix, to ask him what he and Daniel were so concerned about. When she approached the door to his apartment, however, she heard voices. One of them was a woman's voice: Estelle's. Morag stood outside the door, seething, for a few minutes, undecided whether or not to enter. Finally she went away without knocking. It had gotten unnaturally quiet in the apartment and Morag had no wish to witness what might be an embarrassing scene. When she got back to her own room she found herself asking Ben to call on Felix immediately, as the old man had left a . . . a kerchief, yes, there it was. Ben grumbled, plainly puzzled, but did as he was asked.

TWENTY-ONE

A set of caves, similar to those discovered behind Inland, was found in the rock wall in the hinterland of First City. Felix said that it was probable a third set existed behind the City of Beasts. Preparations were made to enter the caves behind First City. The party was to consist of Daniel, Lila Leckmann and Max MacKenzie (two very tough ex-trysts), and Ben. Morag wanted to go too, but Felix advised against it. She was needed where the people could see her. A leader who is continually absent leaves room for others to take her place, warned Felix. Morag was unhappy at this but she consented to remain with the old man when Ben insisted that he was right.

The expedition was gone for three days. When they returned one of the trysts, Leckmann, was missing. She had been lost. The party looked grave and dispirited as it staggered out of the mouth of one of the seven caves—not the one they had entered—and they all seemed greatly relieved to be back. Morag wanted to hold a debriefing immediately but Felix suggested that the explorers needed to rest first, especially Max Mac-Kenzie, whose interest in Lila Leckmann had developed into more than companionship. Morag tried to prise information from her one-armed common-law husband but even he refused to reveal anything before the "proper time" and fell asleep as she was speaking to him. Morag began to feel that her friends were turning against her and a little bitter seed sprouted in her breast. They seemed eager to take each other into their confidence, but whenever she approached the talk would cease and awkward smiles replaced the deep frowns. She knew that something was desperately wrong but she could find no one willing to discuss it with her. Felix stone-walled her questions as the others slept. She was certain Daniel had spoken to him about the expedition's findings but there was nothing she could say or do which made him admit to it.

"I'm *entitled* to know," she said, through hot tears of frustration. "You of all people. . . ." Her chest burned with a mixture of emotions, not least of which was anger, until the meeting was finally called. Somewhere between the Primary giving her undisputed leadership over First City and the discovery of the City of the Beasts, she had lost touch with those who mattered to her. It hurt her deeply and she was determined to get to the root of the cause.

Morag's anger was uncontrollable when she arrived at the longhouse, the meeting hall, to find that the others had all been there for an hour and that the meeting had started without her.

"Felix, what the *hell* is going on? I demand an explanation now, or by God I'll . . . I'll do something for which I know I'll be sorry. Ben—" she turned to her husband—"you left my bed this morning to join these . . . these conspirators. I consider that a terrible betrayal. Loyalty to me as your leader—let alone as your wife—should have dictated your conscience. I'm your *wife*, damn it! You're supposed to be in love with me!"

"Morag—" began Ben, but she silenced him.

"I don't want any, *any* half-baked excuses or lies. If you're not going to tell me why I'm being frozen out, then don't bother to speak at all."

Ben was pale. He nodded at Felix. "I think Felix should be

the one to tell you. He has more knowledge of the situation in any case."

"Felix?" she snapped. She wanted to slap at the old man and pummel the information from him as he stood like a grim, gray rock before her. He appeared inflexible, rigid as he spoke.

"Morag, could I *beg* you to leave it to us? The problem . . . the problem is deeply involved with you. You may even be the cause of it and it can only be solved by trial and error. If we tell you now, it may ruin our chances of escape. . . ."

She was completely taken aback. "You mean . . . you mean you're working *against* me?"

"Not exactly." Felix folded his arms, unfolded them after a moment's reflection, then began pacing the floor. "Not exactly against *you* but something that may be part of you . . . working against us without your knowledge. Using you as an . . . an instrument."

"Mento!" she cried. "You think that the part of me that is Mento is working against you? I must know what it is. I *must* know, so that I can fight against her, surely? Felix, what did they find?"

Felix sighed. "Nothing. Just a labyrinth."

"Is that so bad?" she asked. "We have more caves to try. I would have thought . . . look, Felix, all of you, I'm one of *you*. I want freedom as much as the next person. More! Why should I fight against that? All my life I've been an advocate of freedom . . . even when it was illegal and the penalty was death."

Ben said, "Morag, we're not questioning your personal motives. Listen to Felix. He knows what he's talking about. Let him decide what's best."

"No." Her voice cracked out across the room. "I will *not* be frozen out."

Felix said to Ben, "She'll guess in the end, in any case. I'm going to have to explain."

"Talk to *me*, not him," cried Morag, infuriated. "What am I around here? A piece of furniture?"

"Don't be unreasonable," said Ben, putting his hand on her shoulder. "This is very difficult for all of us."

She shrugged away his hand and stood, staring belligerently, at Felix. In the corner of the room Max MacKenzie and Daniel were silent and seemingly a little embarrassed by the scene. They did not appear to wish to contribute anything, though they were obviously prepared to listen. Felix began.

"Our problem is this... no, let's start with the evidence. Yes, I think that's necessary. You remember when we were trapped by the ice, Morag, and no one had seen the outside world I spoke to you once about Rome... how its ancient streets were paved with marble? You suggested afterward that that was how you would like to see the world outside... a place of flat, pure marble."

"It is...." she interrupted.

"Yes, it is. Also there are only three cities in this marble world. I recall you saying that your mind could only envisage three cities... that three was enough for any world. Further, I told you about Carthage being a place of merchants who deal in colorful textiles and fine things. A bazaar. That would equate, generally, with Inland. Finally we spoke about Egypt."

"Alexandria."

"Yes, Alexandria, a city in a country called Egypt. I told you about its gods... a dog-faced god called Anubis...."

"Well? Get to the point, Felix. What are trying to say?"

"This may be a little difficult for you, Morag, but—I think you're creating those places outside. All my suggestions. They're too close to what we've found...."

Morag was incredulous. "That's ridiculous, Felix. Why would I do that—even supposing I could? I want to get out of here as much as you do."

"Do you, Morag?"

"Yes." She was emphatic.

"But perhaps it's not you... maybe it's Mento?"

A chill went through Morag, but still she could not believe that she was being manipulated to the extent that Felix was suggesting. Surely, if she had the power to form three-dimensional objects—*cities*—then she would be aware of it.

Such power must be accompanied by a release of energy. She said as much to Felix.

"I don't know what the rules are—neither do you. All I know is what we have here—circumstantial evidence that you are producing these places. Remember the dog-faced god? What did we find in the third city? A man-beast with a canine snout...."

"The City of Beasts," she said in despair. "I see what you mean, now . . . I'm creating these places subconsciously, as we go along. Or . . . Mento is. I . . . Oh, I don't know." She buried her face in her hand.

"Now, the labyrinth behind our city. The home of the Minotaur of ancient Greece. Our party—Ben and the others—heard something in those tunnels and Lila was dragged off when she fell behind the rest. I don't think we'll ever see her again. Certainly we can't enter the caves to search for her. It was pure chance the others managed to get out . . . they were completely lost. If we are to proceed any farther we must make sure your mental picture is what we want to find. How we do that, I just don't know, but the MacKenzie in you is losing to the Mento. She was obviously more powerful than her lover, which was probably why he lost the battle. The Primary had a limited life. She left you behind to insure our continued captivity."

"You must . . . you must kill me," said Morag. There was nothing but despair in her heart. Her friends, her people, had been relying on her to deliver them from their prison and all the while she had been working to keep them there.

"Very noble, Morag, but I don't think we can do that. Mento probably knew that too. Raxonberg would have executed you without bothering to think twice, but we are not of his ilk. We're humane people . . . it goes against our nature. The Primary knew what it was doing when it killed Raxonberg.

"You remember we spoke about closed doors . . . ? About there being an infinite range of possible worlds existing behind them? It's my belief . . . ours . . . that you create the scenes behind those doors out of suggestions and, perhaps, dreams.

Mento is working from your subconscious. Of course, there are rational explanations for the existence of those places once we find them... the half-human beasts *could* have evolved from a crossbreeding introduced by the Primary ... by the way, I think the Primary was present in all three cities. *Now that they exist they have always existed.* It's a difficult concept to grasp, but they are as real as First City, now that the door has been opened. This is why we must be so careful when we open other doors."

"What do you plan to do with me?" she asked miserably. She felt wretched. When the ice walls of First City had melted she had felt as if her life was full of purpose. From a poor creature of the streets she had risen to become the leader of a nation. Fulfillment was hers, at that moment. Even her love for Ben had been dwarfed by the high, enveloping emotion that accompanies power. If anyone had tried to take it away from her then, she would have fought like a savage. Now? Now she felt as if she were a disease that was infecting the whole populace. Where they once had needed her, she was now a barrier to be broken down and eradicated. She stood in their way—in the way of freedom. How could they let her live? They had no choice but to cut her out of their body like a canker, so that the remainder could thrive, could live again. She said as much to Ben.

He replied, "But if the *head* is infected, it does no good to cut it off, Morag, because the body dies without it. We can do without a leg... or an arm...." He waved his stump. "That's me ... or Felix. But without a head we cease to function. We *might* not be able to make it *with* you darling, but we are *certain* to perish without you. Don't forget, part of you is MacKenzie, and that part is striving for us, fighting, however unsuccessfully at the moment, against the force of Mento. We need you. We can't do without you. Please, don't *ever* contemplate suicide. Apart from all that, I love you," he said, simply, "and tacky though it may sound, *I* can't function without you."

"Oh, Ben, I feel terrible." She hugged him to her, oblivious of the others in the room. How could she leave such a man behind? But what if he was wrong? What if she was evil, through and through, and the only way they would make it was without her? She would have to consider, coldly and carefully, what was best for all of them. It was her life, to do with as she thought best. Unless they showed her that she was indeed needed by them, that their survival depended upon her, then she might have to remove herself from their path to freedom and their right to a real world.

"What I plan to do, Morag," said Felix, "is to describe to you what the world *should* look like. What the earth once was to us and may be to others at this time. This world is only a trap...a series of traps and layers. If we can forge our own path to the outside world, then we'll have made it...the first step anyway. We must sit down together and I shall discuss with you the world as told to me by the Primary. I'm sure we can get there...we just need your cooperation."

"Anything," she said, wearily. "Just so long as I'm not going to hinder you."

The others left the longhouse, leaving it free for Morag and Felix. She had wanted Ben to stay, but Felix said he wanted her to have no distractions. She listened patiently to what he had to say, all the while aware that part of her, inside her head, was taking this information for possible use as sabotage material. She had to be aware of that, always keep it in her mind. The descriptions undertaken by Felix were very long and detailed. She asked many questions as she fought to master the complexities, long into the night. Mento, her mother, had kept these people down for five hundred years and they deserved their freedom. It was, in a way, a little like the story of Moses, leading his people from Egypt, she heard Felix telling her. After it was all over Moses made certain mistakes too, but he overcame them.

"Then they made it," said Morag. "Moses and his people."

"Yes...." He seemed hesitant.

"*Tell* me," said Morag. "Did they or not? You should always tell me the truth, whether you think it's dangerous or not. Half-truths and inadequate facts have led to our failures so far."

"You're right," he said. "Well, his people *did* see the promised land but Moses had angered God by one of his mistakes."

"Anubis?"

"No, this was the God of the Jews . . . a sort of omnipotent, omniscient character. The one we occasionally make reference to . . . his son was Jesus Christ."

"But these are just exclamations—like *hell* or *damn*."

"They're all part of the same culture, the same religion. It's been lost to us, though some of the words survive in our everyday speech. We must sit down and talk about it someday. There's much for you to learn."

"And Moses? He died before he saw the promised land."

"The story is not an exact parallel, Morag. Don't concern yourself with it too much. This time Moses will get there . . . history never repeats itself to exactitude. You will succeed where Moses did not. I'll make sure of that. Our battle is with another human. A very powerful one, granted. But she is not the Devil. If she were, none of us would be here now. There must be a certain amount of compassion and mercy in her soul."

Unless she enjoyed playing games, thought Morag. Unless she liked putting people in boxes to see if they could find their way out. She must have a penchant for cruelty to lock people away for numerous generations. That did not sound like compassion to Morag. That was anything but merciful, as far as she was concerned. It would have been kinder if Mento had killed her original enemies, since they died in captivity anyway. To make innocent offspring suffer was the work of a sadist.

TWENTY-TWO

A second expedition was planned. They entered the caves beyond Inland, and this time Morag accompanied them. Although they took lights with them these proved unnecessary. Unlike the labyrinthine caves behind First City, the rock walls here glowed with a phosphorescent light of their own. The passage was straight and narrow and led them directly to a huge cavern, not unlike the one they had left behind, only in this place the floor was of gray rock, which curved upward, as if they were standing in a giant bowl.

"Look!" cried Ben, craning his head backward and pointing up at the roof. Morag followed the line of his arm and saw that above them, suspended from a flat, mottled whitish sky, were three cities, upside-down. Two of the cities were circular and situated on one side of a sun embedded like a huge ball in the smooth heavens. They stood away from the sides of the rock-walled valley. The third city sprawled shapelessly along and flush against the rock wall. There were the remnants of stargirdered canopies over all three cities but the ice-shields had been shattered by Time and her agents. They had existed an hour . . . or half a thousand years. Morag felt giddy as she stared at the roofs of the buildings that hung high above her, and the thin towers, with their cupolas ready to drop from the tips and splash like giant tears on the valley floor.

"First and Second Cities," she said, overawed by the strange spectacle. "Replicas. . . ."

"And the City of Beasts," murmured Daniel.

The overhead buildings appeared deserted. Streets of ghosts. There was an eerie silence which seemed to cling to them like a filmy shroud, indicating that nothing and no one inhabited the cities in the sky. Had they ever been populated? What was this place, where whispers echoed in the stillness like voices from the past?

"Daniel, Ben," said Morag. "Let's go back. I think you've found what you wanted, haven't you?" She knew she had failed again, but the worst of it was, she did not know why.

For the past several days she had been building an imaginary world of trees, rivers, mountains and fields . . . an infinite sky encrusted with white lights called *stars*. How difficult it had all been, charting these objects in her mind . . . and for what? For this? It just was not fair. She felt like weeping. A desire to commit suicide swept through her. When she was alone again. . . .

"Well," confessed Ben, "I didn't know what to expect. Don't worry too much. It's not your fault. We'll find a way . . . we'll find a way. Morag, are you still fond of me?" Daniel and Max moved away at these words.

She had been turning from his intense gaze but she looked back quickly. His black features with the white streak of hair snaking back from the brow were so beautiful to her that she ached for him.

She said softly, "Ben, you're the dearest person I have ever known. It's always been a wonder to me that I could attract the affection of a man like you for so long."

"I have my faults. Many of them, Morag. For one thing, I'm a cripple." He shrugged the stump on his armless side. "Oh, I know that doesn't mean anything to you," he continued, obviously reading her expression correctly. "But I have others—personality faults. Some you may not be able to live with. For instance, I'm inclined to moodiness. . . ."

"Everyone has faults. How boring a flawless person would be! Why did you ask me if I still loved you? Are you that unsure of me?"

Ben smiled. "No, but I'm an insecure person, Morag. I need reassurance from time to time. You're so busy with your concern for the future . . . rightly so . . . it's just that I need to know you still think of me the same way you always have. Anyway, I asked if you were fond of me, not if you loved me. Love implies possessiveness and I would not ask you to commit yourself completely . . . I just want you to remember how fond you are of me, and how much I love you, before you do anything. Do you understand me?"

"Yes . . . yes, I understand. I'll try, Ben, but there are more important issues at stake than our love for each other."

"I merely ask you to bear it in mind."

She nodded. She had influenced the geography of the unknown, once again, to the detriment of her people. It was essential that she consider suicide. She realized, now, where the strange cavern had come from. Felix had spoken of a spherical world with antipodean regions. This place was her upside-down world. . . . Somehow she had formed it during Felix's talk, as she had struggled with mental pictures of the true world. It meant she had absolutely no control over her ability to manifest suggestions as solid objects. Mento was skillfully manipulating her again, as if she were a puppet, insidiously pulling the strings of her mind until that terrible woman had her desired false trail. It seemed there was no way out . . . except through death.

Morag was depressed when she returned to First City and told Ben she wanted to be alone. He expressed concern but she said, "You can't watch me all the time, Ben. If anything's going to happen, it'll happen, whether you're there or not."

"Don't talk that way, Morag."

"Please, Ben. Just leave me with my thoughts for a while. I have to be alone."

He was still dubious but did as she asked. She lay back on the rugs in the room and considered their position. They were running out of time and she was the main obstacle to their escape. Mento, that ultimate artist, obviously had the power to create worlds consciously, but she had not passed on the gift to Morag—not in its complete form. Morag had the ability to create but without control, without the capability of shaping things to desired specifications. In fact her talent was completely out of control. Was this her destiny? To be the prisoners' walls?

There were people who were destined to live a prisoner's life, unconsciously directing their energies toward remaining behind walls, while consciously insisting that *freedom* was their desire. Perhaps she was one of those insecure members of society who find it impossible to function unless within an establishment? Yet her prison, First City, had hardly been a place where the inmates were well cared for. Within its limited area were all the aspects of an otherwise normal life. It was certainly not a retreat from the real world.

"I am the great architect," she said to herself, "who works from no blueprints, no plans. I build t'e monstrosities of nightmares and dreams, out of fables, legends and threads of conversation." She laughed. A hard, bitter laugh.

She felt a hundred years older than when she had first met Ben. Really, he was the only one she would miss . . . no, that was not true. Felix was a good friend too, and Daniel, poor Daniel, the willing servant. What made her a leader and Daniel a follower? Surely, anyone had the ability to lead provided they had the belief of others and the belief in themselves. Let Daniel lead the people out of this place. Let him be the Moses of First City. She was tired of it all.

She rose and left the room, climbing the stairs to the roof. There, she crossed to the parapet of the four-story building and looked down to the street below. It was a very easy thing to do . . . one of the easiest acts of her life. All she had to do was to lean over too far. Just let herself fall against the air, let the air support her body for a few moments. She was so tired. So tired. . . .

"Morag."

She straightened and looked behind her. Felix stood in the doorway to the roof.

"Don't come any closer, Felix. I have to do it, you know I do."

"Nothing of the sort," he said, quickly. "There's been a new development."

She studied the people in the street below. She had been noticed now and they began to gather in the shape of a crescent, leaving space on the street for her body to strike. None of them want to come with me, she thought petulantly. They're afraid I'll fall on them.

"Morag, I'm not lying. There is something new. Listen. While you and Ben were inside the Inland caves, I went to those behind the third city. It's the way out, Morag. The exit we've been looking for."

"You can do it without me."

"No! No, we can't. We don't know what Mento has built into that mind of yours. Perhaps when you die there will be terrible physical catastrophes . . . fire, flood, earthquakes? We may be sitting on top of a volcano about to erupt. Who knows what energy lies in your head, awaiting chaotic release. At least while you're alive you control it to a degree."

"So you don't care whether I live, you only care whether I die. I have to die someday, Felix."

"Yes, but *quietly*, in old age. Not like *this*. And of course I care whether you live or not. You're like a daughter to me. You know that."

"Ben would call that tacky sentimentality."

"I'm entitled to be a little sentimental. I'm an old man. Morag, listen, the world . . . it's as I described it, exactly. Beautiful rivers flowing through green fields. Hills covered in flowers. You should *see* it . . . such a place. Better than we dreamed of. I crept through the City of Beasts, risking this tattered old body, to the caves at the rear. Unlike ours their city touches the rock face at its edges, so we can't go round it . . . we have to go through it. We're going to make it, Morag, as long . . . as long as you don't ruin it all for us by jumping."

She began crying. "I *can't* be that important. I won't be. I don't *want* to be."

"Stop being childish. You *are* and that's fact. You can't shrug off your responsibilities just because they're getting too burdensome for you. We need you."

She stood for a while, looking at her stone destination below. It looked so *inviting*.

"Besides," added Felix, stealing her attention again, "you don't honestly believe you created those places by yourself, do you? It took all of us . . . a kind of collective. You were the strongest and your mind was the keystone, but don't make the mistake of thinking you did it alone. That would be pure conceit. And while I'm chastising you, I might as well tell you I don't like the way you keep interfering in my relationship with Estelle . . . that's just plain jealousy. You can't stand to see one of your admirers with another woman, can you? Oh, I know you don't want me *that* way . . . but you don't want anyone else to have me either. You're an egotist, Morag."

"An egotist?"

"Yes. Raxonberg had an ego one could spend a day climbing up . . . you're beginning to develop the same way."

"Don't compare me to that crass boor," she said, angrily. She stepped away from the parapet, then paused. "Damn. You tricked me. I really wanted. . . ."

"I know, but it wasn't a trick. There *is* a world out there and we have to find the best way of getting the people to it." He put an arm around her shoulders and she allowed herself to be led away, down the stairs to the room below.

As they came down the stairs, Morag said, "I'm sorry about Estelle. It was very stupid of me."

"Yes, it was," replied Felix, "but I forgive you anyway. I feel rather flattered, really, which is most unbecoming of me. Two women needing the undivided attention of an old man like me. . . ." He glanced at her as he spoke. "Oh, yes. Estelle was just as stupid as you. But then, we're all possessive at times . . . I know I am. Here we are."

Ben was there. He jumped up when they entered and his eyes were wide and damp.

"Thank God! Morag. . . ." He put his arm around her. Then fiercely, "You silly fool . . . what the hell did you hope to gain by it? I *knew* you would try something like that . . . that's why I went for Felix right away."

Felix said in measured tones, "It's all right, Ben. I've told Morag about the caves behind the City of Beasts. She knows we've found the way out, to the real world."

"What? Oh, yes, but that doesn't excuse her. God, I'm glad you're safe," Ben said, his voice dropping into a concerned note again. "Don't *do* that to me again."

"Will people stop putting their arms around my shoulders?" she said, defiantly. "I can stand up by myself. I don't need any support. I'm not a . . ." There followed an awful silence.

". . . cripple," Ben finished for her. Then he laughed. Uproarious guffaws. Morag joined him. Felix remained silent, watching them release their tension, wishing perhaps that old men could do the same without risking a heart attack. Instead he sang. *"We shall see the hills and the trees of Earth, when we walk again in her gardens."*

All the words of the song "The Gardens of Earth" came to Morag then, and she saw in her mind's eye rolling stretches of green peppered with white and yellow flowers, and tall hills with dark brows of rock whence water gushed as if from mouths, falling sparkling to the valleys below. There were trees with networks of branches covered in leaves that slapped each other gently in the breezes. Below the trees wound rivers like meltwater floods, contained within red clay banks.

"Oh yes," she breathed, "I can see that place, Ben. It's *so long* since I heard the song . . . since I was a child and my father sang it to me." He stroked her cheek with the back of his hand, once.

They were *free*. After centuries in chains, they were free.

What did that mean, exactly? She did not know, but it felt *good*. It felt very, very good. Almost as if she had cheated the mother whom she could never call *mother*—Mento. Had she left them this single door into the garden as a salve to her conscience? Perhaps she had thought they would never emerge sane from the ice, let alone find the single passageway to a world of which she considered them unworthy.

"Ben, I want to see the sun go down. Would you please excuse me, Felix?"

"Of course, but..." He smiled. "The sun doesn't go down here. In our new world it will, but here it just turns..."

Then he left them alone. Ben said, "Morag, I'll walk you to the edge of the city but you're in one of your silent moods again. I can see it coming on, so I don't know why you want me to be with you."

"You'll understand, Ben. We don't need to talk. You'll understand."

They went down the stairs and out into the street. Everywhere they walked people acknowledged them, smiling. Had the shouters spread the word already? Or was it that they were still full of gratitude for the first deliverance?

The people of First City gathered together what few personal possessions they owned and bade farewell to their old city with reluctance. Possibly, at some time in the future, they would look back on their former homeland with nostalgia: when times became uncomfortable, deprived: when some harsh political regime caused them to forget Raxonberg and the trysts and remember only the street-corner speeches and mellow conspiracies: when the crops failed and food was scarce.

To future generations, if there were any, if all went well, First City would be the legend of their birth. There would be no need to look beyond the basic symbol of an ice wall opening like a womb to let out the life within. Morag spoke to the multitude.

"We are about to walk through the door to the world," she told them. "Let's do it with pride. Our ancestors were crammed into a box and left to rot . . . but they survived, just as we shall survive this new adventure. We are a hardy people. We have stamina, if not grace. We have grit, if not gentleness. We have courage, if not fine ways. Later we can look toward manners, culture and artistry. Now let us instill within one another a strength to overcome all that we may meet in the way of adversity."

They cheered her. Their backs straightened and they cheered her. She was happy with them and herself. There would be trials but she would carry them through. The first of those trials they were about to encounter. They had to make their way through the City of Beasts . . . or rather *over* it, for Morag had decided that the safest route would be across the rooftops. That way they might all reach the rock wall undetected by the hybrids. Shod ladders had been fashioned, and portable bridges, to travel from one rooftop to another. Ben had confessed to foreboding over the plan but could offer no alternative. If they went through the streets en masse they were sure to be attacked; if they tried to sneak through in small groups, the discovery of one band would endanger all others, and it would be more difficult to fight when divided. Daniel and Felix were in favor, since they hoped it meant little or no bloodshed.

TWENTY-THREE

They passed the sun, with the monstrous hooded eyelid sliding over its cornea. None could stare directly into its brightness but Morag caught the twelve-hour wink in the corner of her own, more sensitive eyes. Morag wondered how much of the Primary, their erstwhile jailer and their provider, had also been Mento. She would surely have overlaid much of herself, her persona, onto her locum?

Mento seemed to have been one of those enigmatic leaders who twisted historians into knots; she was full of contradictions. She had been capable of much good or great evil. Those who failed to heed her laws came up against wrath as unquenchable as Hell. She had buried fifteen generations under a mountain, in cones of ice, and left them to mutate, inbreed and fester. But in doing so she had left them also, as a small gesture of mercy, the key to their deliverance: Morag.

Walking beside her was the stooped but stately figure of Felix. He was an old man and would not have long in the new world but on his face was an expression of grim happiness.

Joy does not necessarily have to smile gently from within, she thought; it can be a harder, more resilient feeling.

"What do you expect of a new home?" she asked him suddenly.

"An exhalation of stars," he replied, as promptly as if he had rehearsed the answer. "An exhalation of stars from the mouth of the night. And if that sounds false, it's because I'm repeating a phrase once used by the Primary, when I asked it a similar question. I don't even know what stars look like, but you can be sure if the Primary wanted to witness such a sight, it'll be worth seeing."

He added, "You have exchanged the animate architecture of ice for that of the mind."

Morag turned her head sharply. Something in his statement caused a tremor of alarm to ripple through Morag's complacency.

"I don't understand," she said.

Felix stared steadily ahead. Finally he said, "Architecture of the mind. One's mind . . . yours, mine, everyone's. . . ."

Word had been sent to Second City, to tell them of the exodus and that they could join it if they wished. The citizens of Inland met with Morag's people on the far side of the sun. Morag was amazed when she found they had made no preparations and had brought no equipment or weapons.

"You'll have to share ours," she said, in a resigned tone. "Most of my people carry more than one weapon . . . and you'd be better to tie your togas up between your legs as we have, to prevent them snagging. You realize we may have to fight."

"Yes," answered Pougerchov, stiffly.

She relented in her attitude toward him. He was no coward, otherwise he would have stayed at home. Frightened perhaps, but prepared to carry out the wishes of the majority nevertheless.

"Well, we hope it won't be necessary. God help us all if we do have to."

They waited a kilometer from the City of Beasts until day rolled out. The glow from the dim street lights of the city was their guide to the outskirts. They had contemplated climbing up onto the canopy but the enormous height of the stargirders filled them with trepidation. Morag told them there was no logic in their fear—they could die as easily falling from a building—but logic does nothing to dispel a phobia. The roof-tops were familiar to them. The canopy was not. They placed the ladders against the walls of the outer buildings and began to climb to the rooftops. The operation was completed with quiet efficiency. They became silent phantoms: some through fear, others through resolve. A stream of dark shapes flowed heavenward for several hours.

Most of the buildings in the City of Beasts were flat-roofed and four stories high, much the same as in the other two cities. When the first band, which included Ben, Daniel and Morag, was up on the roofs, they clipped a portable bridge, half a meter wide, to the eaves and lowered it with ropes to rest on the ledge of the neighboring building. This operation was re-peated by other bands and by these means they moved swiftly across the top of the city, above its bestial inhabitants. Soon the whole group was swarming like beetles with an urgent mission over the shadowy blocks, toward the blackness be-yond.

In the gloom of the streets below, Morag saw the occasional figure loping swiftly through cones of yellow light. She prayed none of them would think of looking up. In any case, she reassured herself, the humans would be dark against the canopy above them. Periodically, animal-like screams rent the stillness, underlined by loud moans and, once or twice, the harsh cough-ing of the hunter that has caught its prey and has gorged itself beyond mere satisfaction.

Finally the last of the group scrambled down the ladder where the others awaited them. There was a feeling in Morag's stom-ach as if she wanted to vomit. She stood apart from the crowd, trying to marshal her reserves of psychological strength, while Felix and Ben spoke calmly with the people. They were ready to go outside.

Outside.

*   *   *

They gathered at the entrance to the cave and then began to file inside. Felix looked terribly concerned. He and Morag were the last to enter.

"What's the matter, Felix?" she said, alarmed at his hesitancy, "There is a world of . . . trees, grass and open air outside, isn't there?"

"There will be, Morag. There will be, I'm sure of it. Listen. You remember that door in the wall? I said to you that if you hadn't seen behind it, then whatever you wanted could be on the other side . . . until the door was opened and you saw for yourself what was *actually* there."

"Yes," she replied, fearfully.

"Now that the others have *seen* what *is*, it cannot be altered. We are not a figment of your mind. The world does not exist for you only. Nor do these people, the people of our cities. You did not have the power to change the order of what already existed, but while there were areas outside the known world, outside our knowledge, *those* you had the power to form—because they did not then have any form. They were not realized quantities. They were vapors, vacuums, voids without meaning or comprehension. Those places folded themselves around your thoughts, Morag. You were the Maker."

She was shaking. "You haven't been out there yet, have you? You lied to me?"

"The others are there now, Morag. You can't change what they have seen. Happily for you and for us, yours was not a conscious power, Morag. You didn't wield it—you merely possessed it. There is a great difference. The difference between responsibility and . . . You are, fortunately, malleable. I have manipulated your imagination, overriding Mento's spirit in you.

"Things without form take form by suggestion. That suggestion can come from within—as did your marble world with its sky of stone, and its scapegoats, the inhabitants of Second City—or it can come from without. I have described to you the world outside."

"Yes." Her heart was beating fast. Did she want to hear more?

Felix spoke softly, placing his hands on her shoulders.

"No, Morag, I have not seen the world outside. If I had gone there before I lied to you I would have drowned. You told us in your story what to expect, that above our sky of rock was an ocean—an underground sea. Above that, more rock, and above *that* rock *more seas.* Do you understand what you were creating for us, Morag? Prisons within prisons within prisons. Unending layers."

"What am I?" she asked, plaintively. "Why did she do this? My *mother*?"

"You, Morag?" He held her head against his chest for a moment. "Perhaps you are her last weapon. Perhaps she left your seed behind in order to insure we could never escape." He paused, then continued: "Or maybe, just maybe, you are her final, her only act of generosity. Her single gesture of kindness. After all, you can create a prison *or a paradise....* You are Mento's daughter."

"But I had no conscious power, you said. I couldn't command a heaven. I could only form it by accident."

Felix smiled and pulled her to her feet. His face was a map of wrinkles and his eyes captured the light of his torch.

"*You* could not, Morag. But *we* could. I gave you the blueprints of belief. The outside world has been formed ... to *our* specifications. *Whatever lies beyond that wall of rock is the world we've designed for ourselves.*"

"My God," she said with a voice full of emotion. "My God, I hope you're right. I'm trying to think ... I want it to be ... It has to be...." There were lights at the end of the tunnel and cool air touched her cheeks.

They left the exit and joined the others, standing silently, waiting.

It was black outside. A darkness.

"Oh no. Oh my God, no," she said.

They saw lights, glistening in the far distance.

The lights seemed to vary in brightness but they came no

nearer. They stayed remote, swimming gently through the blackness above their head.

"Look!" cried Ben.

Far away, before them, was a red grimace in the night. A thin smile of light that slowly widened, and deepened.

"Is this your world?" asked Morag, anxiously. "Is this the way you want it to be?"

But no one answered her. Their eyes were only for the scene before them.

The sun gradually rose through crimson streaks to reveal a wide, glaciated valley flanked by mountains. The valley sides swept down to a dark river silently flowing to somewhere just below the sun. There were tors and medial moraines scattered over the slopes in untidy heaps and here and there a shrubland or a patch of trees. To Morag it looked totally unwelcoming, but her first reaction was to the space: it was so immeasurably vast. The mountains formed some sort of limit to its expanse but the sky had no roof and seemed to go on forever.

The ground beneath her feet was unstable: soft and spongy. She had to keep adjusting her position to keep her feet. It was also covered in fibrous plants and grasses, making it somehow obscene in its resilience. There was wildlife too, not visible but definitely vocal. The river itself moved like a slick, gray monster, inscrutable in its aspect, and gave her the impression that if disturbed it would turn on them with lightening-fast fury. The whole scene had a worn stained look about it that spoke of age and weary neglect. Was this the place in which they had to make their home? She had expected a shining, glorious landscape, vivid in color but tasteful in form and pattern. This was wild, untamed and riotous. Its texture was too loose and its crazy undulations had a nightmarish quality to their unkempt protuberances. It could swallow them whole, this gargantuan landscape, and leave not a trace of them.

She looked around her at the faces of her friends and they looked pale and frightened. Everything was so strange, so different from that which had been familiar to them in their old world: the smells, fragrant but insistent; the colors, rich but cloying; the distances, awe-inspiring but terrifying. She felt weak at the knees and dizzy at having to adjust her vision to take in the dimensions of this outworld. The weirdest part of it all—of the landscape—was the lack of straight lines, of sharp angles and symmetry. Everything was so *shapeless*, as if it had been tossed together by some blind, maladroit giant, careless of the neatness of his creation. Was *this* the promised land? This heap of rubble? The lack of control was appalling.

"Do you think we ought to go back?" she asked Felix, quietly. "I don't think I like it very much. Do you?"

Felix looked at her with a helpless expression.

"This is not the worst of it," he said after a while. "The Primary once told me that one of the worse things Romans had to contend with was the weather, the elements. Apparently it can change at a moment's notice, from sunshine such as this to dark storms full of rain and electrical discharges from the sky. There is such a thing called *thunder*—a loud crashing in the sky, worse that the biggest fallberg we've had to contend with. If we find this frightening, we'd better go back, because there's a great deal more to experience and none of it very pleasant."

Had Felix been encouraging or insistent that they see it through, Morag might possibly have ordered a return to their own world. Instead she felt her will hardening to the task. They had come this far and they *would* see it through.

"We have to be strong," she said. "If we weaken at the first hurdle we'll never find out whether there's a better life here or not. Let's go down there and see what this place has to offer."

She set off down the slope at a determined pace, and gradually in ones and twos, the others began to follow. As she made her way among the rocks and patches of alpine flowers she wondered whether she had indeed created this immense, forbidding land. Had this world been there all the time, just waiting for them to find the right exit? Or had she, Morag, indeed formed it with her so-called paranormal powers? Had Mento come to this place long ago, seen the cave, and formed their prison behind it with her mind—or had she merely brought with her a group of engineers who fashioned it with their hands, with mundane skills, tools and common craftsmanship, leaving traces of the outworld embedded in racial memory? Perhaps the other aspects, the false trails and hidden traps, had been incorporated from the beginning and finding them first was merely a case of taking the easiest course? One thing was certain—there would always be more questions than there were answers. Therein lay the magic, the mystery.